HISTORY OF THE MOVEMENT
From 1854 to 1890

SCIENCE FICTION IN OLD SAN FRANCISCO
Volume I

HISTORY OF THE MOVEMENT
From 1854 to 1890

by Sam Moskowitz

DONALD M. GRANT, PUBLISHER
WEST KINGSTON, RHODE ISLAND
1980

SCIENCE FICTION IN OLD SAN FRANCISCO
Volume I
HISTORY OF THE MOVEMENT
FROM 1854 TO 1890
Copyright © 1980 by Sam Moskowitz

First Edition — 1980

Printed in the United States of America

CONTENTS

	page
Preface	13
The Aerial Bombing of San Francisco	19
Supernatural San Francisco	25
Scientific San Francisco	33
Fantasy in *The Overland Monthly*	35
Ambrose Bierce	41
William Henry Rhodes: Landmark Science Fictioneer	43
Enter Milne	62
The Argonaut	73
Emma Frances Dawson	78
Milne at the *Argonaut*	83
Milne Tries Science Fiction	86
Robert Louis Stevenson	95
W. C. Morrow	97
Hart Comes to the *Argonaut*	108
The Californian	112
Hart Rebuilds the *Argonaut*	126
Milne Makes It	131
Milne Turns to Drama	137
The Brief, Bizarre Career of Nathan Kouns	140
San Francisco's Greatest Science Fiction Writer	144
The Ingleside and *City Argus*	158
Fantasy and Milne Continue in *The Argonaut*	161
J. Esten Cooke and Jules Verne	168
Milne the Magnificent	171
Fantasy in *The San Franciscan*	180
The Argonaut of 1886	183
The Influence of Milne	187
William Randolph Hearst, Jr. and *The Examiner*	192
The Examiner Turns to Science Fiction	195
Morrow Comes to *The Examiner*	197
Ambrose's Bierce's Dystopias	201
Stevenson Returns to San Francisco	205
Fred Somers Launches *Current Literature*	210
An Unwitting Hoax	213

Morrow Moves Into High Gear	217
Argonaut's Fantasy Quotient Rises	220
Milne in *The Examiner*	230
Milne Takes the "Cure"	235
The Last Flaring	238
The Descent	245
The End	251

I. — Robert Duncan Milne

II. — Robert Duncan Milne

I. — Powered Air Flight, 1869

I. — The only known photo of Robert Duncan Milne, the phenomenally imaginative and prolific science fiction author of 19th century San Francisco, taken before 1893, when he was at the height of his imaginative powers.

II. — This remarkable sketch of Robert Duncan Milne appeared as the only illustration for the last work of science fiction he was known to have written, "The Passing of the Printing Press," on page 22 of the December 18, 1898 edition of *The San Francisco Call.* It was literally sketched from life by the staff artist while Milne was writing on the long, narrow strips used by reporters of that day.

III. — Scientific experiment was part of the San Francisco scene and it is possible that this non-rigid dirigible, invented and built by Frederick Marriott, publisher of the *San Francisco News Letter,* may have made the first successful powered air flight in history. On July 3, 1869, powered by a steam engine and guided by long ropes from the ground, it actually flew in full view of a large audience.

IV. — Fred M. Somers was co-founder of *The Argonaut,* and publisher of *The Californian.* In New York, he founded *Current Literature,* probably the finest journal of literary comment ever to appear in the United States.

V. — Jerome A. Hart deserves the same praise in regard to his fostering of fantastic literature in the 19th century that Bob Davis earned for his brilliant work on *The All-Story* and *The Cavalier.* Hart's *Argonaut* was the most outstanding single source of adult fantastic literature in the United States in the 19th century.

VI. — The genial Noah Brooks may have written the first science fiction yarn to appear in a West Coast magazine. "The Diamond Maker of Sacramento" was published in the famed *Overland Monthly* in July 1868. Brooks went on to national recognition with a book on Abraham Lincoln, whom he knew personally.

VII. — Frank M. Pixley was a journalist and lawyer of independent wealth who co-founded *The Argonaut* as a weekly of political and literary appeal with focus on the San Francisco area. This weekly became the frequent home of science fiction, fantasy and horror tales, and was first edited by Ambrose Bierce.

VIII. — One of the neglected masters of the short story, a friend of and profound influence on the work of Ambrose Bierce, was William C. Morrow, who enjoyed a great prominence in the Greater San Francisco area for his tales of horror, supernatural and science fiction.

IX. — Unquestionably, one of the most distinctive masters in the realm of the American supernatural and horror story was Emma Frances Dawson, a woman of learning and artistic temperament. Dawson lived the life of a recluse in poverty in the San Francisco Bay area. Her work was championed by Ambrose Bierce.

X. — An artist's drawing of Jerome A. Hart, when in his later years, he wrote a book of memoirs and observations of people and events, that included a substantial amount of material on his penchant for the fantastic and those who wrote it.

XI. — In the 1870's, attorney William Henry Rhodes of San Francisco, wrote a series of science fiction hoaxes for the local newspapers that first frightened Northern California and then amused it. These were collected posthumously in CAXTON'S BOOK in 1876, establishing him as an important pioneer of American science fiction.

IV. — Fred M. Somers

V. — Jerome A. Hart

VI. — Noah Brooks

VII. — Frank M. Pixley

VIII. — William C. Morrow   IX. — Emma Frances Dawson

X. — Jerome A. Hart   XI. — William Henry Rhodes

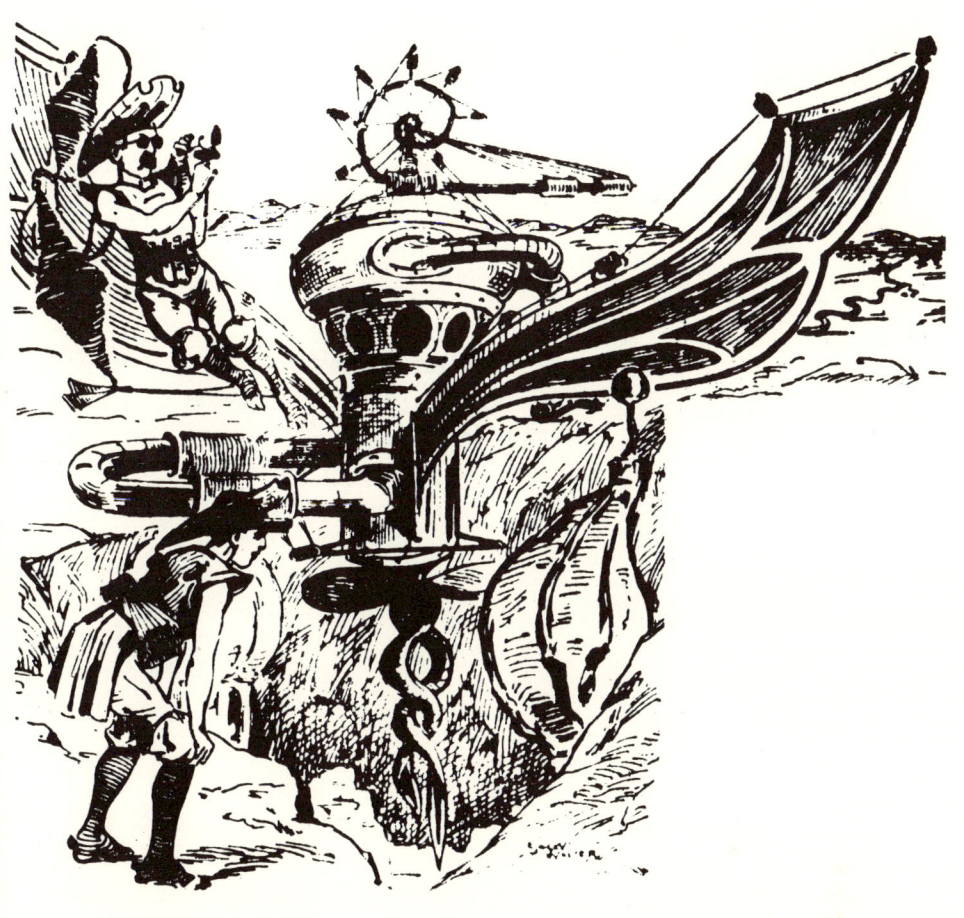

An adroitness in the depiction of speculative machinery was displayed by Solly Walter in this drawing, one of six by him which illustrated Robert Duncan Milne's story of the future: "How San Francisco Looked in 1893. An Archeological Fantasy," of men from the year 3893 excavating in the region of San Francisco Bay. It appeared in *The San Francisco Examiner* for Sunday, January 1, 1893.

To
Margaret Moskowitz

Who, with the fervor of a
dedicated researcher, made
possible this subject's
real potential.

PREFACE

That a truly gifted and accomplished writer of science fiction could have published in American weeklies and dailies as many as sixty bonafide stories in the genre between the years 1879 and 1899 — a candidate for the earliest full-time science fiction writer — and never receive a single mention in any work on the development of science fiction, let alone American literature seems inconceivable.

That this man, Robert Duncan Milne, enjoyed not only unprecedented reader popularity as a writer of science fiction but gathered critical acclaim for his achievements from contemporaries as distinguished as Ambrose Bierce, Gertrude Atherton and Charles Howard Shinn, without prompting further investigation of his talents seems improbable.

That he could have influenced an entire school of San Franciscan science fiction writers, not the least of which was Ambrose Bierce and the entire movement be forgotten, would appear impossible.

That he was cited as having befriended Robert Louis Stevenson during that author's darkest hours in San Francisco and not even receive a footnote in literary history seems incredible.

That he was hired by William Randolph Hearst as part of that notable's plan to use science fiction as part of his formula for building his first newspaper The *San Francisco Examiner* is certainly astonishing, since it never has been previously mentioned.

Nevertheless, that was the case.

Just as Edgar Rice Burroughs was the dominating figure in the creation of the scientific romance school of writers in the Munsey Magazines (See UNDER THE MOONS OF MARS, "A History and Anthology of the Scientific Romance in the Munsey Magazines 1912 to 1920" by Sam Moskowitz) so Robert Duncan Milne

HISTORY OF THE MOVEMENT 14

was the key figure in the creation and promulgation of the San Francisco school of science fiction which flourished during the last decades of the 19th century and had been interred almost without a trace.

This book is the documented history of that movement with special emphasis on its prime mover, Robert Duncan Milne. It tells the *comprehensive* story of the contributions by San Francisco's writers not just to science fiction but to the literature of the supernatural, occult and horror, detailing the movement from its earliest beginnings in 1854 through to 1890. Robert Duncan Milne's story is carried through to his death in 1899.

Detailed attention has also been given in this account to the lives and extraordinary works of William Henry Rhodes, W. C. Morrow and Emma Frances Dawson and this book quite literally presents the only important critical and biographical information on those important literary figures that presently exists. Rhodes story is complete but there is more to come in a later volume which proposes to carry the history of the San Francisco science fiction movement from 1890 through to 1906 (when it rejoined the national mainstream) about W. C. Morrow, certainly one of the most unique story tellers in American history and also on the final years of Emma Frances Dawson. There will, of course, be complete data on the development of the school of science fiction which Milne championed.

This volume contains substantial material on Ambrose Bierce which has never previously been published and there will be more forthcoming. Up until 1890 he was less a leader in the development of science fiction, fantasy and weird fiction than an enthusiast of those who worked at it. This volume precisely pinpoints his transition into a writer of satiric dystopias, supernatural and horror stories. By 1890 he had at last begun to write the short story masterpieces that would swiftly win him international recognition.

The role played by the editors and publishers of the San Francisco newspapers and regional magazines in the fostering of science fiction and fantasy is fastiduously covered, in the process presenting information about those newspapers and periodicals not previously known.

Since the majority of the stories mentioned in this work have never been reprinted, an outline of the plots of virtually all of them as well as a critical evaluation of their worth is included.

A companion book that appears simultaneously with this one has been composed entirely of a selection of the stories of Robert Duncan Milne. It was imperative that a good cross-section of his science fiction be published immediately or his work might be lost forever. A suitable selection from the work of his contemporaries, imitators and admirers is planned for a later date.

Only a very few were aware of my years of research to establish the existence and validity of the San Francisco school of science fiction, the sometimes ingenious and at other times painstaking efforts to locate, assemble the stories themselves and information on their creators. I asked for confidentiality and it was respected for six long years, even after the "diggings" began to pan out.

There were three people who had any clear idea of what I was working on. The most important was Margaret Moskowitz, the wife of my brother Maurice. They lived in California, so she was enlisted to do research and soon became completely absorbed and fascinated by it. For the best part of a year, she would receive letters of instruction from me, supplemented by long-distance telephone calls, itemizing what to look for and where. As she turned in her findings, the information permitted me to more definitely zero in on pay dirt or determine whether a particular vein of research was played out. Thousands of pages of photocopies of material flooded back and thousands of dollars were forwarded to pay for the expense of it all. Together, we broke the back of this project and that is why she richly deserves the dedication in this book.

A second major figure was Joseph H. Wrzos, for a period editor under the name of Joseph Ross of *Amazing Stories* and *Fantastic* when they were sold by Ziff-Davis. A life-long enthusiast, he pursued on his own what references were available in the New York area but even more important, he was, for the entire period of research, my confidant, evaluating my findings and offering advice and even more important *enthusiasm* for the continuation of the project. Many of the stories were printed in microscopic type, unacceptable to a printer and he volunteered to put selected stories into manuscript form. For his intellectual as well as his practical support — as well as his silence — the fictional companion to this history is dedicated to him.

The third man who knew of the project from its very beginnings and as a trusted friend literally began to research it with me in the early stages when we naively thought that the material we required would be sequested somewheres in the Library of Congress, was Lester Mayer of Silver Springs, Md. We spent a frustrated weekend at that exalted American institution before we were forced to concede that the materials we were looking for must reside elsewhere.

Though he did not have the slightest idea what was on my mind, retired New York City science fiction enthusiast and dealer Milton Spahn was instrumental in securing for me many invaluable books, magazines and references which gave me a positive direction on where to look.

A misdirected letter resulted in an offer by Charles Townsville to tie up some loose ends of research after my sister-in-law had moved from California. Though he had no particular interest in science fiction, he became intrigued by the research and succeeded in locating stories and special information that had eluded me even when I suspected their existence.

To obtain genealogical background on Robert Duncan Milne, I employed Sheila Pitcairn in Scotland who provided material that would have been impossible to obtain in this country.

Presiding at the finish was Rhea Finkelstein, who started typing my manuscripts 20 years ago because she needed the money and has continued to work on them out of friendship because she gets a kick out of being the first to read what outlandish new discoveries I have come up with this time and how the publishers will treat them.

That is not very many people for a book of this type and to all of them I am considerably indebted not just for their efforts but for providing companionship on what would otherwise have been an extremely lonely, costly, seemingly endless but incomparably enthralling search.

Sam Moskowitz

HISTORY OF THE MOVEMENT
From 1854 to 1890

SCIENCE FICTION IN OLD SAN FRANCISCO

I. THE AERIAL BOMBING OF SAN FRANCISCO

The year is 1892. A pilotless helicopter hovers over San Francisco. A missile drops from its bomb bay and the City Hall goes up in smoke.

The helicopter has been launched from a Chilean warship, anchored beyond range of the shore guns. Ransom is demanded or the entire city will be demolished. Wagons begin carrying the gold from the San Francisco mint house to the docks.

An American cruiser arrives to give combat. The first Naval bombing from a heavier-than-air-craft in man's history is attempted upon her. Out-gunned, out-armored, she appears to have little chance against these new forces of modern science. Though the enemy ship is completely invisible in the fog, the cruiser launches a torpedo in its general direction. Unerringly the torpedo homes in on the Chilean vessel, guided by a newly invented magnetic warhead. There is a tremendous explosion and San Francisco is saved.

That story, "A Question of Reciprocity," a novelette serialized in two installments and appearing in William Randolph Hearst's *San Francisco Examiner* for November 15 and November 22, 1891, was the latest in a series of literary triumphs by Robert Duncan Milne, the first writer in the history of the world to devote virtually full time to the writing of science fiction. It confirmed Hearst's wisdom in luring to the pages of *The Examiner*, four years earlier, the man who had become a household name in the San Francisco area after 40 consecutive science fiction novelettes and short stories, involving literally every major gambit of the art from reprogramming the genetic structure of the human cell to a series of close-up views of the civilization of Mars. Not even the stories of Ambrose Bierce — his co-worker and fierce defender — were more eagerly sought after by San Francisco publications.

The most literary magazine of the period in San Francisco was *The Wave*, edited and published by John O'Hara Cosgrave. It was a magazine to which Milne had contributed two stories in 1891. One of the most popular columns in the publication was "Splashes" by "The Witness," which Cosgrave used as a pen name. That column for November 28, 1891 commented: "'A Question of Reciprocity,' Robert Duncan Milne's story, that appeared in the *Examiner* of the past two Sundays, was a remarkably clever effort, worthy of a better finish. But from first to last it was told with the interest-holding ability that Mr. Milne has to such a marked degree. The writer has a strong enough hold on science to make it useful to him in stories; and he can construct a theory of invention as well as any writer at present engaged in entertaining the public. In 'A Question of Reciprocity,' the characters are not expected to do much, but what they do is natural, and if one happens to know the men one is quite sure they are made to do the circumstance of the story."

Cosgrave was a good friend of Bierce's, who was also a contributor to the pages of *The Wave*. Normally it would have appeared that Cosgrave had been complimentary enough to have satisfied any reasonable man, but Ambrose Bierce had never been noted as a reasonable man and co-worker Milne on *The Examiner* was a much-admired Sacred Cow. In his famed "Prattle" column in the Sunday edition of *The San Francisco Examiner* for December 6, 1891, Bierce came roaring back in justification of Milne:

> "What under the seven suns does the *Wave* man mean by finding fault with the conclusion of Mr. Milne's story, 'A Question of Reciprocity'? It is hardly possible to think how it could have ended more impressively. Two warships are fighting, watched by the population of a great city. One has sent an automatically guided torpedo feeling for the other in a fog which has drifted over both and suspended the battle while concealing them from

the multitude on the shore. A dull, thundering sound is heard, the fog clears away, the people strain their eyes seaward. "Far as the eye could reach from Point Bonita to the Farallones, nothing could be seen but one white object, glistening like a swan upon the dancing waters — the *Charleston* was alone upon the ocean." The thing is dramatic inexpressibly! Did my good friend of the *Wave* wish to gloat upon the shattered hull, the flying masts, the hurtling marines, variously impaired and fitfully surprised by the mischance! Did he want to be shown a flapping and flinging about of tangles of entrails, the sky bombarded with un-assorted viscera and the sea splattered and be-slubbered by a sparent diffusion of gore! One wouldn't think him that kind of a man; he doesn't look it when you see him close to!"

Ordinarily, one might have credited Bierce with mock seriousness, but evidently it was "for real," because Cosgrave took enough offense to reply almost immediately in his column in *The Wave* for December 12, 1891.

"Ambrose Bierce, the Apostle of the Opposite, to whom the Queen's English is indebted for many a word that long ago would have sunk into the oblivion of misuse, is not always unfair. Since the death of Frank Pixley, Bierce has not crowded him into a corner of his grave, or brought to light acts that were better hid, to cover his lonely resting place with posthumous infamy. But I should like to ask Bierce what obvious and unblushing fault I did not see in Robert Duncan Milne's story that he should attack me so generally for my expressed dislike to the end of it? I sincerely hope my Prattling companion-at-Pens does not think that I believe that he came to the rescue of the Pope's nose of a 'Question of Reciprocity' because that was the only part of it that needs defense.

"Bierce must have found some seriously

humpbacked perversion of literary license in the story that may or may not have showed its deformity under the eyes of somebody else, or he would not have refused so eagerly to dispute my right to say I was not enamored of Mr. Milne's ending. I was not ambitious of gazing on the shattered carcasses of Hessians, whether drawing money from America or Chile, discoloring the pale air with their gore; I have no eager craving to watch the gentle marine blown into bits, four bits or six bits; nor do I want to see the useless inside of the enemy thrown up among the rafters of heaven, there to tie themselves into knots, and hang for their better curing; as Ambrose Bierce has said, I'm not that kind of a fellow. But I did desire to see Mr. Milne end his story in some manner than the only manner possible. I think Mr. Bierce will agree with me that is the way to finish the story."

Milne did not know it, but the year 1891 was to mark the apex of his popularity. He was credited with simultaneously being the West's most brilliant scholar and most unrepentant alcoholic and the latter did not allow adequate time in the years remaining to him to forcibly demonstrate the former. Still, Gertrude Atherton, even then gaining recognition (her later novel, THE CALIFORNIANS [1898], would receive national acclaim), was an enthusiastic supporter of Milne. In her article "The Literary Development of California" which appeared in the January, 1891 issue of *Cosmopolitan*, she ranked Milne third in importance among contemporary California writers, just after Ambrose Bierce and W. C. Morrow, and said of him: "Robert Duncan Milne has an extravagant imagination, but under it is a reasoning and scientific mind. He takes such a premise as a comet falling into the sun and works out a terribly realistic series of results; or he will invent a dream for Saturn which might well have grown out of that planet's conditions. His style is so good and so convincing that one is apt to lay down such a story as the former with an anticipation of nightmares, if comets are hanging about. His sense of humor and literary taste always stop him the right side of the grotesque."

There were virtually no dissenting opinions on Milne's brilliance. Wherever and whenever he was mentioned, it was with high praise for his extraordinary imagination, writing skill, erudition and incomparable command of science and scholarship. This was to remain true right through to his obituaries.

Milne was the quintessential heavy science writer of science fiction. Hal Clement, whose "Mission of Gravity" *(Astounding Science Fiction*, April to July, 1953), has become the supreme symbol of a story based on the most credible extrapolations of a basic scientific premise to its extreme potentialities, would have been incredulous at the artistically involuted and rhythmically sustained variations on scientific and philosophical backgrounds that Milne employed to explain and rationalize the inexplicable. He sidestepped or glossed over little. His fund of knowledge seemed inexhaustible and was unquestionably up to the minute for the period in which he wrote. The scientific explanations and background compete with the plotline for reader fascination, because they are not double-talk or evasions, but extraordinary expositions of science and logic.

By the late 1880's and 1890's his type of science fiction had become so popular that he influenced an entire school of science fiction writers — some of them already famous for other types of fiction — into following his lead, including Ambrose Bierce, W. C. Morrow, C. D. Willard, Geraldine Bonner, E. C. Clough, Edmund Stuart Roche and Julie Classon Kenly. The remarkable thing about this school of writers of science fiction and the factor that connects them beyond any chance of argument is not that they wrote for the same magazines and newspapers as Milne at the same time or immediately following (which they did), is not that some of them repeated his plots with variations (which they did), but that in all but a very few of the stories, *San Francisco and its environs was the basic locale.*

If a comet destroyed the earth and there were any survivors, it was in San Francisco. If astronomers found a means of observing life on Mars, it was in San Francisco. If a scientist discovered the secret of changing the genetic trigger of human cells, it was in a San Francisco laboratory. If the United States was invaded by a foreign power, they landed at San Francisco. If men from the future searched for momentos of past civilization, it was in San Francisco. When a man is found who has been frozen in a block of ice for 10,000 years, he is thawed out in San Francisco. Quite literally, San Francisco was the center of the universe. Not only do these stories represent as rich a lode of undiscovered literary science fiction that ever focussed on a single city — bowing only to New York and London as the all-time champions — but represent an archive of the life and times of San Francisco before it was destroyed by the earthquake of 1906 of considerable historic value.

II. SUPERNATURAL SAN FRANCISCO

What was all the more remarkable about this movement was that San Francisco was not truly a scientific community at all. If anything, it had been noted since the Gold Rush for its prodigious appetite for the occult, providing fertile ground for spiritualism. For every science fiction story published there were 10 of the supernatural, horrible or grotesque. The result was that San Francisco in the decades before and after the turn of the century cultivated a remarkable group of superb literary stylists, dealing heavily in the "forbidden" lore and the dark side of man's conscience. Among the better known were Ambrose Bierce, Frank Norris, Gertrude Atherton, Gelett Burgess, and W. C. Morrow. Not as well known was the admirable stylist Emma Frances Dawson; the vivid supernaturalism and off-trail character of Nathan Koun's tales of the South; the unjournalistic ghost stories of the great reporter Henry Bigelow; the ghostly and ghastly westerns of Y. H. Addis, rivaled by those of Addie J. Holmes; the colorful occult stories of Thomas J. Vivian; the incredibly competent efforts of famous editor Arthur McEwan and the equally effective work of fellow editor Frank Bailey Millard, to name just a *handful* of the practitioners.

Those supernatural tales, written by the foregoing writers in residence, most frequently, like the science fiction, had their locales in San Francisco. Easily as many stories of the supernatural were picked up from other U.S. and foreign sources and reprinted locally as were written by Californians, making for a substantial number.

The truth was that the quantity of science fiction to appear in San Francisco in the last quarter of the nineteenth century was predominantly due to the power and effectiveness of Milne's work. Without him, all the authors who followed him would still have written, but it is highly unlikely that they would have written science fiction.

Yet it was in a remarkable occult work of fiction that, deliberately or not developed into a much-publicized hoax, that the devoted recorder and historian of Californian writers, magazines and newspapers, the late Ella Sterling Cummins, saw the beginning of the school of science fiction writers that would fascinate San Franciscans of the eighties and nineties. The work she spotlighted was "The Eventful Nights of August 20th and 21st" by Ferdinand Cartwright Ewer, serialized in the October and November, 1854 issues of *The Pioneer*, the first true magazine to be published in San Francisco.

"This may be considered the first of those wonder-stories," she said, "which seem to spring into growth so naturally in our climate, and which formed, afterward, the fields chosen by W. H. H. Rhodes (Caxton), in which to make himself famous and to-day is represented by their prototypes, Robert Duncan Milne, Ambrose Bierce and William C. Morrow, who present the choicest flowering of the literary orchid."

Born a Unitarian Quaker in Nantucket in 1826, Ewers embraced Episcopalianism and then became for a time a rabid atheist. He was a publisher as well as a writer and launched two ephemeral papers, *Pacific News* and *Sunday Dispatch*, before taking a flyer at a bonafide literary magazine for the West Coast in the form of *The Pioneer*, which began publication in January, 1854 and expired in December, 1855. There is every indication that his effort may have been written as a straight-faced spoof against the rage for spiritualism prevalent in San Francisco and also as a means of entrapment for the claims of its leading proponents.

The story opens with considerable narrative skill. The author has been delivered a note from a dying man, John F. Lane, by his child, Jane, bidding him to come to his bedside immediately. San Francisco was a wide-open city with literally no law at the time, to venture out after dark involved a very calculated risk. The author leaves his valuables at home and, fortifying himself with a pistol, starts for the address on the note, accompanied by two friends. They reach the home of Lane and find he is dying from tuberculosis. He claims he is a medium who has made contact with the spiritual world and has deliberately selected Ewer as the receipient of what he has to demonstrate, because he has heard that Ewer is an atheist with no belief in spiritualism. He then proceeds to write a message which he claims to come from the spirit world, whose purport is expressed in the lines: "The time is ripe... 'the gates of Death are open...'"

Ewer, skeptical, asks for proof of authenticity. The spirit message continues, promising that Lane will converse with him prior, during and *after* death. The promise is kept, Lane babbles as he dies, fearing that he may be going to hell, crying out at the fearful loneliness of death, and then abruptly breaks off in the middle of a sentence. The table rises from the floor and presses against the bed. Ewer takes up the pencil, and as he does so, the dead man's hand moves on top of his hand and guides it, writing upside down.

Then ensues a dialogue where Ewer questions the dead man aloud and in response his hand is manipulated across the paper. Question follows question on the nature of the dead man's impressions, as well as the character of the spiritual world itself. The dead man replies that death releases the spirit into an intermediate state, followed by a final passage to its ultimate haven, which is incomprehensible to us. Some of the questions are not answered.

The story ends with the corpse abruptly *speaking:* "Great Heavens! — I am — I am — *leaving my Universe!* My out-creations die from around me! — I am passing to the next — O Where! — *where!* — I am Dying! — dy---Fare---"

A cyclone of letters descended upon Nos. 111 and 113 Montgomery Street, San Francisco, where *The Pioneer* was now published by Messrs. Lecount & Strong who had bought into the company. A very heavy percentage of the letters were convinced the story was *absolutely true* and among the believers was the editor of one of the leading spiritualist magazines of the day (there were at least a dozen of them, including *The Christian Spiritualist, The New England Spiritualist, Spirit of the Age, The Oneida Circular, Bizarre, For Fireside and Wayside, Spirit Messenger and Harmonial Guide, Spiritual Telegraph,* and others).

J. W. Edmonds (commonly referred to as Judge Edmonds, though whether he was a real Judge or whether that was actually his first name was never quite clear), reprinted "The Eventful Nights of August 20th and 21st" in the November and December, 1854 issues of his magazine *The Sacred Circle,* asserting it was irrefutably true and that Ewer was an "unconscious medium," who had been granted the great gift of being able to communicate with the spirit world. He said that in his own right he had contacted John T. Lane in the spirit world, conducted several interviews with him, and could authenticate everything that Ewer had written. In view of his own experience, he asserted it would have been "utter folly" not to have believed it.

The Sacred Circle was published in New York City (1854-56) with the assistance of a Dr. Dexter and O. G. Warren. *The Christian Spiritualist,* another New York publication, edited by Mr. Toohey, also *confirmed the story as true* and in addition there were reprintings in several magazines and newspapers across the country.

Because the two leading proponents of the factuality of the story published in New York, the focus of events shifted clear across the continent from San Francisco to New York City. That was why Ewer wrote a letter of explanation to the renowned editor of *The New York Herald,* James Gordon Bennet, which was published in the March 12, 1855 edition of that newspaper. In his letter he stated that his story was pure fiction, that several of his friends had watched him working on the story. That it was never presented as anything other than fiction. That there was no such person as John T. Lane in San Francisco and had never been. He pointed out that Edmonds had for years alleged to have very carefully weighed all "testimony" concerning spiritualism and had gained the confidence of a great number of people. This situation had confirmed beyond any hope of contradiction that Judge Edmonds was "incapable of judging testimony touching spiritualism carefully and not only one whose mind can be easily tossed about by the designing, but, as in this instance, to be one who is anxious to deceive himself."

In a bravely pathetic admission, Judge Edmonds wrote from his offices at 85 Chambers Street a reply which appeared in the March 14 edition of the *New York Herald.* In it he freely admitted that he was completely taken in. In defense he said that he was a victim of entrapment. Copies of *The Pioneer* with the article had been deliberately hand-delivered to him. He had received a letter from Lecount, whom he later found to be one of Ewer's co-publishers, attesting to the integrity and veracity of Ewer, that "he was a gentleman utterly incapable of perpetrating a fraud." Edmonds failed to explain how he had twice gotten in touch with the spirit of the imaginary John Lane. A short time later in a letter dated April 16, 1855, Ewer refused to let Edmonds off the hook, asking why his "theories" of spiritualism clearly presented as *fiction* had to be falsified into fact?

A short time later Judge Edmonds died and some felt that it was as a direct result of the complete and utter humiliation he had received at the hands of Ewer.

To add some whip topping to the pudding, on April 16, 1855, *The San Francisco Chroncile* published a letter signed merely "A", which asserted there was indeed a man named John F. Lane, his brief biographical sketch could be found in the list of "graduates of the Military Academy" published in 1850. This man served as a Colonel in the Florida War commanding a regiment of Mounted Creek Volunteers and died by his own hand, October 19, 1836 at Fort Lorane, Florida. Possibly *that* was the Lane that Judge Edmonds had communicated with in two seances.

Milking the situation for all it was worth, Ewer reprinted in the May, 1855 issue of *The Pioneer,* "The Eventful Nights of August Twentieth and Twenty-First," together with the most pertinent correspondence relating to it. He even wrote a brief sequel titled "Flown: A Reverie," in which he has taken in the little girl Jane and raised her as his own. The child had grown to be very happy and loved him, but illness took her away: "When she had passed, it seemed like the ceasing of exquisite music."

There were now accusations that Ewer had derived his idea from Edgar Allan Poe's "The Facts in the Case of M. Valdemar," first published only nine years before in *The American Review* for December, 1845 and since collected in book form. Ewer claimed never to have read that particular Poe story and on looking it up conceded that there were indeed points of similarity, but Poe's story was scientifically explained, whereas his was a true tale of the occult and spiritualism, developed in a completely different manner (which was true). However, he did admit that he had gotten the idea from an essay of Poe's, "The Philosophy of Composition," where Poe describes how he planned and wrote "The Raven." Ewer said he copied Poe's method in writing his story.

In an abrupt about-face Ewer turned back to Episcopalianism again in 1857, was ordained, became a priest, and built Grace Church in San Francisco. So aggressively did he pursue his new calling that he was offered and accepted a position as rector of Christ Church in New York City. He became an advocate of elaborate ritual, condemned both Catholicism and Protestantism, and exulted Episcopalism because of its enlightened view of scientific progress. As far as he was concerned no argument existed between science and religion.

He moved so far to the left (in a religious sense) that he was almost removed. Indignantly he established his own church, St. Ignatius. He was always in the midst of things, even having been arrested as a spy in France in 1870.

When he died at the age of 59, while preaching a sermon in Montreal, he was given one of the most ostentatious funerals ever received by a man of the cloth in the United States. So many clergymen, others faiths as well as Episcopalian, attended, that *hundreds* had to be turned away. His most famous sermon was that in which he fervently implored his fellow men never to give the church the tiniest vestment of political power or permit it to use political influence of any type for its own ends. "There is a blasphemous impertinence in the priest either dictating in prayer to God the will of his people, or, on the other hand, in his ignorance, substituting his own crude, political notions for the great, hidden perfect will of God, and then dictating them as though from God to his people. It is a high crime upon the sacred political freedom of the people and a daring insult to God himself."

Devastating as Ewer's expose of the fallaciousness of the precepts of even the most reputable spiritualists had been, the subject manifested itself in whirlpools of excitement in many metropolitan centers of the United States during the 1850's and San Francisco was one of the most active. San Francisco had undergone two periods when the citizens formed vigilante committees to deal with an unbearable wave of criminality that innundated the city in the wake of the Gold Rush. The first was in 1851 and the second in 1856. Two prominent members of the vigilantes were Col. J. P. Manrow, a colorful character who would ride forth daily with the hounds dressed in an English riding habit; and the other was William H. Rhodes, a well-liked attorney who spent more time writing under the pen-name of Caxton for the California press than attending to his legal duties. Rhodes was to eventually achieve fame in the seventies as the West Coast's leading science fiction writer.

Manrow conducted seances at his home, making extravagant claims as to the goings on. He invited Rhodes and a mining engineer named Almarin Brooks Paul to attend one on the evening of September 19, 1856. Robert O'Brien in his book THIS IS SAN FRANCISCO (1948) reported on the extraordinary results. "Together with three female members of Manrow's family they sat in a circle holding hands. Suddenly, knocks were heard in all parts of the room. The table rose a foot from the floor and swung about in mid-air. Sofa cushions flew in all directions, books leaped from the shelves, the doorbell rang violently, and all six present were simultaneously struck on the head with invisible hands or kicked by invisible feet. A book hurtled across the room and struck one of the ladies."

That was scarcely a prelude. The book kept opening to pages containing cryptic passages without the help of any outside agency. They managed to get in touch with the ghost of an old Hawaiian woman named Capitana, who, as a sign of her spiritualistic integrity, caused a bush to begin trembling outside the window and a shadowy apparition momentarily appeared before them. As evidence that they weren't going to be shortchanged, "another shape materialized out of the ground. Its countenance was so hideous and repulsive that everyone but Paul fled from the room in terror" (including our great science fiction author-to-be, Rhodes!).

When they got the courage to reassemble at the table, "soft hands carressed and patted their cheeks... and as many as twelve were counted hovering about the head of a single person."

Regaining their skepticism, Rhodes and Paul returned two more nights in a row and claimed that the same thing, with embellishments, was repeated. O'Brien reports that they never again doubted the authenticity of those events for the rest of their lives, and the Manrow family asserted that peculiar happenings continued for months. Their house became known to the locals as "The House of Demons."

Against this background, two things became evident. The first, the backdrop of spiritual activity and publicity that would understandably cause people to believe that Ewer was telling the truth. Secondly, that his story belongs to the great tradition of hoax stories exemplified by Richard Adams Locke's "The Moon Hoax" *(The Sun,* August 25 to August 31, 1835) and Edgar Allan Poe's "The Balloon Hoax" *(The Sun,* April 13, 1844), though the evidence is inconclusive that Ewer intended a hoax. This "style" of hoax depended upon the story being presented as truth, often in the form of a news feature, with typical headlines and decks.

III. SCIENTIFIC SAN FRANCISCO

Despite the prevalence of spiritualism, scientific inventiveness was also on its way to San Francisco in the form of Fred Marriot, Senior, the founder of the *London Illustrated News* and editor of the London *Morning Chronicle,* who made his way to San Francisco in 1856, and in July of that year published the first issue of *The News Letter.* He had patented a steam-driven flying machine in England 14 years earlier and felt that the United States, particularly near the gold fields, was the place where he could raise enough money to build it. It took years, but he made money and began the construction of his flying machine, which he named the *Avitor.* He formed a corporation called the Aerial Steam Navigation Company in 1866 and in 1869 had obtained a United States patent on his invention. Stock was sold in the company and among its investors was the creator of the San Francisco cable cars, Andrew Hallidie.

Marriot was no hare-brained inventor. He issued invitations for a trial flight and several hundred turned out at Shellmount Park race track on July 3rd, 1869. The *Avitor* was a non-rigid lighter-than-air machine, shaped like the later dirigible with wings as stabilizers. Suspended from the dirigible was a steam boiler and steam engine. The bag was filled with hydrogen and was 37 feet long and 11 feet wide, with the propulsion units on a frame extending down eight feet. A full description of it appears in John Bruce's book GAUDY CENTURY (Random House, 1948). Bruce said of it: "The wings were five feet long and came to points like those of a swallow. They were white cloth on a frame of heavy wire. At the rear was a rudder and elevator, four moveable planes set at right angles. The steam boiler and engine weighed about 84 pounds. Spirit lamps were under the boilers. There was a crank connected by cog wheels with tumbling rods that in turn went to two four-

HISTORY OF THE MOVEMENT 34

foot-long propellers. The propellers were on the wings. There were 1,360 cubic feet of hydrogen in the 'cigar.' " A photo of the *Avitor* appears in MIRROR OF THE DREAM by T. W. Watkins and R. R. Olmstead (1976).

Marriot did not trust any men in the contraption. He started the steam engine and it began to turn the props. The control of the ship was from the ground, via ropes attached to the rudder and elevators. The *Avitor* rose from the ground and flew twice around the race track at about five miles an hour and then was brought back down to the ground.

This was all a prelude to the sale of stock in the company for the following day, appropriately enough, July 4th, 1869. The performance was again repeated in the Mechanics' Pavilion. Marriot planned on 10-day flights to New York and was partial to a bid by engineers Miller & Haley to build a larger vessel capable of carrying 2,500 pounds. He raised only $750 in stock, but the next day a carelessly lighted match blew up the *Avitor* and apparently Marriot abandoned his project.

We say "apparently" because the November 19th, 1896 issue of *The San Francisco Call* devoted an entire page to a flying machine, shaped like a dirigible, with four screws (or propellors), possibly with wings and sporting a bright searchlight, that quietly soared about despite wind and rain. It was seen in Oakland and Sacramento on successive nights and was even said to have landed and ascended again. Some of the stories about the vessel could have been imaginative extensions of the facts, but one thing is incontrovertible: seventeen years earlier Fred Marriot, Senior had successfully conducted several limited, unmanned, powered flights viewed by hundreds, and reported in the press. He was now dead but his son was alive and the technology (and patents) existed to duplicate his *Avitor* and improve about it. It cannot be ruled out that some unknown Frank Reade, Jr. of the late 19th century actually built and flew a powered, lighter-than-air craft with at least limited success. It is also worth mentioning that patents expire in 17 years!

IV. FANTASY IN THE OVERLAND MONTHLY

The most acclaimed West Coast magazine and one of the longer-lived ones was *The Overland Monthly*. Its fame resulted predominantly from the fact that Bret Harte was one of its trio of editors and in its second issue, August, 1968, it had run "Luck of the Roaring Camp," the story of the rough-and-ready miners working at raising the child of a prostitute. This made his reputation and that of the magazine. The appearance of "The Outcasts of Poker Flat" in the January, 1869 issue left no doubt that here was a voice of the West of considerable talent.

The magazine was patterned after *Harper's* and *Atlantic*, carried very few illustrations but quite a readable content. One of the editors was Noah Brooks, who had previously edited the famed San Francisco newspaper *Alta California*, a daily. Born in Maine October 24, 1830 Brooks had come to California and established himself as a newspaperman. Extremely likeable, he was popular with almost everyone. He was to go on to contribute to the leading magazines of the period, including *Century*. Within a few years he became a regular contributor of boy's stories to *St. Nicholas* magazine, and these enjoyed a great popularity in hard cover, THE BOY EMIGRANTS (1876) being highly regarded even today. He was a friend of Abraham Lincoln and was to write an important book on him, ABRAHAM LINCOLN AND THE DOWNFALL OF AMERICAN SLAVERY (1894). He would return east and become prominent as an editor as well as a writer. He died August 16, 1903. All this introduction is because it is just possible that he wrote and had published the first science fiction story on the West Coast, "The Diamond Maker of Sacramento," which appeared in the very first, July, 1868 issue of *Overland Monthly*.

In "The Diamond Maker of Sacramento," a young man builds

a laboratory-model machine in which he *succeeds* in artificially manufacturing tiny diamond crystals. He forms the California Diamond Crystallization Company, and begins construction of a production model. Considerable believable detail on the theory and physical construction of the machine is woven into the story, lending a willing suspension of disbelief. When the Grand Machine is finally completed, the eight major stockholders travel to the location of the machine in a lone and desolate secret spot. A gigantic battery holds the electric power to motivate a giant sphere of bubbling compound. The lever is turned and the machine blows up, almost killing the inventor. He realizes he has not built the apparatus strong enough to hold the sudden and tremendous release of electricity, but his backers are no longer interested in another try. They desert him, and after years of illness, he dies while trying to give his wife the formula that will produce diamonds.

The story was more prophecy than science fiction, because we *can* produce diamonds now. The story is little known and probably has never been reprinted, despite its excellent quality. If one needs a diamond-making short story for an anthology, they select "The Diamond Maker" by H. G. Wells *(Pall Mall Budget,* 1894) or a novel for discussion, THE DIAMOND MASTER by Jacques Futrelle (1909). The most fascinating sidelight to the story was the comment of Noah Brooks in his article "Early Days of 'The Overland,' " *(Overland Monthly,* July, 1898) that it was "founded on the actual experience of a California genius who actually did produce diamond dust by exploding carbonic acid gas under enormous pressure."

"The Haunted Valley" by Brooks which appeared in the September, 1868 *Overland Monthly* was a pastoral fantasy and extremely well done. George Wilder, an artist, goes into the Sierra mountains to sketch, hunt, fish and "botanize." He wanders into a remote valley, with a beautiful waterful, behind which is a cave. Entering and looking out from the cave, he sees a gigantic shape, the face of a man bearing a noble forehead, white temples and hair, blue and tender eyes, with a face both stern and kindly, indicating great vigor despite advanced age. The impression is one of "goodness." The immense face and shoulders fill the mouth of the cave and then dissolve.

The artist sees the face and shoulders several more times, once floating above the tree tops. He meets a trapper, Mariposa Bill Williams, and while speaking to him, the shape materializes above a cascading waterfall, but Williams sees nothing. One final time the shape appears above a waterfall, with its mighty dignity, winning smile, glorious beauty, air of Godliness and suggestion of deep humanity. He runs toward it, a rotting wooden bridge collapses beneath him, and he plunges to his death. Noah Brooks was a fine writer and had he continued to write science fiction and fantasy the field would have been richer by a number of excellent stories.

"A Pioneer of 1920" by Harwood Lathrop in the April 1870 issue of *Overland monthly*, was another tale of fascination to science fiction lovers. In the opening of the story, Lathrop mentions "The Arabian Nights, Gulliver's, Munchausen and 'Hale's Syborean-stay-at-home-theory,' " indicating the derivation of his approach. The story is told by a man in the year 1920, looking back on the destruction of San Francisco by an earthquake in 1870. It is hard to find historical data, for there is a general suppression of books of the old days. A new quake tosses up the remains of several old railroad cars, and he rides one down the river to San Francisco, which is now an island in the center of a lake.

The people there call themselves "The Pioneers," and those left alive after the quake and their descendants have grown ever larger in size and enjoyed a prolonged life which brings about boredom. There is an acceleration in rate of growth and size of vegetables and fruits. Peas planted in February are ready to harvest in two weeks. Apples are so large that they are sold by the slice. Taxation is extremely heavy, but it is not used for anything in particular, merely piled up in the treasury. "The Land of Sundown," as the place is called, feels isolated and wishes that it had more contact with the outside world. Continuing his travels, the protagonist interests the King of Honolulu, who promises he will send forth an expedition. Despite the foregoing, the story was mediocre, and Lathrop only had one other contribution to the magazine.

The Overland reinforced the observation that San Francisco during that time was much more interested in spiritualism, occultism and the supernatural than in science fiction. "Hu Huwan's Ghost" by Samuel Williams (January, 1869), tells of the spirit of a Welshman which returns to reveal the name of his murderer; "The Water-Witch" by George F. Emory (July, 1869) relates the powers of a Mexican peasant to find water with a dowsing rod; "Jem Catherwoods' Spirits" by Mrs. J. J. Robbins (January, 1870) deals with the refusal of the title character to participate in a seance. He had attended one with a family in San Francisco at one time and envisioned his friend dead with blood on his shirt in the foyer, then also viewed the same friend battered to death by a highwayman. This last vision repeats itself at another seance and recurs almost nightly in his dreams, so he will have nothing further to do with seances, thank you; "A Phantom Tragedy" by Josephine Clifford (February, 1871), is a well-told story of a young man visiting an uncle in an old castle and witnessing the phantom re-enactment of an old family fight and murder; "An Unexplained Mystery" by Mrs. J. J. Robbins (March, 1871) finds a couple, because of finances, forced to stay in a house for a month where *every* night there are terrible noises on the second floor, furniture is thrown about, stealthy footsteps descend the staircase, and bloody hand prints appear on various objects; "The Spectre of Nevada" by John Manning (May, 1871) tells of a New York visitor staying with a friend in Virginia City who is visited by a smiling household apparition who does not leave until she makes them understand that she was the first wife of his friend, and in the process frightens her murderer, a jilted suitor, into committing suicide.

 The Overland Mcnthly also had as a regular contributor Leonard Kip, who had visited California in 1849 by way of Cape Horn. He had a brother, Bishop Kip, in residence, and had lived in the San Francisco area for a number of years before going to Albany, N.Y., contributing to *The Argus* of that city. In recent years he has been rediscovered and it is now understood that he is a minor figure in the development of science fiction of the nineteenth century, several outstanding examples having been included in his collection HANNIBAL'S MAN AND OTHER TALES, published by The Argus Company, 1878.

 All the stories in this volume are science fiction, fantasy or supernatural, but the imaginative masterpiece is "The Secret of Apollonius Septrio," which anticipates Olaf Stapledon. Appolonius Septrio was a man killed by members of the inquisition because he claimed he had lived 600 years and knew a way to extend it to 1,000. He had prepared a description of his method in a book, of which a copy survived. The man who discovers it puts its information to use on himself and his wife, and they live on for thousands of years, watching not only changing events but a continuing evolution of man to the point where they grow wings and bear no resemblance to the species of origin. Tired of merely living the years through, he makes quantum leaps into the future by putting himself into suspended animation. His wife does not accept his method, and on his final awakening, he is so different from the rest of mankind that they regard him as a new species and lock him in a cage. Among those who view him curiously is his wife, who has evolved and is now eight feet tall, of darker hue, and sports drooping wings!

Kip was an *Overland* "regular," and among his stories were two that were harbingers of some of his later fantasies. "An Unincorporated Association" had certain of the elements that would make the work of Edward Page Mitchell and John Collier so popular. A man with a perfect darling of a mother-in-law living with him, a woman loved by the children, cherished by himself, moves into a new town. Everyone there shuns him for no apparent reason, and it appears that the result may be disastrous to his business. He is finally told it is because he has a mother-in-law and that everything will be different if he gets rid of her. He kills her in the most kindly fashion possible and finds that the attitudes of everyone in the town change toward him. He is taken into the "Association," which is composed of the finest people, all of whom have killed their mother-in-law. *Non-members* who are known to be about to kill their mothers-in-law are not hindered, but are arrested and suitably punished afterward. The story ends when a nearby town asks for a charter and aid to form their own chapter of the Association.

Very close to science fiction is "Treasure Trove" (June, 1870). An appreciative alchemist gives two vials of chemicals to a Burgomaster who has done him great favors. One imparts youthfulness and the other turns matter it comes in contact with into gold. An

80-year-old servant drinks the youth potion and the Burgomaster inadvertently washes down a dinner of sliced cucumbers with the formula for conversion of matter into gold. Within a couple of days the much more youthful servant runs off with the maid, and the doctor conducting an autopsy of the Burgomaster puzzles over how he swallowed so many gold chips resembling slices of cucumber.

Kip had already moved into better-paying markets, his novelette "A Pompeian Enigma" appearing in the April, 1870 issue of the nationally-known New York-based *Putnam's Magazine*. It was a tale of the discovery of a well-preserved figure in the volcanic ash of Pompei, of which a "modern" girl is not only a replica, but a reincarnation.

V. AMBROSE BIERCE

Though Ambrose Bierce had been an active journalist on the San Francisco scene for a number of years, his first credited work of fiction, "The Haunted Valley," was to appear anonymously in *Overland Monthly* for July, 1871. It dwelled on a drunken saloon owner, with a fearful prejudice against the Chinese. He had killed one who worked for him with an axe, and had been exonerated. The story turns on the point that the "chinaman" was a woman he had won in a San Francisco card game, and the axe was wielded against a man he thought was "making" her on the grass of a valley near where he was building a home. The man was actually removing a tarantula from the sleeve of the woman, and its bite caused him to move out of the way of the axe as it descended.

Though there were elements of horror in the story, and irony, too, the supernatural element upon which Bierce's final reputation would rest was not yet present. Bierce was born June 24, 1842 in Meigs County, Ohio. He served with the North in the Civil War with distinction, emerging as a Major. He liked military life while in action, but his observed after-effects of the Civil War on the country and the participants contributed towards his subsequent black and bitter moods. Moving West, he was one of the few honest treasury agents sent to the South after Reconstruction. He saw and endured enough to make him permanently and bitterly cynical about all men and all causes. His confidence in the concept of democracy (which he would later satirize), was undermined by laws passed in the South giving only Negroes, carpetbaggers and those Southerners who had remained provably loyal to the Union the right to vote in city and state elections. That was the period when scores of Negroes who could neither read nor write were elected as mayors of cities and sent to the legislature in Washington, D.C., because most Southern whites were deprived of the vote. The later Jim Crow laws grew out of these actions and the ill-considered advantages the Negroes took of them, as much as any other factor.

Bierce, after the Civil War, traveled to Panama, worked under his old Army General in Congressionally-funded surveys westward from Omaha for logical railroad routes, ending up in San Francisco. His work with the Treasury department in the South enabled him to secure a job as night watchman at the San Francisco mint. Up to this time, Bierce boasted only one year of higher education at a military school, and his diaries display word usage and spelling weaknesses that made it seem that journalism was the last career he could aspire to. But he instigated a continuous program of self-improvement and began creating and polishing writing skills. He also became a passable professional cartoonist before he ever sold anything of prose or poetry. His first placements were poetry in 1867, and by 1868 he was a contributor to *The Golden Era, The Californian* and the newspaper *Alta California*. He assisted Bret Harte in putting out the early issues of *Overland Monthly,* but his first big break, which came in 1868, was securing the editorship of the *News-Letter,* published by Marriot who was to later build and fly the first powered lighter-than-air vessel on the West Coast and possibly in the country.

Bierce was to abruptly leave the San Francisco scene following his courtship of Mollie Day and marriage to her December 25, 1871. His father-in-law, Captain Holland H. Day, had given the couple a $10,000 wedding gift. Bierce's last "Town Crier" column for the *News-Letter* appeared in March, 1872, and he was off to England, where, utilizing letters of introduction from Marriot, he quickly involved himself with the literary and Bohemian set and soon became a frequent contributor to *Figaro* and later editor of the magazine *Lantern,* which lasted only two issues. He enjoyed London, despite the ill-effect upon his life-long asthmatic condition, but his wife did not and by the end of 1875 had returned to America pregnant and thereby forced his own permanent return.

VI. WILLIAM HENRY RHODES: LANDMARK SCIENCE FICTIONEER

The first West Coast giant in science fiction was William Henry Rhodes, the San Francisco lawyer who had been writing under the pen name of Caxton since 1852, though not science fiction. Caxton wrote stories, poems and essays in the grand Victorian manner. The editor of *Overland*, Bret Harte, in his own fiction and in that of his contributors, strove for a more regional, American, colloquial style. He decided that Rhodes was not for his magazine. This was no mistake, considering the wordy Victorian-style material Rhodes had been writing for *The Golden Era, The Pioneer* and *The Hesparian*, but it probably lost *Overland* the distinction of being the birthplace of Californian science fiction. Up until 1871, Rhodes had published no science fiction, though the June, 1855 issue of *The Pioneer* had included his fantasy "A Pair of Myths," the first a pastiche of Washington Irving's Rip Van Winkle, wherein Black Hal, addicted to "Nine-Pins," bowls a game against a forty-foot giant from the Norse Myths; and the second a parable in which Adam and Eve figure as the chief characters.

The Sacramento Daily Union, one of the most prestigious and influential of early California newspapers, on page 3 of its edition for Saturday, May 13, 1871, in the first column, published an account headed simply: "The Case of Summerfield." It was prefaced by an introductory note: "We are indebted to a correspondent at San Francisco for the particulars of the most interesting case that has ever come within our observation as public journalists — that of Gregory Summerfield, or, as he was called at the time, 'The Man With a Secret.' This was immediately followed with a letter to the Editors which stated: "A few hours previous to the death of that distinguished lawyer, Leonidas Parker, of this city, he placed in my hands for publication the following manuscript, requesting me, at the same time, to select a journal of the widest circulation for its publication. Yours, etc., W. H. R."

A report was "reprinted" from the *Auburn Messenger* of November, 1870 (when the story was later published in book form, the date was made more specific as November 1, 1870) telling of a case brought before Justice of the Peace James G. Wilkins, concerning Leonidas Parker, who was believed to have pushed Gregory Summerfield, a man of about 70 years of age, to his death from the platform of a train of the Pacific Railroad "overlooking the North Fork of the American River, at the place called Cape Horn." After questioning Parker in a secret session for more than two hours, the Judge discharged the prisoner with no further comment.

The secret document now purported to give the reasons behind the Judge's strange decision. Summerfield had visited Parker in his offices and given a demonstration of a chemical he had discovered that would cause water to burn and create a chain reaction. If it were thrown into the Pacific Ocean, it would literally spread until it had burned up the world. He pours a liquid from a vial into a bowl of water on the table and combustion instantly takes place and every drop of water is consumed.

Summerfield states he will destroy the planet if not paid a huge sum of money. Before the leaders of San Francisco's institutions he duplicates his experiment, burning up a small lake near the city.

The leaders of San Francisco are only able to raise half the money and they ask Summerfield to go with them by train to New York to secure the rest. He agrees and it is on this trip that Parker deliberately pushes him to his death, so as to free the world from future blackmail. It was upon hearing the foregoing story that Justice of the Peace James G. Wilkins released Parker on what amounted to justifiable homicide.

The story was copied by *The Sacramento Reporter*, a competing paper, that same afternoon and other California papers followed. The result was alleged to have been creation of panic in the populace, as most accepted the story as true. The very thought that such an invention could exist caused widespread consternation.

Over the weekend reporters on *The Sacramento Reporter* figured out the identity of the author from the initials "W.H.R." and exposed it as a "Caxtonian Triumph" in the May 16, 1871 edition. Instead of issuing a horse laugh, the *Sacramento Union* replied on May 18, 1871, with a solemn note from "W.H.R." offering to show any "honest inquirer" to his offices at 21 Wright Street, San Francisco, "positive proofs of the chief facts stated therein. I have the original draft of poor Parker's confession in my possession, with the names of the committee in full, and also a list of subscribers to the "Summerfield Fund." He tossed off a few names with their affiliations, as a teaser.

The matter was not dropped there but a headline appeared on the first column, page 2 of *The Sacramento Daily Union* for Saturday, June 10, 1871, reading: "The Summerfield Case Again." It shook the masses to their respective footwear by presenting a series of documents, depositions and statements which indicated that the notorious bandit Black Bart had gotten to the body of Summerfield before the authorities and was believed to have removed a vial of the chemical that could turn the oceans aflame.

Had Rhodes been welcome at *The Overland Monthly*, it is doubtful that he would ever have written the type of science fiction he did. It is also possible that even if "The Case of Summerfield" had appeared in *The Overland Monthly*, it might not have had the spontaneous reaction from the public. On the other hand, it is entirely conceivable that such material might have given the declining *Overland* the boost that could have avoided the hiatus that occurred in December, 1875. For Rhodes had now found his forté and would vigorously continue writing science fiction until Bright's Disease cut his life short at the age of 53, April 14, 1876.

Rhodes was born at Windsor, Bertie County, North Carolina on July 16, 1822, son of Col. Elisha A. Rhodes and Maria Ann Jacocks. His mother died when he was but six. He first attended Princeton, but was removed when his father was appointed United States Consul at Galveston, Texas, before that country became part of the United States. He returned to Princeton, leaving it for Harvard Law School in 1844 at the age of 22, terminating there in 1846. While at Harvard he had published in 1846 THE INDIAN GALLOWS AND OTHER POEMS, from Edward Walker, New York, in a handsome, illustrated edition. He regarded the book as a salute to the Indians, whom he felt were "rapidly passing away."

Upon leaving Harvard, he returned to North Carolina for a short time to practice law and then shifted to Galveston, Texas, where he received an appointment as Probate Judge, undoubtedly through the influence of his father and their mutual acquaintanceship with Sam Houston. That he knew Houston extremely well was underscored when he ripped to shreds a book titled THE LIFE OF SAM HOUSTON, published anonymously by J. C. Derby, New York, in the September, 1855 issue of *The Pioneer*. He proved the book a self-plagiarism by C. Edwards Lester of his book published in 1847 and tore apart its authenticity stating: "Knowing Sam Houston, as I have known him for the last fifteen years, in the varied characters of President and Senator, inebriate and teetotaler, Indian and madman, I had been led to believe that his wardrobe was at length exhausted; and I confess my astonishment to behold him appear in a new dress, aspire after wider notoriety, appropriate yet more extensive honors, affect still sublimer titles, and with his usual effrontery, after deluding his biographer with the *ruse*, attempt to foist himself upon the world as *the one* hero of the Texian revolution, and the sole bulwark of the American Union. . . . In his happier hours — for even Sam Houston has had sober moments — he has been heard to award to Stephen F. Austin those honors . . ." In an impassioned, bitter review, Rhodes denounced Houston for pocketing Indian funds while in Congress and being brought up on charges for it, and starving the Indians, bludgeoning a fellow legislator and being fined for it, hobnobbing with the Indians so he could double-deal them, working *against* annexation and when it was an accomplished fact claiming it was due to his efforts. In the papers of Rhodes, there is undoubtedly information if not already known to historians at least confirmatory of what they have found concerning Houston.

He left Texas for New York, went back to Windsor, then moved to California in 1850. He began the practice of law in San Francisco and the contribution of poems, essays and letters to the local newspapers. He gained fame with a series of political letters to the *Daily Alta California* beginning in 1853 and continuing through 1854 and

1855, dedicated to the American Party of California, a fusion party of Whigs and Democrats, "Fraternized for the first time since the Revolution, for the perpetuity and prosperity of the union," and published under the name of Caxton. These letters were collected in a brochure of 18 pages in small type, probably in 1855.

The year 1856 found him one of the most active members of the San Francisco Vigilance Committee. The Law again proved incapable of coping with the rampant crime and the citizens took justice into their own hands. History records that they did a phenomenally good job of it, acting decisively but without excesses and temporarily sent the worst elements in the community seeking a safer haven. A friend of Rhodes' was the Chief Justice of the State of California, David S. Terry. The two of them had worked in the same law office in Texas. A Sergeant of the Vigilance Committee, Stephen A. Hopkins, with two soldiers, attempted to arrest Reuben Maloney, who was wanted as a witness in the illegal seizure of government arms entrusted to him by an unauthorized party. Judge Terry drew a gun, and Hopkins tried to wrestle it from him. Terry then pulled a knife and stabbed Hopkins. The wound was so severe that it seemed it would be fatal. The Vigilance committee seized the violent Judge, held him prisoner for seven weeks, until it appeared certain Hopkins would recover, then put him on trial.

The Committee wanted to either hang or banish the Judge from the community in disgrace. Rhodes went to work to save him. As a power in the Masonic order, of which Terry was a member, Rhodes convinced them to bring all their influence on his behalf. He kept his fellow journalists from crucifying Terry in the press and with his own persuasion as an unquestioned loyal and active member of the Vigilantes, secured Terry's release. Far from being grateful, Terry never spoke to Rhodes again.

Rhodes' actions on behalf of Terry gained him an enemy in the form of the *Daily Evening Bulletin.* Its publisher, James King, had been murdered for trying to reveal the corruptness of the San Francisco scene, and it was his death that caused the re-forming of the Committee of Vigilance. Rhodes, who was editing the short-lived paper, *The Daily True Californian* published by Washington Bartlett (May 26, 1856 to July 23, 1856), came under fire from

Thomas S. King, the brother of the murdered man, for his activities to save Judge Terry, in the June 26, 1856 edition of the *Bulletin.* Ironically, Rhodes wrote a memorial song with music by R. Herod to the memory of James King, which was published and sold by W. H. Oakes in 1856. The sheet music, handsomely printed, was titled "He Fell at His Post Doing Duty. Words by Caxton. Written on the Death of James King of William." He had also written a poem asking for vengeance for the murdered King in the Saturday, May 17, 1856 *Daily Evening Bulletin.*

Blasting Rhodes on a regular basis was the *Daily California Chronicle,* edited by Frank Soula. The two fired literary salvos at one another. Lack of support found Rhodes' *Daily True Californian* in bankruptcy. The *Daily California Chronicle* survived it by only a few weeks, but like a sinking battle ship, kept blasting away in prose and poetry at Rhodes, until bankruptcy stilled its militancy.

Though Rhodes had enemies in the political arena, he could have gained grass-roots support from the people of Northern California had he ever run for office, because his literary proclivities made him a mixer. Wherever there was a special occasion, there was Rhodes giving a speech and writing a special poem for the event. He was said to be an excellent speaker, with fine diction and voice, an excellent head of hair, an Uncle Sam beard and fine features. When he spoke he never relaxed but remained as tense as a coiled spring. This was sometimes discomfiting to the listeners who half expected him to take off. He appeared at most rallies of the Irish, writing poems to their past glory for each event and rendering them with every ounce of emphasis he possessed. He showed up at agricultural meetings in Sacramento, with a poem to the bounty of California soil. If a ship was to be launched, Rhodes was there with an appropriate verse. When an Atlantic Cable celebration was held in San Francisco in 1858, Rhodes' muse rose to the challenge. Wherever there was a women's club in need of an inspirational bit of verse, Rhodes was always available.

California bred a substantial crop of women writers, so many able ones, in fact, that by 1890 The Pacific Coast Woman's Press Association was a large and vigorous organization. The first magazine published by a woman on the West Coast was *Athenaeum,* a weekly that lasted a single issue. *The Hesperian,* published twice a month by Mrs. F. H. Day, beginning with the April 1, 1858 issue, was to last a bit longer, continuing into 1862, and considering the state of San Francisco publishing, be regarded as a modest success. Subtitled "A Journal of Literature and Art," it attracted the attention of Rhodes, who, writing as Caxton, contributed some solid pieces for it, including "The Discovery of the Pacific Ocean" (March, 1859) and "The Two Georges," August, 1859 (contrasting George Washington with King George the Third). Certainly his most interesting is "Prophecies" (July, 1860), where he attempts to interpret the predictions in a work called "Les Prévision d'un Solitaire," written by a monk named Philip Olivarious and published in 1544. These prophecies are very much like those of Nostradamus, possessing great ambiguity and some near misses. They extend through to 1903, and since the article was published in 1860, it gave Rhodes a great topic to expound upon. Most of the predictions dealt with events in France and apply particularly to Napoleon, one of the forecasts stating: "But never will the warrior bear up against the state of the weather, and behold the third part, and again the third part of his army has perished by the cold of the almighty. Two lustrums have passed since the age of desolation; the widows and the orphans have cried aloud to the Lord, and behold God is no longer deaf. The mighty that have been humbled take courage, and combine to overthrow the man of power. Behold the ancient blood of centuries is with them, and resumes its place and its abode in the great city. The man of power returns humbled to the country beyond the sea from which he came. God alone is great."

A notice in the April, 1859 issue reported that Rhodes had completed a play founded upon the rise of Mormonism. It was not produced but Rhodes read it under the title of "The Mormon's Prophet" at Tucker's Academy of Music on September 8, 1860 specifically, and through published hints probably before and after that date. Another unproduced play titled "Lucky Miners, or, the Old Dominion and the New" was read at the Metropolitan in Sacramento, September 18, 1860, so we see the range of Rhodes' literary interests knew no boundaries.

It is entirely within the realm of possibility that Rhodes' frequent contributions to *The Hesperian,* in effect a woman's literary magazine, either reflected or contributed to a more serious interest in the opposite sex. Objectively he would have seemed to rank high on the list of eligible bachelors: a lawyer by profession, an author, newspaperman, poet, orator, with a manly build, handsome and distinguished features. Despite this, he was married relatively late. He was 37 when he took the hand of Susan Harrison at Oroville, California on December 29, 1859.

There were four children, Ann H., the oldest, who was already teaching at Valencia Street Grammar School in 1877. The second child, a son, was named Arthur Pym, after Edgar Allan Poe's uncompleted novel, and he was working as a clerk by 1881, entered college as a law student in 1883, and by 1886 had law offices at 16 Montgomery Ave. in San Francisco. By 1891 he had evidently failed at the practice of law and was working as a clerk again, then in succeeding years was a real estate agent, a weigher at the San Francisco Customs Houses, a salesman and a deputy registrar. William Henry Rhodes, II, began his working career as a clerk and bookkeeper in 1882, and remained in that capacity until 1897 when he became Superintendent, Vault Dept., California Safe Deposit and Trust Company, finally entering the insurance brokerage business in 1919. Raleigh began working as a clerk in 1885 and set up as an attorney in 1892, in the same offices at 417 Montgomery with his brother Arthur Pym, who was then in real estate. No record of Raleigh can be found from 1893 on, so he either died or moved from the city. Virtually all birth and death records were lost in the San Francisco Earthquake of 1907, making people difficult to trace.

The family name was carried forth by the family of Arthur Pym, for he had a son Arthur Pym, Jr. and named a second son Caxton Pond. At this writing Caxton Pym Rhodes, II and Caxton Pond Rhodes III still reside in Southern California, living monuments to their distinguished ancestor.

Rhodes found supporting four children no easy task. His predilection for literature detracted from his law practice, and while he was paid for some of his efforts, the amounts were not great. Writing a memoir of Rhodes in *The San Francisco Bulletin* for January 2, 1897, George E. Barnes, an old friend of his, said: "I recollect, while sitting at lunch one day, Rhodes complained about the meagreness of business, and mentioned his failure to obtain a court commissionership, for which he had applied, and which was given to a comparative stranger in the State.

" 'Can you tell me the reason why I am thus overlooked?' he inquired of a friend. 'I am posted in the law; I have been in the State since 1850, and why am I being let alone where business is concerned?' "

His friends gave him a straight answer: "There is no money in California, my dear fellow, for literature, as you very well know, but there are large rewards in the law when closely pursued, and when you have gained a reputation for application."

In 1871 on the occasion of his 12th wedding anniversary, like any other special event, he wrote a poem for his wife titled "Our Wedding Day," which included the revealing stanza:

> 'Tis true, our home is humble, Sue,
>   And riches we have not,
> But children gambol round our door
> And consecrate the spot.
> Our sons are strong and brave, dear Sue
>   Our daughter fair and gay,
> But none so beautiful as you
>   Upon our wedding day.

The poetic muse did not fail him in 1869 when Marriot successfully tested his powered lighter-than-air-craft, The *Avitor*. The poem, quite appropriately titled *"The Avitor,"* foreshadowed his imminent notoriety as a science fiction hoaxer, concluding with the lines:

> No longer shall earth with her secrets beguile,
>   For I, with undazzled eyes
> Will trace to their sources the Niger and Nile,
> And stand without dread on the boreal isle,
>   The Colon of the skies!

> Then hurrah for the wings that never tire —
> For the sinews that never quail;
> For the heart that throbs in a bosom of fire —
> For the lungs whose cast-iron lobes respire
> Where the eagle's breath would fail!

Rhodes managed to get a political position as Secretary to the Governor of California, J. Neely Johnson in 1855 when the Know Nothing Party was in vogue. He was not discreet enough to temper his political writings and the party members forced his dismissal. In 1857 he joined his law practice with that of E. W. Sloan, a former judge, who like Rhodes hailed from South Carolina. They worked together for about six years, with a relatively good practice. It was this "security" that probably made Rhodes feel in 1859 that he could take a wife.

For two years, beginning in 1863, he moved to Virginia City, Nevada, primarily at the behest of the Comet Mill & Mining Company, which was defending itself against a suit which alleged they did not own the ground they operated from. Rhodes received $6,000 for his work on their behalf and on its completion moved back to San Francisco to set up law practice. In the period after his return to San Francisco he also managed to swing an appointment as Court Commissioner of the Twelfth District Court, to supplement his income.

Rhodes' immense popular success with "The Case of Summerfield" in 1871 aroused public interest in the man. It was discovered that the sciences were his passion and he was widely read in them, particularly astronomy and chemistry, and that further he had a small chemical laboratory of his own. It was also self-evident that he should follow up on his success and he did, turning out a series of highly original and well-constructed works of science fiction. The major problem with them has been to discover their place and precise date of publication. All were published between 1871 and his death, and all were published in San Francisco papers, but microfilm is great in saving space but not in preserving text. Most literary works are not microfilmed until they are badly worn and yellowed. The microfilm is subject to constant wear from continuous movement on spindles and deterioration from the heat of the viewer, literally making even the enlarged works unreadable. Add to that the fact that a great deal of newspaper and magazine files were destroyed in the San Francisco earthquake of 1906 and there are often great gaps in the runs that do exist and the problem comes much more sharply into focus than does the type on microfilm.

Clues are sometimes provided by internal evidence of the stories. "The Earth's Hot Center" leads off with a memo dated December 12, 1872, indicating that it appeared in the very early part of 1873. It is close in style to "The Case of Summerfield," for the entire story is also an attempt at a hoax, containing no plot or special characters, but is presumed to be extracts from a report of Gen. Flannagan to the Hon. Hamilton Fish, Secretary of State of the United States. It tells of the formation of the International Board for Subterranean Exploration by France, the United States, Great Britain, Russia and Belgium to determine the exact nature and depth of the earth's crust. Year after year digging continues with diamond drills, nitroglycerine, compressed air, with specially insulated chambers to protect the shovelers from the heat. By November 1, 1872, a depth of 37,810 feet had been attained, but underground detonations forced all work to stop. On November 5th, lava oozes up from the borings and destroys a Belgian town. Two hundred homeless families are financed to emigrate to the United States. It is predicted that eventually all of Holland, Belgium and Denmark will be covered and a natural bridge will connect England with the continent.

The scientific detail was erudite and impressive. The story was intended to be credited as true and was another in the chain of hoaxes.

"Phases in the Life of John Pollexfen" was cast in the format of a story, but strove to give the impression of one based on truth. Like "The Case of Summerfield," it was laid in San Francisco. John Pollexfen is a scientist working on the secret of color photography. He makes a contract with a young girl that when she comes of age she will sell him one of her eyes for $7,500, because he believes he can perfect a color camera using a human eye for a lens. A hitch appears when the girl takes the contract to a lawyer to test its legality. He claims it is against the law but she insists on keeping the contract. Her eye is removed and through its use Pollexfen does discover the secret of color photography. Her fiance comes to kill Pollexfen, but decides to have one of his eyes removed instead so that the girl will not feel inferior to him. Everyone lives happily ever after, including Pollexfen, who even is awarded a pension by Emperor Napoleon the Third for his great invention.

There is a note of the sardonic in the ending of the story, which distinctly separates Rhodes from Victorian moralism. It is a long novelette, well written and developed, centering about a single theme of the unusual while keeping all else in a normal setting.

Probably Rhodes' single best work of fiction is "The Aztec Princess," a 25,000-word novelette, which has to be one of the finest lost-race stories ever written. Inspired by the reports of the discovery of the ruins of the lost Central American ancient Aztec cities Uxmal and Palenque, a young American, Stephens, sets out with an old friend, a Judge, to explore these finds. An apparition of a beautiful Aztec princess appears to them following an earth tremor and she utters a single word: "Palenque!" She then folds her arms across her breasts and disappears.

They take a steamer across Lake Nicaragua, just as the volcano Ometepe erupts. The ship is set afire and it seems they will all perish, when a tremendous mass of water falls on the ship, extinguishing the flames. The volcano in its eruption had belched a vast quantity of water into the air and it had saved them. A guide, Pio, is hired to conduct them to the ruins. Stephens is amazed that Pio can apparently read the hieroglyphics of the ancient Aztecs which have defied the best efforts of the finest scholars. Pio takes them through six miles of underground chambers to the ruins that they seek. The earth trembles and the Aztec princess again appears. She touches Stephens and the two of them rise hundreds of feet into the air and speed across one of the world's vastest forests. Rhodes does not consign himself to fantasy, but devotes a page and a half to a theory of the neutralization of gravity as an explanation. Finally they reach "the white walls of a magnificent city." Thousands of people throng its streets, dressed in garments no white man had ever seen before, but corresponding "precisely with that of the figures in *bas-relief* on the sculptured monuments at Palenque."

The people of the city are baffled as to how he arrived and whether he represents a menace to their civilization. He is taught their spoken language, but not the reading of hieroglyphics, which is a musical language, taught only to royalty. Pio, the guide, abruptly shows up garbed as the others. Pio makes arrangements to have Stephens taught the royal hieroglyphics. He translates segments from their manuscript, including one that states that once the South American and African continents were one mass. That they broke away and were carried by the continental drift great distances from one another. Also in the city is a French explorer, Armand de L'Oreille, sent out on the same mission of discovery as Stephens. The French explorer is sacrificed, but Stephens escapes with the secret of decipering hieroglyphics. He attempts to return once again to the site of the ruins where he had experienced the Aztec princess' visitation and discovers her precise features carved in ancient marble in the moldering stones. Evidently he and the Frenchman had been carried into the past in a time warp and only he had escaped.

The story is extremely well written, displays an extraordinary knowledge of the region, and offers, possibly for the first time, a half-dozen variations on the lost race theme, which have since become cliches. Despite its age, it strikes sparks of imagination and orginality that mark it a classic of its type.

A tale which opens with references to "the palaces of Uxmal and Palenque," labeling it as of the same period, is "Legends of Lake Bigler." It is divided into two parts; the first, an Indian legend, "The Haunted Rock," tells of two tribes that inhabited the opposite shores of what is today known as Lake Bigler. One is the Ako-nitas on the Western shore and the other the Gra-so-po-itas, in what is now the state of Nevada. Marriage between the tribes is forbidden. When the love trysts of the son of the chief of one tribe and the daughter of the chief of the other tribe is discovered, they are sealed in a rock chamber to starve to death. When the chamber was eventually opened, so eerie a sound issued forth that the braves were rendered too fearful to enter.

The second tale, "Dick Barter's Yarn; or, the Last of the Mermaids," claims that human beings once lived in Lake Bigler and that they breathed under water. There was also an amphibious Indian race which was called the Pol-i-wogs, which were a hybrid between the Pi-utes and the lake people. They were few in number and the movement of other Indian tribes destroyed them. A description of the life and habits of the Pol-i-wogs is given, as well as a war they once had with the underwater people. None of them are known to any longer exist. Prepared with a special whistle which is supposed to attract the underwater people, two men venture forth upon the lake. On the third day a giant water serpent appears, chasing a bonafide mermaid. They shoot the mermaid, but the serpent swallows it destroying the evidence, and the dreamer awakes. Despite its ending, it is well told.

"The Telescopic Eye" could have been the last work of science fiction that Rhodes ever wrote and had published, because the story is told in the past tense and is derived from documents dated as late as February 17, 1876. Rhodes died of Bright's Disease, a very serious kidney condition, April 14, 1876 at the age of 53. The reference of his friend, William H. L. Barnes, gives the publication in which "The Telescopic Eye" appears as *The Evening Post*, but research has been unable to locate it there. It again belongs to the hoax school of science fiction, where the extraordinary event is the main focus of the story, with the interleaving of precise dates, names of well-known people, careful scientific explanation, offering the reader the option of regarding it as true, if he is so inclined.

A nine-year-old boy named John Palmer, living in South San Francisco, is believed to have been born blind. He is kept in a darkened room for fear light may damage his eyes beyond the ability of scientific advance to some day remedy them. One night, when the window blind is left up in the room, a full moon makes its appearance and the boy, turning towards it, utters a "sudden, sharp scream." When his parents run to his side, they are told that he can see every object on it, that he has phenomenal telescopic vision. Scientists are called in and the boy describes, in minute detail, a civilization on the moon and the utterly alien, wheel-shaped inhabitants. The "vegetation" is a metallic form of life.

When asked to view Venus, Jupiter and Mars his vision is cloudy and indistinct. It is determined that his eyes focus at 240,000 miles. They set the only major telescope in the city so that it views Mars as it would look at a distance of 240,000 miles and have the boy look through it. "One cry of joy, and unalloyed delight told the story!" Everything on the surface of the Red Planet is now clearly visible to the boy. The story abruptly ends as the reader is imparted that knowledge and no question at all remains that there will be a sequel in an early issue of the paper, describing the wonders of that world, and if the public proved sufficiently receptive, the same technique would be used for the other planets. The derivation of the literary device from Richard Adams Locke's "The Moon Hoax" is too obvious to elaborate upon. There was no question that, in utilizing his technique of the newspaper hoax, Rhodes followed in the footsteps of Locke.

When Rhodes died, he was still a practicing attorney and held the position of Court Commissioner at the Twelfth District Court, 420 California Ave., San Francisco. He resided at 212 Fair Oaks near the corner of 23rd St. Among the papers that ran stories on his death were *The Daily Alta California* for April 15th and 16th, 1876; *The Daily Evening Post,* April 15th; and the *Sacramento Daily Record-Union* for April 15, 1876.

The Twelfth District Court adjourned the entire day April 15, 1876 and three members of the court, including a Judge Blake, eulogized his poetry, his strong style, his deep interest in the sciences, and reaffirmed his honor and integrity.

The Daily Alta California for April 15th noted: "About five years ago, he began to write scientific hoaxes, or accounts of imaginary discoveries, and in their class they rank high.... Much knowledge, a careful regard for scientific probabilities, and study of the laws of evidence — and each made a lively sensation. We shall not be astonished if they were considered worthy of republication in book form."

Already friends, not only of the legal profession but of The Bohemian Club, of which he was a founding member in March, 1872, and where he had delighted the members with an endless stream of occasional poems, were making arrangements to have just such a book published. Whether they guaranteed the financing is not known, but the publisher, A. L. Bancroft of San Francisco, was the largest on the West Coast, and its namesake one of the greatest bibliophiles of all time, who single-handedly collected and saved for posterity every available book, manuscript, city record, letter or script having any bearing on the history of Western America, from Central America on up. He hired an entire team of full-time bibliographers, built a fire-proof, earthquake-proof library on the second floor above his book shop and spent possibly millions of dollars on the accumulation of data, which he eventually issued in 40 volumes, representing the most comprehensive work of its type ever done by anyone at any time. His entire collection was preserved and still exists as a national resource at Berkeley University.

In Volume 38, he stipulates that of a "higher grade are the weird tales of W. H. Rhodes, partly collected in CAXTON'S BOOK, whose ingenious and scientific heft, with many a humorous thread, partake both of Poe and Verne, and have like them found imitators in different directions." This indicates that he may have published the volume on its merit alone. Daniel O'Connell, the 300-pound San Francisco poet and short story writer, who produced features for *The Evening Bulletin* and was with Rhodes one of the founders of The Bohemian Club, undertook to edit the book, appropriately known as CAXTON'S BOOK. All the science fiction and fantasy tales, essays and poems mentioned here, along with other non-fantasies, were collected there. The book must have enjoyed a reasonably good sale, because more than 100 years later copies still turn up in antiquarian bookstores.

"In Memoriam," an informative introduction to the volume, was written by his legal friend William H. L. Barnes. Among other things, Barnes claimed that Rhodes had written science fiction at Harvard as early as 1844, stating: "His fondness for weaving the problems of science with fiction, which became afterwards so marked a characteristic of his literary efforts, attracted the especial attention of his professors; and had Mr. Rhodes devoted himself to this then novel department of letters, he would have become, no doubt, greatly distinguished as a writer; and the great master of scientific fiction, Jules Verne, would have found the field of his efforts already sown and reaped by the young Southern student."

That sounded like an over-expansive build-up by a friend, but in point of fact it had some basis in truth. Nothing by Verne appeared in the United States until 1869 and that was but a limited printing of FIVE WEEKS IN A BALLOON from Lippincott, Philadelphia, which received little attention. It wasn't until AROUND THE WORLD IN EIGHTY DAYS was copied on a daily basis from *Le Temps*, a Paris newspaper, in 1873, that Verne became famous in the United States. *Le Temps* was reported to have tripled its daily circulation during the period it ran the serial, and each chapter was transmitted by transatlantic cable to the United States where it was picked up and run by newspapers across the entire continent. As the novel drew to its conclusion with the journey across the United States, the interest in this country mounted to a feverish pitch and publishers in Boston, New York and Philadelphia scrambled to hastily translate Verne's works and rush them into print. The books were usually pirated with no one paid except the translator, though Scribner's did make arrangements for authorized editions.

A new translation of FIVE WEEKS IN A BALLOON, published by James R. Osgood & Co., Boston, in late 1873, was reviewed in the *Overland Monthly* on the West Coast in the issue of February, 1874. The reviewer stated: "The author of this amusing work has created what may almost be called a new kind of fiction writing, which consists in narrating, with the utmost detail and *varisemblance* of circumstance, utterly impossible adventures — such as his journey of TWENTY THOUSAND LEAGUES UNDER THE SEA, and his present FIVE WEEKS IN A BALLOON.... We are reminded by M. Verne's most entertaining writings of such works as GULLIVER'S TRAVELS, PETER WILKINS, and ROBINSON CRUSOE, but more especially of the two first named, which equally depend for their effect upon an ingenious grafting of the most extravagant fancies upon the soberest realism. But M. Verne adds to his imaginary incidents an imposing familiarity with modern science, which excites special interest if it does not defy incredulity." A review of the authorized Scribner, Armstrong & Co., New

York, translation of FROM THE EARTH TO THE MOON followed in the April, 1874 *Overland Monthly*. Had Rhodes seriously tried to market works of science fiction which he is alleged to have written in his college years as early as 1844, and if his skills reasonably approached his later works, he should have been able to create a reputation, because "The Moon Hoax" had appeared less than a decade earlier in 1835 and Poe's "The Balloon Hoax" the same year (1844), and the public as well as the publishers would undoubtedly have been receptive to such works.

Barnes concludes by saying of Rhodes: "His writings are illumined by powerful fancy, scientific knowledge, and a reasoning power which gave to his most weird imaginations the similitude of truth and the apparel of facts. Nor did they, nor do they, do him justice. He could have accomplished far more had circumstances been propitious to him." Barnes saw clearly and with great regret, that Rhodes possessed an immense untapped potential for this special area of fiction and that everyone lost when he failed to take the plunge and tackle it wholeheartedly.

Despite the diffusion of Rhodes' science fiction works, their collection in book form was to ensure a minor reputation. There is no way to trace the reprinting and copying of his work. It is certain that "The Case of Summerfield," at the time of its first appearance was copied widely by California papers as well as newspapers in other parts of the country and abroad. The story was selected as one of six Western Classics to be reprinted in small, deluxe, hardcover editions by Elder, San Francisco. It appeared in a limited edition of 1,000 copies in 1907 (the year after the San Francisco earthquake), with a frontispiece made into a photogravure from an oil painting of the fictitious Summerfield demonstrating his discovery, executed by artist Galen J. Perrett, and an introduction by the then well-known California authoress Geraldine Bonner. She had read Caxton's book and saw in his stories elements of Fitz-James O'Brien and Edgar Allan Poe, but, of all of them, she felt "The Case of Summerfield" was the one most worth preserving.

This was also the opinion of The Book Club of California, which in 1939 published for its members "Six California Tales," each as a separate, handsomely printed brochure. The second in the series, issued in April, was "The Case of Summerfield," printed by The Windsor Press of San Francisco in a limited edition of 650 copies, with a brief biographical note.

The story was discovered by Anthony Boucher, then editing the new *Magazine of Fantasy and Science Fiction*, and he reprinted it in his third, Summer, 1950 issue, terming Rhodes "in this and other stories one of the great pioneers of modern science fiction."

In England, "The Case of Summerfield" was paraphrased and run in the widely-circulated popular *Pearson's Weekly* for December 3, 1892, printed anonymously under the title of "The Finger of Fate."

In a special Sunday section on California's past literary achievements, *The San Francisco Examiner* for June 4, 1893 reprinted "The Case of Summerfield" complete, as one of the classics worth rereading.

Most important, in 1974, the Hyperion Press, Westport, Conn., reprinted CAXTON'S BOOK with a new introduction by myself, making it available in both hard cover and paperback form for those interested in perusing this early pioneer.

The early death of Rhodes cut short the writing career of a figure who might have eventually scored high in the pantheon of science fiction greats. But the publication of CAXTON'S BOOK was to influence other West Coast writers.

VII. ENTER MILNE

It was less than two years before the death of Rhodes that Robert Duncan Milne first became prominent on the San Francisco scene. What brought him into the city of San Francisco was the Mechanics Institute Fair of 1874, which opened August 18th and ran for 30 days. The Fair was a major event in the city, being held periodically. That year a lot covering four acres of ground, with 550 feet on 8th Street and 275 feet on Mission and Market Streets was leased. A building was erected in which to exhibit the latest the West Coast had to offer in the way of new inventions, machinery, manufactures as well as scientific knowhow. One firm alone displayed 28 steam engines. In addition to the machinery and equipment, tobacco, cotton, home woolens and silks, advances in horticulture, and even a display of local artwork were shown. It was not sponsored by the city but financed by private loans from local manufacturers, businessmen, mine owners and the railroad.

Dressed in the height of European fashion, sporting a mustache, trim, well-built and tanned in appearance, was Robert Duncan Milne, stuttering in the finest Oxford accents, with an occasional interjection of Western lingo. He was billed as an Engineer and he had a *working model* of a rotary steam engine of his own invention on display, in hope of interesting investors. In reporting on it, later accounts stated that it was "pronounced to be the wonder of the fair. This engine was composed of only five castings, two being the cylinder heads; did not occupy more than one cubic foot of space; weighed a little over a hundred pounds, but developed energy enough to run an eight-horse-power shingle machine to which it was belted, the shingles being sawed from the block night after night before the visitors at the fair. It failed, however, to obviate the universal defect inherent in steam engines of the rotary type — namely, leakage, no practical method having yet been discovered of taking the wear and tear of the friction surfaces."

Rotary steam engines were not new, even then, but Milne had invented a more efficient method of gaining compression that proved different enough to enable him to secure a patent. The February 13, 1877 issue of *Specifications of Patents,* published by the U.S. Patent Office, includes as patent 187,402 one called "Compensating-Cranks" issued to Robert Duncan Milne, then of Santa Barbara, California, filed on January 15, 1877. There were nine men to whom he assigned part rights in the patent and they were Edward Graham, W. W. Holister, J. V. Hart, H. S. Greeley, W. S. Chamberlain, E. B. Hall, D. P. Hatch, J. B. Redfield, and H. McLellan. The filing of the patent was witnessed by Olwyn T. Stacy and Frank A. Brooks and included two sketches showing a cross-section of the operation of the compensating crank. The sketches were witnessed by George H. Strong and John L. Boone, and carry, in addition to their signatures, that of Milne. Deway Co. were the attorneys. Of the names that could be checked of those who had been assigned rights to Milne's patent, W. W. Holister was a sheep rancher residing in Santa Barbara, J. V. Hart was a merchant tailor in the same town, and H. McLellan was a Los Angeles insurance agent. Evidently all of these men helped finance the building of Milne's steam engine.

In filing the patent, Milne stated: "The object of my invention is to provide a novel method for the conversion of reciprocating rectilinear motion into rotary motion by a mechanism by means of which the inequality of crank-power is equalized and balanced, in such a manner that the direct pressure of a piston or other motor is transferred to the crank with greater uniformity of action than in the case of an ordinary crank." He claimed two patentable points: 1. The method of equalizing and balancing the varying pressure exerted by a piston or other motor upon a crank during its revolution; 2. The method for utilizing the independent motion of a connecting rod between a crank and its reciprocating motor."

It was obvious that Milne was a man of practical technical application as well as a theoretician. Had Hugo Gernsback been publishing science fiction at that time, he would have found it reassuring to have such a man writing for him. But that was scarcely all that

Milne could have put on his resume. As far as his ancestry and education was concerned, his credentials were impeccable.

Robert Duncan Gordon Milne was born June 7, 1844 at Carlslogie House, described as "a baronial castle which had existed before the days of Robert the Bruce," two miles west of Cupar, in the county of Fifeshire, Scotland. He was the second son of the Reverend George Gordon Milne, M.A., F.R.S.A., who baptized him on September 14, 1844 in the St. James' Episcopal Church in Cupar, a parish his father acted as spiritual guardian to for 40 years. His mother, Elizabeth Anne Kay, was descended from royalty, but not just any obscure bit of royalty. Through the Breadalbane family, here antecedents trace back to King Robert the Bruce, the Scottish king born July 11, 1274 and who died June 7, 1329. As Robert VIII, Bruce was initially loyal to Edward I of England. He began a battle for the liberation of Scotland in 1298, had himself crowned as Robert I of Scotland in 1306, and the same year was defeated by Edward I and exiled to Ireland. He returned in 1807, and following Edward I's death while on the way to confront him, in a brutal and bloody series of battles took most of Scotland from the English and had the independence of Scotland recognized in the Treaty of Northhampton in 1328, after defeating successive British kings Edward II and III. He died one year later of complications brought about by leprosy. In 1333 Edward III reconquered Scotland.

The first Earl of Breadalbane (1635 to 1716), named John Campbell, represented the branch of the family from which Milne's mother had her geneological link to King Robert the Bruce. He was a somewhat unsavory Scottish politician, a traitor employed by the English to bribe the Scottish chiefs into submission to England. He unsuccessfully tried to upend the male heir to the earldom of Caithness; was credited with planning the destruction of the MacDonalds of Glencoe.

The family money seemed to reside in the person of Duncan James Kay, born May 16, 1816 (from whom Milne received his second name) the brother of his mother. Kay, a resident of Drumpark Estate, Parish of Kirkpatrick Iron Grey, Scotland, held the titles of Justice of the Peace and Deputy Lieutenant of the Stewartry of Dumfries (a town) and Kircudright (a county) in Scotland. He was also a Liverpool merchant.

The head of the family, George Gordon Milne, was born March 23, 1801 in Keith Banffshire, son of James Milne and Helen Dean. His wife was born January 13, 1807 at Kinclaven, Perth, the daughter of the Reverend Robert Kay, minister of that Presbyterian parish, and Louisa Stewart. At an undetermined time previous to their marriage George Gordon was an Episcopalian minister at Glasgow, but on the date of their marriage, August 9, 1837 in Cupar, Fife, he was already installed in that parish. The marriage seems to have resulted in enhanced economic status, undoubtedly from the Kay side, for the family lived at Carslogie Castle in considerable affluence.

There was a nursery for the children, of which there were five in addition to Robert Duncan, and the census records show that in 1851 there were also three full-time servants on the premises. The other children were Stewart Spenser, born May 2, 1838; Eliza Margeret, born August 7, 1839; Harriet Madelina, born March 28, 1841; George Gordon, born March 10, 1846; and James Erskine Gordon, born May 2, 1848.

The indications are that the father was not close to his children, for years later Robert Duncan Milne spoke of almost ritualistic procedure where "about the ages of six or seven the children used to be figged up in the nursery and brought by their nurses into the dining room for dessert after dinner." Milne states that he was bundled off to a private school at the tender age of 10.

When it came time to move onto more advanced education, he was enrolled September, 1858, Michaelmas Term, at Trinity College, Glen Almond Valley, Perth, Scotland. Trinity College was Scotland's first independent English-style public school, opened in 1847, and is still in existence. The college was less than 100 miles from Cupar-Fife, which made it convenient, but another reason for sending Robert there was that the school was strongly founded in Episcopalianism and offered lower tuition for sons of clergymen.

Theology was not Robert's forte, but when it came to other subjects he was absolutely brilliant. He attained the Skinner scholarship as the finest Latin student for three years running and in 1860, when he was only 16, entered an inter-school competition for the best student verse written in Latin and won the Knox prize, the top award for the achievement. His prize-winning poem "Clades Variana," all 112 lines of it in virgin Latin, was later printed in *The City Argus* (a San Francisco weekly paper) for December 27, 1890.

He not only was among the most notable scholars in the school, he was also evidently the most popular among the students, for he won the Buccleuch gold medal as a senior in 1862 and was elected Captain of the school. At Trinity he also was captain of the Rugby team, so his interests were athletic as well as academic.

His two brothers also were enrolled at Trinity College, George Lewis Gordon entering Trinity Term, 1860, and James Gordon Milne registering Lent Term, 1861. His two brothers both left the school Christmas, 1862, never to return and with no evidence they were enrolled elsewhere. Robert, though, entered Lincoln College of the prestigious Oxford University on November 6, 1862, at the age of 18.

James, the youngest son, went to sea and rose to the position of quartermaster petty officer in charge of navigational devices and flags. His life was to have a tragic end, terminating at the age of 35, when a ship he was sailing on, the *Drummond Castle* owned by the Castle line, sank off the Franch channel island Usant on June 16, 1869, and out of 250 ship's men and passengers only three were saved.

Robert Duncan Milne had entered Lincoln College with high hopes, but something went wrong. In 1864 he obtained a third in classical moderations, with honours, but apparently left school at the end of that term. He never obtained a degree, for to have conferred upon him a B.A., it was necessary to pass three examinations, but he did not take the last two.

At Lincoln he played on their Rugby team and also was on the school's rowing team, so he obviously was a superior athlete.

The reason for his leaving school without obtaining his degree, according to newspapermen who worked with him in San Francisco, was believed to be related to excessive drinking. There is powerful evidence of this in autobiographical passages in some of the later articles that Milne himself wrote. Despite this, between his time at Trinity and Lincoln, Milne became quite proficient in both Greek and Hebrew, as well as Latin, achievements verified by those who later wrote of him.

It is obvious that something happened in the Milne family in late 1862 when Robert Duncan's two brothers were removed from school after only a few terms. Circumstantial evidence seems to point to the fact that Elizabeth was separated from her husband and taking her daughter and one son, George Gordon with her, left Scotland altogether.

The reason for believing this is that no marriages are recorded for any of the girls in Scotland, nor is there any record in that country of the death of the mother, the girls or the "missing" son. They might have all left Scotland. On the other hand, the death of the Reverend George Gordon Milne occurred October 4, 1872, at the age of 71 of presumed heart disease. He was no longer connected with the Cupar-Fife parish and his address was 3 Rathelpie Row, St. Andrews Parish of St. Leonards. The 1871 census recorded George Gordon Milne living at that address as a *lodger* with two elderly, unmarried retired housekeepers, Margaret and Mary Montiply. The information for the death notice was supplied by his oldest son, Stewart Spenser Milne, then resident in Blairerno, Drumlithie, Fordoun. His mother was then shown as still alive but not in residence. Stewart died on March 15, 1900 in Glenverview, Kincardine of cardiac failure at the age of 62. His occupation was given as Bank Clerk. He had been living for at least 10 years with a distant relative, James Milne, a farmer, as a boarder, and had earlier been listed as an Annuitant, indicating he had been left money by someone.

"Someone" was still taking care of Robert Duncan Milne after leaving Lincoln in 1864, for he attended in 1865 a series of lectures the famed British biologist Thomas Henry Huxley and the British physicist John Tyndall delivered in the British Association lecture hall in London. Huxley placed his stress on chemistry and Tyndall on electricity. Both men were agnostics, advocates of Charles Darwin against the church. Milne reported the impact of those lectures on him in an article titled "When I Heard Huxley" which appeared in the Sunday, July 14, 1895 edition of *The San Francisco Examiner.*

He described Huxley as "tall, angular, abrupt of motion, awkward in gesture, but with a wealth of candid honesty beaming from out a rather heavily bewhiskered face. . . . Tyndall would have his electrical apparatus; Huxley his chemical. . . . Both were brimful of meat and illustrated with all the apparatus that modern techniques can bring to bear upon the oft times shadowy domain of science." He also praised the lectures and writings of Herbert Spencer, noted for his astronomical work. A skepticism about religion was clearly apparent when in the same article he remembered attending a lecture in a parlor room at Canon Pusey, Christ Church, Oxford, on the subject of Noah's ark, "and many and varied were the ideas as to how the carnivorous animals in the gigantic whaleback were supplied with their proper rations of flesh, the gramnivorous ones with their accustomed fodder." It was evident that these lectures had put him in conflict with his father's teachings.

Respect for the proper nuances and meanings of words was instilled in him at Oxford, for as late as April 7, 1895, in *The San Francisco Examiner,* Milne was rebuking Ambrose Bierce for praising the lines of a local poet, Flora MacDonald Shearer. Particularly onerous to Milne was the passage: "A flash fell from the wings of night."

"Flashes don't fall," Milne doggedly insisted, "if they are flashes worthy of the name they don't waste any time in falling."

At an undetermined date after 1865, Robert Duncan Milne came to the United States and spent years roaming through Mexico and Southern California. He could not have come to the United States without the financial assistance of his parents and relatives. This raises the question of why a distinguished family would finance and maintain a classical scholar in the semi-lawless frontiers of Western North America. Circumstantial evidence points to the fact that Milne was on his way to becoming an embarrassing alcoholic in his early twenties, probably sacriligious as well, and his family wanted him out of sight.

Writing in *The San Francisco Examiner* for January 17, 1892, Milne revealed: "For the last quarter of a century, at least, I have been what is generally termed a 'regular drinker' and as a rule a moderate one. There have been one or two periods, not many, during that time when I have abstained from the use of distilled or fermented liquors, and I can't say that I look back to those periods with any complacent self-satisfied feeling and unalloyed happiness. No; I can't indulge in self-gratulation in this instance, as I am free to admit that the only reason I abstained from alcoholic stimulants upon the occasions in question was because there were none to be had. Such perfunctory and enforced sobriety as this cannot surely be counted unto me for righteousness, and I have no desire that it should be so. I think that I can safely say that for the last 10 years there has very rarely passed a day that has not been signalized by the casting of more or less incense upon the shrine of Dionysius."

Then he proceeded to give the history of his introduction to alcoholic beverages. While still under the care of nurses, after meals "dessert included a glass of sherry, consequently I think you would be chronologically safe in assigning the date of my introduction to the alcoholic habit to a period not earlier than thirty-five years ago.

"At the school to which I was bundled at the age of ten, half a pint of small ale was the invariable concomitant of our 2 o'clock dinner. By the age of fifteen the regulation half pint assumed the dimension of a whole pint. When I went to the university at the age of eighteen, the functionary who presided over the buttery of the college of which I was a member was only too glad to honor the orders conveyed to him by my scout for either strong or bitter ale, and as the buttery was open for an hour at a time at stated intervals during the day, the facilities for the imbibation of malt liquors may be said to be unsurpassed at any educational institution of ancient or modern times. Of course this is supplemented by a private cellar in one's own apartments, stocked more or less with those celebrated, but indefinable liquors known as university port and sherry — liquors sufficiently fiery in their nature to satisfy the most exacting palate."

The evidence is strong that by the time he had left Oxford University Milne was, at the very least, on his way to becoming a lifelong alcoholic. How he came to America, whether around the Horn to the West Coast, or to the East Coast and then across the continent by train, is not known. Transcontinental rail travel had become a reality in 1867, so it is quite possible Milne landed in an Eastern port and traveled west by train.

The implication is present that Milne never again returned home, though this has never been definitely established. He was what the Westerners used to call a "remittance man," which meant that periodically a draft for a substantial sum of money would arrive through the firm of Faulkner Bell & Co., San Francisco. Later references seem to indicate that these drafts were on the order of $200 to $300 per remittance. In the 1860's, a sum of $300 could easily keep a frugal man alive for six months and with care an entire year. Needless to say there were many such checks. When Robert Louis Stevenson was first in San Francisco in 1878, he literally came close to starving to death. The final agreement of his father to send him the equivalent of *$750 a year was then considered adequate to remove his financial worries.* The trouble with Milne was that when he received a "remittance," he tended to celebrate. He did not like to celebrate alone, so he invited everyone around to lift glasses with him. Frequently, by the time the spree had ended nothing at all remained.

This may account for the periods he spent in Southern California and Mexico, trying to stay alive between drafts from abroad. Sheepherding was a favorite refuge of his during financial stress and he wrote a series of articles on the occupation that mark him without question as California's most literate expert on the subject. Since sheepherding was an important Scottish industry, he may have had basics in animal husbandry in England. The late Olaf Stapledon makes note of the fact that when he went to primary school at Euttoxeter, Derbyshire, before World War I, he was taught, in addition to Latin, how to wash sheep! Most of Milne's sheepherding activities seem to have been carried out closer to the general region of Los Angeles than that of San Francisco. Old books on California underscore that Scots frequently went into sheepherding and were regarded as the elite of that occupation, so Milne's proclivity for that work was not unique. Sheepowners frequently supplied 10-gallon kegs of wine as fringe benefits. Milne became an adequate cook, not only to feed himself on the long nights with the flock, but to earn extra money cooking at *rodeos*. (Rodeos were roundups and branding of calves by cattle herders, not exhibitions.) He did not stay put, but continually wandered around, sometimes with money and at other times penniless. He was a horseman and occasionally owned a horse, but usually the mount was sold between remittances. When on foot and roaming, he carried blankets, some food and cooking equipment, and literally thumbed rides on passing caravans.

In 1873, Southern California was plagued by a small but murderous band of Mexican bandits headed by a short man named Vasquez, who made up what he lacked in stature through the savagery and slaughter of his raids, one of the most gruesome being that at Tres Pinos. He was mentioned by Robert Louis Stevenson, and has become the principal of many tales. Following his capture and execution near Los Angeles, his atrocities became the subject of legend. During the summer of 1873, Milne was herding sheep at a watering hole surrounded by three shacks, on the border of San Bernadino and Los Angeles County. The nearest human habitation was at Willow Spring, 20 miles away. He was alone, but there was a 10-gallon barrel of wine. His boss, a man known only as Walker, would be gone 10 days at a time to get supplies from Los Angeles, and during this period Milne was completely isolated. The only thing of real value was the bales of hay, difficult to come by in the west and worth $5.00 a bale.

While chopping up some dry branches to cook supper with, Milne observed four Mexicans, with soldier overcoats, mounted and armed with navy guns and knives, ride up. They questioned Milne and, satisfied he was alone, said their horses were hungry and they had no money.

Milne offered them a bale of hay and said he would put it on their account. This seemed to strike them right, so they asked for food. He had only bacon, beans, potatoes and coffee, and could bake some bread. Not satisfied, they looked around and saw a small group of rangy cattle in the distance. They lassoed one of them, slaughtered it and began a barbecue. Milne prepared the side courses and coffee and a feast began. When all seemed in a jolly mood, he tapped the 10-gallon barrel of wine and the Mexicans began to get talkative, claiming they were "rancheros" from Lake Elizabeth, rounding up some of their wandering cattle. In the morning, the Mexican leader, a small man, left Milne a quarter of beef to pay for the hay and expressing "mutual esteem and good will," took off. After Vasquez was captured and hanged, Milne saw a picture of him and "it was the same little man who had led the jolly group that dined with him alone in the desert."

A good part of the time Milne was what the Westerners could have termed a "saddle tramp," except that he infrequently owned a horse. He walked from place to place, hitched rides, picked up work where he could and then periodically showed up at a location where he could check to see if money had come from home. There is no indication of any published material in the United States before Milne's showing at the 1875 San Francisco Mechanical exhibition. That he had a literary predeliction was evident from his Latin poetry prize in school. Milne seemed more interested in actual applied mechanical science at this time than writing.

VIII. THE ARGONAUT

After the issuance of the patent on his rotary steam engine failed to ensure a sale, Milne returned to San Francisco. Los Angeles and San Bernardino were only small towns, with few newspapers that had little or no need for outside journalism. San Francisco by 1877 had grown to a Western metropolis of 200,000, the leading port, business and manufacturing center on the West Coast, the terminus of the transcontinental railroad and the center of culture of the entire West. It had so many newspapers that the names of many of them have been swallowed up in history, even the titles having been forgotten. Printers and journalists had a market for their wares and could drift from one newspaper to another.

Milne began working around on newspapers, and since that profession had a reputation for enjoying liquid refreshment, his excesses were taken as part of the tradition of the trade. Newspapers were not publishing Sunday editions in those days, though there were seven dailies: *The Daily Alta California*, the oldest; *The San Francisco Chronicle, The San Francisco Examiner, The Evening Post, The Morning Call* and *The Evening Bulletin*. The lack of Sunday editions also meant that there was a minimum of material about the literary world or even art, music or the theatre.

Two men, Frank Morrison Pixley and Frederick Maxwell Somers, thought this offered an opportunity for a weekly with a political and cultural tone. Pixley had come to San Francisco in 1848. He was born in 1825, son of a New York State farmer. His maternal grandfather, a wealthy lawyer, saw him through law school. He had been editor of the *Daily Herald* in the fifties and had worked on the *Chronicle* later. His writing was particularly strong on politics. A controversial man, he left the *Chronicle* because of differences with Charles De Young, the editor, and continued to have differences with a wide cross-section of people all of his life. In his case, he could afford them, because through the successful practice of law, engagement in politics and real estate deals, he had become a man of wealth. His complaint was he often found his writings in newspapers subject to censorship as indeed they should have been. He married Amelia Van Reynegom in 1853, practiced law, was City Attorney, and for a time Attorney General of the State of California.

Fred M. Somers also worked on the *Chronicle*. He helped convince Pixley to join with him and even had the name for the proposed publication, *Argonaut*. Somers, born in Maine in 1850, was a school teacher who chanced into newspaper work and finally ended up in San Francisco in 1875. He was accused of not being a truly creative editor by Jerome Hart who was to buy him out. Hart stated that Somers predominantly concerned himself with the "eclectic" side of the paper, selecting material for reprinting from domestic and foreign sources and doing the nitty gritty.

There was a need for someone with both creative writing and editorial ability and an aggressive personality, Hart asserted. That left an opportunity for Ambrose Bierce, who had returned to San Francisco the Fall of 1875, in the midst of a depression. Unable to find any literary work, he had secured a job at the San Francisco United States Mint, partially through the influence of his brother Albert who was working there. When Pixley and Somers offered Bierce the Associate Editorship of the proposed new weekly, he was delighted to accept. He wrote a great deal for the paper, editorials, stories, poems, articles, and both solicited or passed upon new material submitted to the paper.

The *Argonaut* began publication as a weekly with the issue dated March 25, 1877. It stabilized to a 16-page tabloid format with three and four columns of microscopic type to a page. The pages measured 15¼ inches high by 11½ inches wide. There was no illustrative matter at all, except for a stock cut of a bear above the editorial page and a stock cut of a Shakespearean actor above the drama column. The paper was printed on a cheap book stock.

A standard issue would lead off with a work of fiction on the front page, either an original work by a West Coast author or a reprint (foreign translations from German, Russian, French, Italian and other languages were frequent) and often another shorter work of fiction somewhere else in the issue. Poems of all lengths, original, reprint, foreign and domestic, were found every week. There were standard columns: "Individualities," about current doings of world-famous people in every walk of life; "The Alleged Humorists," short squibs excised from hundreds of sources, foreign and domestic; "Society," which is self-explanatory; "Art Notes," which dealt heavily with local artists; "Literary Notes," which included brief book reviews and items on literary personalities; "Vanity Fair," society items ranging across the world; "Storyettes," brief vignettes excerpted from many sources; "Nebulae," a column written by Robert J. Burdette, of humorous anecdotes; "Correspondence," a letters column; a New York gossip column, and various others, as well as individual articles and essays.

The most dynamic and controversial pages of the paper were the two devoted to editorials. Pixley was unquestionably one of the most trenchant and effective editorial writers of his time, Bierce not excepted. The only trouble was that he was a bigot and racist of the vilest sort. An Episcopalian, his primary target was Roman Catholicism, specifically the Irish, and he excoriated them years on end with scant mercy, until he died. His second favorite target was the Jews, his most incredible editorial appearing in the issue of September 15, 1883, where he applauded the decree by the Russian government forbidding Jewish firms from hiring any Christian employees (they were also forbidden to hire Jews!) because that was a form of exploitation. He claimed that the Jews in Russia owned all the liquor and pawn shops and through these businesses they had fleeced the Russian workers of the scant wages paid them and almost destroyed the Russian economy. He further stated that "nearly all the disreputable trades that thrive on prostitution, debauchery, intoxication and crime are in the hands of the Jews." From that point on he became abusive! Quixotically, only weeks previously, in a series of editorials, he had vigorously defended the Jews against the "vile accusations" that they ever had as part of their religion the sacrifice of a Christian child on the Passover.

When he wasn't dealing with Catholics and Jews, he was tearing into the Negroes and the Chinese. The most incredible thing was that he was frequently observed at lunch or dinner with prominent Catholics and Jews in outward manifestation of great camraderie. It was theorized that his militancy against the Catholics was because the Irish formed a political power base which he wished to neutralize, and his battle with the Jews waxed and waned in intensity according to the advertising support they gave the *Argonaut*. Charles de Young, the newspaper editor with whom he had quarreled was also Jewish.

Perhaps because it was well financed, distributed, and reasonably priced at 10 cents, and had a substantial quantity of lively and varied editorial content, *Argonaut* became profitable from the first. Not necessarily a money maker to arouse the envy of the leading national magazines, but any publication which made a consistent profit with a predominantly regional circulation had to be treated with respect. The strange part was that while the *Argonaut* was regional in sale in the United States, it enjoyed European circulation.

To these pages contributed Ambrose Bierce, who was frequently liberal on racial matters, particularly to the Chinese, and would express contrary opinions both on the editorial page and in his column "Prattle" which he commenced to those of Pixley. Bierce also favored slanting the *Argonaut* culturally. He had no prejudice against a fantastic tale of science, horror, terror or the supernatural.

The first fantasy run by *Argonaut* was obviously picked up from a British source. It was written by George Robert Sims, English journalist and playwright who became best known for his tale "Puss in Boots" as well as a successful series of detective and crime novels. Titled "My Little Dog Pickle" it appeared in the May 19, 1877 number and dealt with a highly advanced system of mesmerism that permitted a dog to be hypnotized in such a manner as to permit the animal to learn, to understand and talk human speech. Another reprint, this an anonymous translation from the French, was "Love in the Clouds," subtitled "A Wild, Weird Romance," which appeared in the June 16, 1877 issue, in which a young man proposes to a beautiful French girl, who tells him she can never marry him.

She relates a story of being drugged and carried off on a wild balloon flight with a former suitor. As the story reaches the point where the balloon is rent and they are descending into the sea, she begins to demonstrate ballet steps. He realizes she is mad and terminates the romance.

"The Spirit Wife" which appeared as a two-part serial in the July 21st and July 28th issues was noteworthy because, though it is a tale of the supernatural and published anonymously, it was obviously written by a San Francisco writer for it had its locale in that city. In it, the spirit of a man's dead wife, in all her youthful radiance, returns to live with him. Only a close friend can see her and as she passes a mirror no reflection is shown. Her business advice to her living husband brings immense wealth, which on his death is left to the narrator of the story. Its San Francisco background is highly authentic.

IX. EMMA FRANCES DAWSON

"The Spirit Wife" indicated that a magazine that was receptive to local talent and paid something for their efforts would begin to attract them. Surely enough it did. Fred Somers bought a story titled "Shadowed" which he published in the January 14, 1878 issue from Emma Frances Dawson. It told of a man who shot his wife to death when he caught her with another. Her image came back to lure him to his death beneath the wheels of a wagon on the streets of San Francisco. The plot was nothing unusual in the way of supernatural stories, but the writing was extraordinary. The woman had a richness of imagery then associated with only the best European writers. There was a touch of the exotic in her style yet she managed her transitions from dialogue to narrative with such skill and naturalness that there was no question that she was a literary technician of the highest order. Though her tales were exceedingly complex and ornamentally wrought, she had an unfailing sense of how far she could go without losing the reader. Yet, "technician" is a grossly unfair term to apply to her, because there was such richness of feeling and sureness in the handling of the most powerful of human emotions that left no question that she deserved to be ranked with the world's great specialists in supernatural and horror fiction. She was an experimentalist, inasmuch as a poetess, she blended complete poems — a number of them — into the appropriate context of virtually every story. It was almost as though she was writing a musical and working the lyrics in at intervals of the story. The trouble was not only that her fiction was far superior to her poetry — which was good enough for the period — but that the poetry almost seemed discordant. It stopped the flow of the story. Edgar Allan Poe carried it off successfully in classics like "The Fall of the House of Usher" and "The Assignation," but he was a master of both forms and he did not overdo the technique. Dawson would frequently throw three or four long poems into a single story. Despite this, she accomplished outstanding work and Ambrose Bierce, thinking that "Shadowed" was her first published story, waxed estatic in his "Prattle" column: "It is not my custom to set 'the cover of praise upon every head that is presented, but of Miss Dawson I should like to be understood as affirming with whatever of strength resides in forthright sincerity that in all the essential attributes of literary competence she is head and shoulders above any writer on this coast with whose works I have acquaintance. And on this judgement I gladly hazard my small possession and large hope of reputation for literary sagacity.

"Here is a young woman who is a perfect surprise in the extent of her reading, by her precocious instinct, the delineation of character, and what is still rare, a balanced reserve of power in finishing her sketches with the fewest possible touches." All that can be added to Bierce's statement is that he was right! All his life Bierce remained her staunch advocate, willingly writing testimonials or introductions to her works.

The apearance of "An Itinerant House" in the April 20, 1878 *Argonaut* was the story that helped make whatever reputation it was possible to make on the West Coast for Miss Dawson. In that story, the wife of a Mr. Anson of San Francisco arrives by boat, and the Mexican woman who has lived with him, Felipa, who thought she was the only woman in his life, falls apparently dead from the shock of it all. An electric current passed through her body restores her to life. She curses all around her and curses the very walls of the house she has "died" in. Participants of the scene return to San Francisco and at different locations death and tragedy occur in rooms that turn out to be the same that Felipa cursed. Each location has an unsavory reputation of many families moving in and out, as frequently as five times a year. It finally develops that it is the accursed room in the same house, literally moved twice from its location and once even rebuilt with a store on the first floor. Truly an itinerant house.

Bierce was wrong in believing Dawson to be a new discovery. Two of her stories had appeared anonymously in the *Overland*

Monthly before it closed its initial series with its December, 1875 issue. The first, "The Romance of a Lodger," was printed in the January, 1875 issue and the second, "A Dead-Head," in the issue for May, 1875. "The Romance of a Lodger" was a powerful tale of horror, telling of a young woman who comes to San Francisco and rents a room in a strange house which seems to be run by a single old lady. The woman lets her have the room of her son who is away. Seeking to pay the rent at the end of the month, the roomer wanders into a room where a bestial looking man with an evil-looking parrot is literally chained where he sits. The landlady calms her but offers no explanation. Soon afterward she awakens with a handsome young man lighting the gas in her room. It is the landlady's son, returned at night with no idea that someone is now occupying his quarters. The young man becomes deeply enamored of her, but she offers no encouragement. One night, the man she has seen chained appears in her room, accuses her of spying on him and threatens to throw her out of the window. The son intervenes with a gun, but in the struggle he is killed with his own weapon. The police arrive to take the madman away, but the mother of the dead youth demands to know why the girl led her son on if she did not care for him. She replies to the landlady that she *did* care for her son.

"That is more of a puzzle. Why did you repulse his advances?"

The girl refuses to explain, leaves the tragic house forever, but she does tell the *reader* the answer: "And I? I returned to the East, to my husband."

"A Dead Head" is an atmospheric weird story of the opening of a book store in San Francisco by a man having a collection of books but no trade at which to earn a living. He is losing ground, his chief companion a Russian, Terentieff, who pores through the books, endlessly, never buys any, but discusses supernatural literature and philosophy and keeps urging the shopowner to write a ghost story. The bookowner writes a light play for a young actress, which is a success. He then works on a tragedy for her, but is tormented by another admirer, Thornton, into a duel. He kills Thornton and faces a heavy jail sentence and fines. Throughout the situation Terenteiff figures strongly, even loaning the bookstore owner a special ear trumpet which enables him to gain the information from Thornton's lips that incited him to the duel. The story ends as he tries to find Terentieff, only to learn that the man has been dead the entire period of their friendship and philosophical debates.

There is no question that had these two stories been published under Dawson's name, she would have gained notice three years earlier. As it was, though she quickly received not only a local but an international following, she hindered her own progress by the fact that she was a recluse. Born in Massachusetts August 16, 1851, she had received a superb education, the type of education usually reserved for women for whom culture is an ornament to enhance their cultural position. Whatever Dawson's antecedents, few, if any, knew. She was so fluent in German that it was virtually a second language, but she was also good enough at Spanish and Italian to make excellent translations for San Francisco publications, and she sometimes took a crack at Russian and Persian!

She gave her occupation as "Musician," but what instrument or instruments was never clear, though it appeared to be the piano. That she had a superb grounding in music and the various instruments was apparent from the internal evidence of her fiction and verse. She also had taught in public schools in the San Francisco area. Even after she had been in San Francisco for 20 years, few people claimed to have ever seen her. Those who did know her said she was extremely approachable and unaffected, but for 12 years she cared for a slowly dying, invalided mother. Those were also the years when she did most of her writing to provide an additional source of income and, when her mother died, living in seclusion had become a habit. Her companion for 50 years was a splendid white cockatoo, which *survived* her, and in her later years she had a large green parrot. A photo of her as a young woman shows well-formed features which do not add up to beauty, possibly because she did not strive for it.

Emma Frances Dawson made one major appearance in the *Argonaut* in 1879 with "The Second Card Wins," which ran in the May 17th and 24th issues. It was not one of her most successful stories. Mark Dillon angers an Indian Fakir when he laughs at some of his most impressive tricks. The Fakir gives him a fan and states, "When *her* hands hold it, will be when your sun sinks behind a golden mist!" This prophecy comes true when the first wife of his closest friend, whom he has loved for many years, comes looking for the man who deserted her and finds him married to another. She accepts $100,000 to leave and never return again, spurning Dillon's renewed overtures. He shoots his brains out and his spirit returns as a chill wind to pull the fan from the hand of his friend and dash it to pieces. In this story Dawson is at once too direct and too subtle. The directness makes the story seem obvious and the delicate innuendos are missed and the point of the story lost. The omnipresent poems in the text further destroy concentration.

X. MILNE AT THE ARGONAUT

Dawson's contact on the *Argonaut* was Fred Somers. Whether in person or through the mail is not certain. Aside from the editorials of Pixley, the *Argonaut* had Ambrose Bierce whose forte was cutting, merciless criticism in his "Prattle" column, devastating epigrams, witticisms and poetry. He was not yet noted as a short story writer. They had added Dawson and now into the office drifted Robert Duncan Milne, working in stints on some of the San Francisco papers and having been apprised that the *Argonaut* was financially viable and actually *paying* for material. Milne was not a handsome man; he possessed a large, fleshy, somewhat curved nose, and through a good part of his life a mustache. When his finances were good, he was photographed in Europe's most stylish formal dress, with a shiny stove-pipe hat, gloves and a gentleman's thin walking stick. When a prolonged bout with alcohol had him down, he would don the shabby clothes of a sheepherder. He was thin, of average height, but was hampered by a stutter of such severity that it often hung him up in the middle of a word, fighting and gasping to finish it. Later, *Argonaut* editor Jerome A. Hart said that he had never encountered a man with a worse stutter.

His earliest associations at the *Argonaut* offices in 1877 and early 1878 were with editors Fred Somers and Ambrose Bierce. At that time Bierce was working in the San Francisco offices and had not yet retired to the wilds to nurse his asthma. Bierce knew Milne, brought material from him, edited his copy and later would work on newspapers with him, and of course lifted elbows with him at local bars. A friendship of many years played a part in Bierce's later 1891 defense of Milne in the pages of the *San Francisco Examiner*.

Milne had undoubtedly done considerable work on local newspapers before his first story appeared in *Argonaut*, but no *bylined* stories have yet been uncovered or anonymous ones identified.

HISTORY OF THE MOVEMENT 84

His first article of record was "In the Cow Countries" in the *Argonaut* for March 2, 1878, which told of his riding and guiding two mules from the Salinas area up to two Mexican ranches where a *rodeo* was in progress, describing his trip, the country, the Mexican cooking and the roundup of young calves with great accuracy. The following issue, March 9, 1878, he had a nine-stanza poem, "A Shifting World," in the style of Tennyson, starting:

> I rose in a dream of morning —
> Sublimely I rose — and far
> Earth's planet revolved beneath me
> Faint lit by the morning star
> Gleaming fair upon China. Pagodas
> Reflecting the spirit of man,
> Light, graceful, took shape in the shadows;
> But their idols perverted the plan

Commenting in verse on the lands as the planet revolved beneath him, Milne was readable, effective and thoughtful.

"A Mexican Family on the Move" appeared in the same issue and is actually a continuation of "In the Cow Countries." He had been drafted as a cook at the Mexican *rodeo*, and getting fed up with it, packed his bed roll and his belongings and begged a ride on a wagon accompanied by a group of horsemen. In the wagon there is also a woman and a young girl. He rides with them, camping out at night, describes the food preparation in the most minute detail. His relation of Mexican family life on the move is superb and his account ends as he leaves the group closer to Los Angeles than San Francisco. He continues his autobiographical pieces with "A Reminiscence of Vasquez" in the March 16, 1878 issue (previously described) and in this piece he shows not only excellent powers of observation but considerable narrative skill. He has a precise date, "the summer and fall of 1873," and it seems probable that the events of the two earlier pieces occurred in the Spring of 1873.

The implications of being constantly on the move were expressed by Milne in a poem in Western vernacular, almost a full column in length, "A Spirit Tramp," in the April 13, 1878 *Argonaut,* told by the ghost of a hobo who fell between the wheels of a freight car he was riding on and was killed. Like much of Milne's poetry, it was light and free of the erudition of his prose. The hobo has wound up in a sort of heaven, where he feels very uncomfortable:

> But you see it ain't walkin'
>   That helps a man here,
> Nor yet flyin' with wings —
>   Thar ain't no sech gear;
> But it's wishin' that hystes
>   You along — ain't that queer

He finally concludes with the lines:

> So I'm off on a scout
>   Do you see that there star?
> Well, somehow by wishin'
>   I think that up thar
> There may be what I want —
>   Will you come? It ain't far.

Though his article in the December 21, 1878 issue of *Argonaut*, "A California Sheep-Shearing," is loaded with literary allusions ("Arcadian idyls have been chanted by Theocritus and Virgil, and attempts made to realize them in the pleasure-parks and palace lawns of the Bourbons"), it is the most precise and detailed description of how sheep are divested of their fleece to be found outside of a specialized trade journal. He is very specific as to where it occurs, citing the Cerritos rancho in Los Angeles county.

Most of the articles and poems bear the date of composition, and some are just three days before the date of issue! This would seem to indicate that Milne was called upon to fill gaps in the *Argonaut* just before press time. Ever since *The Overland Monthly* had established the policy of giving its material a Western slant, this was also the policy of publications that followed. The articles and poems of Milne, full of local and regional color, adhered to that precept, though they appeared to be no more than a bit overwritten fillers by an itinerant newspaperman.

XI. MILNE TRIES SCIENCE FICTION

The abrupt metamorphosis of Milne into a writer of fiction with "A Modern Robe of Nessus," a long short-story that ran in the February 1st and February 9th, 1879 issues, is inexplicable. The *Argonaut* always included at least one work of fiction in every issue (though the editors complained about the difficulty of locating suitable stories). Was "A Modern Robe of Nessus" also a last-minute assignment, born out of editorial desperation? If it was, the editors of *Argonaut* had lucked into something good, because Milne had the art of storytelling down to a "T." He began, appropriately enough with a Basque shepherd in the California hills, telling Milne the story over a cup of wine, of why he left France. Milne entices the reader with his first sentence. Then, as the action shifts to Paris of 10 years earlier, his knowledge of the language, customs and life is apparent. A French noblewoman of 35, married to a man of 50, becomes infatuated with one younger and more charming. For a plan to incapacitate her husband long enough for them to run off together to America without being apprehended, they have selected the night of a grand masquerade ball. A special robe like that of Mephistopheles is woven for her husband to wear. This robe is impregnated with a chemical which the heat of his body will cause to enter the pores of his skin. The wearer will be rendered paralyzed, though completely conscious. The robe must be removed after a specified amount of time or death will occur.

Her younger lover will then enter in an identical-appearing robe, and they will leave together. Before her husband can recover they will be on the high seas with transferred funds from his accounts waiting their arrival in the New World.

The Basque shepherd, then a servant in the family's employ, overhears the plot and informs the husband. The robes are switched and the lover falls victim to the paralysis. A fire burns the house and one charred body is found. The lady is never seen again, though the records show that she and a man booked passage on a boat to America and a logical assumption is made.

The story is handled with considerable skill both in narrative and dialogue and moves with great speed. The description of the effects of the chemical impregnated into the robe are superbly delineated. This is a scientific murder mystery, utilizing a chemical that does not exist. Milne was on his way to becoming a science fiction writer, and the *Argonaut* had added to its literary stars Ambrose Bierce and Emma Frances Dawson, the name of Robert Duncan Milne.

"A peculiarly observant eye might have noted on Clay Street, San Francisco, during the spring and summer of '78, a slight thread or cord shooting up into the firmament from the roof of a semidetached two-story mansion...," was the way "The Great Electric Diaphragm" by Milne opened in the May 24, 1879 issue of the *Argonaut.* This remarkable story is about Baron O, a meteorologist, who has invented a system based on the findings of Thomas Alva Edison, for transmitting two or more signals on one wire simultaneously. In recent years, this has been one of the greatest advances in our telephone system, making it possible to transmit scores of messages almost simultaneously over the transatlanic cables, making it unnecessary to keep adding new cables to accomodate the increasing load. Baron O hypothesizes that the rotation of the earth and the effect of the sun have created a magnetic or electrical current in the upper atmosphere of extreme tenuousness. What he has done is send up a small balloon, with a wire attached, to the region of this current and through the means of a telephone device communicates with his servant in Berlin, who has a similar device. With a single balloon and wire, utilizing Edisons's system of multiple impulses operating at the same time, thousands of phones can be linked in similar operations with countries around the world.

That is all of the story. Merely the description of the invention and questions and answers concerning its operation, but Milne's elaborate, ingenious, imaginative, fascinating and seemingly logical rationalizations and scientific buttressing of his theories is unique in the entire history of science fiction. Certainly many authors, particularly under Gernsback, stopped the action of their stories again and again to throw in their scientific lectures and double talk, but Milne is not lecturing. He is giving a brilliant exposition of a scientific concept in fictional form, examining its ramifications, exploring it and fabricating logic out of it. The failure of Milne to render a story places this in the category of the fictional hoaxes of Robert Adams Locke, Edgar Allan Poe and William Henry Rhodes. In fact, Rhodes was obviously well-known to the staff of the *Argonaut* because they reprinted his poem "The Love-Knot" in their earlier, March 9, 1878 issue, with the comment: "Scientific prose fiction was his forte. 'The Case of Summerfield,' 'The Telescopic Eye' and 'The Earth's Hot Centre,' are as wild and imaginative as anything Jules Verne has written."

"The Earth's Hot Centre" provided just the format that Milne had taken off on, possibly with the contrivance of the editors. "The Great Electric Diaphragm" was even set up like a news story with the sub-title "Some Account of the Telegraphic System of the Baron O--" beneath it. It is by these standards that this and other early works of Milne must be judged. They were written as though they were extraordinary interviews or happenings, with the locales on named streets in San Francisco — to give them the touch of verisimilitude.

The concept of turning baser metals into gold had been the preoccupation of alchemists for centuries before Milne came on the scene and stories of those experimenters who succeeded had been a standard plot among literary workers who preceded him and would be utilized by scores who followed him. One of the most renowned American stories of his generation was "The Golden Ingot" by Fitz-James O'Brien, originally published in *The Knickerbocker, or New-York Monthly Magazine* for August, 1858, copied by many publications across the country, collected in THE POEMS AND STORIES OF FITZ-JAMES O'BRIEN (1881) and reprinted often since then. It tells of an alchemist in the United States who believes he has transmuted baser metals into gold, but all the time he is being fooled by his daughter who has purchased a single gold ingot and places it in his crucible after each experiment to keep his mind from snapping.

"A New Alchemy" by Milne in the *Argonaut* for July 12, 1879, deals with the artificial creation of gold, but displaying profound "Knowledge" of alchemy, disproves its tenets and proposes a modern scientific method of producing the much-sought-for metal. The story introduces the character Philip Hall, who would appear in other Milne stories, a brilliant inventor described as "a man apparently of about forty-five years of age, tall, rather lean, somewhat stoop-shoulder, hair long and black, nose aquiline, complexion pale, beard long and straight — black like his hair — eyes bright and piercing: his *tout ensemble* conveying the impression of a man of good abilities and education, and tolerably good breeding, but one on whom fortune had not showered her brightest smiles."

By profession he was a civil engineer from the east coast and he and a partner had been experimenting with creating gold as nature had, using as a clue the fact that gold formations were commonly found intermingled with those of quartz. His partner perfected the process while Hall was away, refused to share it with him and left. Hall has tracked him down to San Francisco and wants the process of producing gold published, so as to destroy its value and thereby prevent his "friend" from realizing anything. In his story, Milne goes into elaborate and absorbing detail on the new theory of the production of gold. The narrative had begun with a newspaper story of an explosion in the basement of a building on Stockton Street, near Broadway, in San Francisco. In the basement are found elaborate machinery and the dead body of Hall's former partner. But also in the debris are found quantities of pure gold mixed with quartz. Hall and Milne had been observing the final successful experiment through auger holes outside of the building penetrating through to the basement, and had been saved from death or injury by the intervening wall.

If the plot were not so old today, this would be a rich and rewarding story. Milne preceded H. P. Lovecraft in the theory of the short science fiction story that: "The true hero of a marvel tale is not any human being, but simply a *set of phenomena.*" Therefore, all of his considerable talents center about satisfying the reader's curiosity of how gold might be artificially manufactured. To him, *that* was the story, not the situations that might grow out of it. Milne was writing in a day when the ideas were thrilling and new and contriving original situations from them would be left to the next generation of writers. Science was creating new marvels on every side. Alexander Graham Bell had invented the telephone in 1876, the same year that Robert Koch discovered the anthrax bacillus. Thomas Edison had produced a successful phonograph in 1877. Giovanni Schiaparellis had excited the imagination of mankind by observing "canals" on Mars the same year. David Hughes announced a successful microphone in 1878. Electrically powered trains were demonstrated in Germany in 1879 and the following year Thomas Edison's electric light would thrill the world.

These marvels were so far beyond what had previously been accomplished that the public did not want them utilized as icons to symbolize the future, they wanted to know how such marvels could be fulfilled. This Milne understood and this his editors agreed with, because "A New Alchemy" was 8,000 words long, complete in one issue starting on page two. Milne was telling them what might be achieved by science tomorrow, the theory of its probability and the mechanics of its accomplishment. What Milne possessed, more than most writers of science fiction before or since, was a fine education, a remarkable fund of knowledge and a continuing personal scholarship between drunken debauches that he was to continue to the last days of his life. It was said of him that he was probably the leading scholar on the West Coast and there was absolutely no question that he was at the very least the leading scholar writing for popular publication.

That Milne's "A New Alchemy" must have been extremely popular is not recorded in any reader's column, competitor's notices or editorial statements, but is implicit. Another story titled "Philip Hall's Air Ship," featuring Philip Hall, began on the opening page of the *Argonaut* for October 11, 1879 and ran one column short of three solid pages, or 8,000 words. Casually observed, the title sounds almost like a juvenile. "Frank Reade and His Steam Man of the Plains" had been serialized in *Boys of New York* February 28 to April 24, 1876, and was the first of a long series which would still be running in the twentieth century. Luis P. Senarens, author of all but the first four Frank Reade stories, was especially noted for his pioneering fictional aircraft, particularly helicopters. There is no question that copies of *Boys of New York,* an immensely popular weekly, penetrated to San Francisco. There is also no question that Luis P. Senarens' *first* story of an aircraft, "Frank Reade, Jr. and His Air Ship," did not appear until more than four years after "Philip Hall's Air Ship." What is more, Milne's aircraft, which was hauled aloft by the helicopter principle, is the earliest so far discovered in fiction utilizing this flight principle, obviously preceding Senarens' and anticipating Jules Verne's "The Clipper of the Clouds" which initially appeared in 1886 by even more lead time. Still further, while Senarens gives a very adequate description indeed of his air ship in about 300 words, then goes on to creating adventures for his characters in its use, Milne writes a scientific text on the theory and construction of aircraft, down to the stress of metals, engine testing, torque of the blades and methods of propulsion.

Philip Hall has gotten back in touch with Milne. Through straight business opportunities, he has made a fortune which permits him to invest in inventions. His first will be a flying aircraft utilizing the helicopter principle, with parachutes for the passengers' safety in case of power failure. Since the steam engine is too heavy to provide the power needed to turn the helicopter vanes, he has devised a unique form of internal combustion engine, in which a stream of powder-filled cartridges provides continuous explosions (like a machine gun), which energy keeps the pistons of the engine moving up and down, supplying the power for flight. A sample of Milne's explanation for this engine is excerpted:

> "The generator was used in the following manner: The holes in the revolving disk revolved, passed in rotation over the mouth of a larger hole in the head of the cylinder in the same manner as the chambers of a revolver pass over the breech of the barrel. The generator was used in the following manner: The holes in the revolving disk were charged with cartridges filled with compressed gun-cotton, the size of the charge being accurately gauged to the contents of the cylinder and the

pressure desired. These cartridges as they passed in rotation over the breach in the cylinder automatically closed the circuit of an electric battery, the spark from which ignited the cartridge. The explosive force thus acquired acted directly against the free piston in the generator, which was driven to the further end of the cylinder, compressing the air in its progress and forcing it through the valve which opened into the receiver at the same time closing the valve which opened inward from the outer air. The piston having reached the other end of the cylinder, and the force of the explosion becoming spent, a partial vacuum was left behind it, which was immediately taken advantage of by the outer air rushing in through the valve in the top of the cylinder, and forcing the pistol back to its original position at the other end; at the same time filling the generator with air to be compressed at the next explosion; while the pressure of the compressed air in the receiver against the valve which opened from the generator did not permit its escape.

Milne then went on to describe in exact terms devices for feeding the cartridges, regulation of speed and even casting of metals. He employed aluminum (later adopted by Senarens and Verne) for all his metal castings because it was one-third as light as iron. His moving parts were constantly coated with a hydraulically forced film of oil to prevent fiction. Quite literally, Milne, part by part, built his aircraft in front of the reader's eyes, giving previous history, physics, engineering and theory for each key segment of it.

Before a flight is made, the machinery is tested part by part for the reader's edification and adjustments made. Milne, who has previously written so detailed a treatise as to make the reader wonder whether he might not be actually describing a real invention, manages to get a touch of tenseness into his description of the testing of the various parts of the vessel, discovers errors and corrects them while the reader waits. It is 7,000 words before the machine has finally risen from the ground and the story ends at 8,000 words with Hall asking a passenger, Auchincloss, if he would like to take the world's first powered air voyage with him. "Auchincloss' answer was characteristic of the man. He looked at me fixedly, took his pipe from his mouth, blew a cloud of smoke, spat, blurted out emphatically the simple words, 'To hell, if you like,' replaced his pipe, and relapsed into silence."

Milne then informs the reader that if no further communication is received, it may be assumed that all passengers have died on the flight.

In a sequel titled "A Flight To the Pole" or "How Philip Hall Reached the Extremity of the Earth's Axis," Milne receives another communication which he passes on to the readers beginning on the first page of the very next, October 18, 1879, issue of the *Argonaut*. The flight is commenced and the speed will average 200 miles an hour. The goal is the North Pole and return, a distance of over 8,000 miles from San Francisco, and the precise time the ship passes over key towns and geographic landmarks is related, as is the route and altitude the aircraft must operate at for each region. Clothing against the cold, a *wood* stove for cabin heat, a tarred pole with the American flag and the Union Jack, and champagne to celebrate the reaching of the pole are all brought along.

Including a landing at an eskimo village to exchange whisky and tobacco for warmer clothes, the entire round trip is accomplished in 38 hours.

To follow, understand and remain interested in Milne's stories, the readers had to average a very high level of education and intelligence. Despite their titles, these were not children's stories (to underscore that fact, one of the character says "damnd" not once, but *twice)*. In fact, the *Argonaut never* published a children's story. This was a magazine aimed at the intellectual elite in content but not in appearance. Despite its low price (10 cents) its mass appeal therefore had to be circumscribed. The fact that it survived, made a profit and continued into the next century (It had a half-page on The World Science Fiction Convention in San Francisco in 1954!) indicated that the *Argonaut* must have counted a very high percentage of the West Coast educated among its regular readers.

Milne followed his science fiction successes with a story of

Mexico, "Love's Dashing Horsemanship," which ran in two parts in the *Argonaut* for November 29 and December 6, 1879. The early part of the story is almost reportorial in its account of the narrator landing in Vera Cruz, Mexico in 1866, where the invitation of a prominent resident near Hermosillo to spend a week at his hacienda is accepted. A beautiful girl at the hacienda is engaged to be married to a young caballero, Don Felipe, but one night disappears on horseback with a dashing Frenchman, riding towards the port town of Guaymas, 112 miles distant. Don Felipe and the narrator give pursuit on horseback, and the story of their pursuit is vividly told. They almost succeed in overtaking the two, but are stopped by 70 soldiers outside of Guaymas, because it is their fellow officer who has made off with the beautiful senorita at *her* consent.

The main feature of the easy-to-read story is the authenticity of the Mexican background, which underscores Milne's quite real observations in that country.

Milne finished the year with an essay "Elegies and Idyllic Sorrows" in the *Argonaut* for December 20, 1879, discussing with apt quotations how differently great poets — Milton, Pope, Poe, Byron, Shelley — treated the subject of grief. Another filler essay, "The Disposal of the Dead" (February 15, 1880), dealt with how various cultures disposed of the corpses of the deceased.

"A Symposium of Tramps," which ran in two installments in the April 3 and April 10, 1880 *Argonaut*, written by Milne, was subtitled "By One of Them." Any doubt that he had indeed spent probably years of his life roaming around Southern California was dispelled when he detailed a variety of stories told around wine bottles of tramps and hoboes, related in their various vernaculars and not only giving insight into their lives but exposing the lies expressed in the stories they told while in their cups to their fireside companions of the road, of adventures and love affairs that never happened. The first installment led off the front page of the issue, underscoring the editor's belief that it was special. This would be reprinted as "The Tramp's Story" under Milne's own name in the *San Francisco Examiner* for June 4, 1893, giving examples of the greatest regional writers in a 100-page special section titled "The Story of the Golden west."

XII. ROBERT LOUIS STEVENSON

It was somewheres during the period of early 1880 that Milne made the acquaintance of Robert Louis Stevenson. References to this fact appear in 1899 San Francisco newspapers, but no historian of Stevenson and in fact no book of any sort has ever mentioned it, yet alone attempted to research the matter. The source of the stories was Milne himself and there seemed little doubt of their authenticity, because when Stevenson returned to San Francisco a great success in 1888, it was common knowledge that one of the men most frequently invited to his hotel was Milne.

Stevenson had gone from Monterey, California to San Francisco a few days before Christmas, 1879. He had a lonely and difficult time, and by January, 1880, his letters reveal that he was living on 45 cents a day, and he minutely describes his daily menu for that period. In his 1920 M.A. thesis "Robert Louis Stevenson in California," researched for the University of California at Berkeley, George R. Stewart, later to become the renowned bestselling author of FIRE and the science fiction winner of the International Fantasy Award of 1951 for EARTH ABIDES, an "after the plague" story telling of the lives of the few survivors in the San Francisco area, states "From just what source his want was at length relieved does not appear; his letters throughout February, however, are in a much more cheerful strain." The probability is that it was Milne who came to his aid.

Stevenson had shown up at some newspaper offices attempting to sell a few items. Indeed, biographers have continued to search for two pieces that were claimed to have been sold by him during this period and have never been pinpointed. Milne asserted that he peddled Stevenson's pieces to the existing "weeklies," which would have included the *Argonaut,* "but none were so poor as to do the great Scot reverence."

They had much in common. Both were of good Scottish families. Milne was born at Cupar, a small town of less than 5,000 within 50 miles of Stevenson's birthplace at Edinburgh. Both were then struggling writers.

The question might be asked: "Just how could a frequently impoverished and itinerant Milne obtain the resources to help Stevenson?" The answer is simple. If one of his $200 or $300 remittances had come through during that period (which after Christmas and New Year's was a quite reasonable probability), and knowing the prodigality of his generosity when he had money, he might quite easily have assisted Stevenson during this most difficult time. After all, if he went to the trouble to peddle Stevenson's stories, would he have stood by and permitted his fellow countryman to starve? To a man living on 45 cents a day, the loan of even a $20 bill solves the food problem for a month. It is that simple.

The following month, in March, Stevenson overexerted himself caring for his landlady's sick child and his tuberculosis flared up. Fanny Osbourne, a married woman with whom Stevenson was in love and for whose divorce he was waiting, found out about his condition and took him to her residence in Oakland, nursing him back from a condition of imminent death. His parents, who were well-to-do, found out about his situation and began sending him money, ending the most critical economic condition of his life.

XIII. W C. MORROW

Few San Francisco writers came to be held in higher esteem locally than W. C. Morrow. Bierce was lavish in his praise of Morrow, particularly complimenting the more horrifying stories. Gertrude Atherton mentioned him favorably in a number of her books, saying of him also in her article "The Literary Development of California" *(Cosmopolitan,* January, 1891): "he is equally a dramatic and interesting storyteller, with a clear, forcible style; a man of fine and peculiar gifts, who is destined to make a mark in literature."

When his collection of short stories, THE APE THE IDIOT & OTHER PEOPLE was published by Lippincott in 1897, it received widespread critical acclaim and sold well for a book of short stories. It was reprinted in 1898 by Grant Richards in London, where it impressed the British. Morrow's forte was for ingenious short stories of explicit physical and psychological horror of extraordinary gruesomeness, though only occasionally actually supernatural or science fiction. How he was regarded by California readers may quite accurately be surmised from a short note in the January 24, 1891 issue of *The Wasp*, a San Francisco weekly:

> "Thinking of San Jose one is necessarily reminded of a former resident of the place, W. C. Morrow, who writes stories which make one feel as if a stream of electrified lizards from ice were streaking it up his back and hiding in his hair. San Jose is never long without a ghost, and a few years ago the immortal part of Vasquez, the illustrious bandit, was holding nightly revel in the jail, and has been seen, too, at lonely spots about the ragged

edges of the town. There were no electric lights in those arcadian times, and it is putting it mildly to say that San Jose was afraid to be out o'nights.

One particularly dismal night some friends of brother J. J. Owens, the well-known newspaper man and spiritualist, talking loudly to keep up their courage, met that gentleman walking along in the most unfrequented and gruesome place inside the city limits.

'Hello, J. J.' said one of the party; 'what in thunder brings you here? You told me youself this was one of Vasquez's favorite haunts, and you're a believer. Such a good night for him, too! Aren't you afraid to be out?'

'My dear fellow,' replied Mr. Owens, with a drear, autumnal cadence in his voice, like the moan of a leaf-laden wind, 'I am afraid to be in.'

'Why, how's that, old man?'

'I have one of Morrow's infernal ghost stories in my pocket, and I don't dare to go where there's light enough to read it!'

Because Morrow was for many years close to Ambrose Bierce, it became appropriate to claim that he was strongly influenced by Bierce. Both wrote a similar type of horror story, at times delving into the beyond to obtain their results. Both wrote stories of the old South and the Civil War, both were magnificently sparse and effective prose stylists and both were masters of the shocking surprise ending. It is more probable they influenced one another, because when Morrow began publishing in 1879, Bierce had only sold a handful of serious stories, whereas Morrow had published a score in a period of two or three years, displaying extraordinary facility with the language, tremendous reserve power and all the qualities that were to earn him well-deserved praise. Just in terms of time-sequence, the evidence is overwhelming that Bierce learned to write from Morrow. The reason biographers have been fooled is that they regard the 1897 date of the publication of THE APE THE

IDIOT AND OTHER STORIES as the time frame for Morrow. That would place him just slightly later than the publication of Bierce's key short story collections TALES OF SOLDIERS AND CIVILIANS (1891) and CAN SUCH THINGS BE? (1893). They are unaware of the original dates or place of publication of most of Bierce's or Morrow's work, so they use the hardcover publication dates as a guide, rendering their observations invalid.

William Chambers Morrow II was born the son of William Chambers Morrow and Martha McCreary in Selma, Alabama on July 7, 1854. The nature of his early life has not been researched, though the fact that he first attended Howard College and then the University of Alabama indicated that his parents were passably well off. The French short story writer, critic and poet Guillaume Apollinaire, who much admired Morrow's work, claimed that he was of French descent, the family's original name having been Moreau. He went further to make a so-far unsubstantiated claim that H. G. Wells had named THE ISLAND OF DR. MOREAU after Morrow, having received the inspiration for his novel from Morrow's science fiction story "The Surgeon's Experiment" (later published as "The Monster Maker") in the April 11, 1896 issue of the English magazine *Pearson's Weekly*, the publication in which Wells' "The Invisible Man" would first appear. Since THE ISLAND OF DR. MOREAU would be issued the following year, in 1897, the possibility that Apollinaire's statement about the origin of THE ISLAND OF DR. MOREAU has some substance cannot be discounted.

The type of life Morrow lived in the South before he came to California, the attitudes he held, can probably be roughly pieced together from his stories which have some autobiographical elements and a realism in their descriptions of Southern life and customs that could not have been obtained from books. Morrow, in his stories, displayed singular sentimental feeling for certain of the "good" negroes described in his stories and almost fiendish mercilessness in his fictional disposal of "bad" negroes. His work has a nuance rarely found in works of the Old South, written by a man expressing his honest feelings, unaware that they are anything but natural and universal. Strangely, from all of this, he does not emerge as a bigot and through a form of social naivete offers an extremely valuable perspective on Southern attitudes immediately after the Civil War.

Fragments of his college life and the behavior patterns of the students are present in his early stories. He also seems to have traveled widely in the South, showing great familiarity with Louisiana, Georgia and Kentucky as well as Alabama.

William C. Morrow, Senior, was a Baptist minister born June 6, 1815 in Pulaski County, Tenn. He moved to Alabama as a boy and prepared for the Presbyterian ministry while still in his teens. He left the Presbyterian church for the Baptist in 1814 and took charge of a congregation in Turnbull, Monroe County, Alabama. He married Martha A. McCreary, an Alabama girl, in 1844, when she was only fourteen. William C. Morrow, Jr., was the last of three children. He was preceded by Sarah, born in 1845, and Georgiana, born in 1848. In 1850 the family was living in Conecuh County in a house assessed at $400. The year of William's birth, 1853, they were resident in Selma.

In 1869, Morrow's father became so ill that though he lived another 10 years to October 16, 1879, he never again was able to carry on his calling. Despite this, his son was sent to Howard College and had completed his final term there by 1876.

There is the possibility that Morrow's mother, still a young woman, supported the family by maintaining a boarding house, for following Morrow's leaving Howard College, the mother, the two sisters and the son took charge of the Gulf City Hotel in downtown Mobile, Alabama. *The Alabama Baptist* for January 2, 1876 ran this notice concerning it: "This hotel, now under the charge of W. C. Morrow, Jr., formerly a student of Howard College, will be found an agreeable home to the stranger in Mobile. It is very convenient to the railroads, street cars and commercial houses of the city. The dining room is under the direct supervision of the gentlemanly proprietor. The table is tempting to the dullest appetite. The servants are prompt and polite. The accomplished mother and sisters of Mr. Morrow will see to it that ladies visiting the hotel shall have a pleasant time."

Apparently they failed at that particular hotel for the November 2, 1878 issue of the *Alabama Baptist* reported: "W. C. Morrow,

Jr., formerly of the Gulf City Hotel of Mobile, has opened a hotel in Meridan, Miss. We could only advise anyone who may visit Meridan to put up at Morrow's Hotel. Mr. Morrow knows how to make guests comfortable and will do it."

The death of Morrow's father occurred in Evergreen, Alabama, so it must be assumed the family was living there at that time and the Meridan hotel had closed or been sold. That was the same year Morrow graduated from the University of Alabama. Apparently, following the death of his father in late 1879, he left for California. It can only be assumed that his mother and sisters (if they had not married), sustained themselves by operating some sort of small hotel or boarding house.

Morrow arrived in California in late 1879 and settled in Oakland, across the bay from San Francisco. A friend from San Jose, writing in the paper *Library and Studio,* gave a physical description of Morrow some years after he had established a reputation: "W. C. Morrow ... is a tall, handsome man, measuring over six feet — in height, of course — a decided blonde, and one of the most delightful companions in the world. In years gone by Morrow was so thin that it was necessary to look the second time to make sure of his presence, but now he weighs one hundred and ninety pounds." Ella Sterling Cummins, the West Coast authoress and poet, said of him: "There is a certain something about Mr. Morrow — a reserved power, an inner self apart — which makes his presence felt as if he approached the size of greatness. He is one of the few writers whose personality is equal to his name. Worthy of mention, also, is the comradeship existing between himself and his wife, Mrs. Morrow, who is his chief critic and assistant. Mrs. Morrow herself is gifted and able to write a first-class story."

A newspaperman Morrow met, E. H. Clough was to provide his entry into the general magazines. Clough had contributed excellent stories with a Western background, involving the mines, cattle ranches and early settlements, to the *Argonaut.* He took Morrow around and introduced him to Fred Somers, who was understandably impressed by the stylistic talent of his new find. Morrow never forgot what Clough had done for him and remained his close friend and correspondent until death.

The first story Somers published was written by Morrow in Oakland on June 23, 1879 and appeared in the July 5, 1879 issue of the *Argonaut*. It was titled "Punishing A 'Shacker,' " with the note, "An Episode of Southern Life," beneath it. Morrow still used the "Jr." to his name at this period, signing the piece W. C. Morrow, Jr. The short piece was more a vignette than a story, and purported to have taken place in the eastern part of Alabama while a railroad was being built. Most of the laborers were negroes and they had their own method of handling "shackers," a slang term indicating a man who used every subterfuge to do the minimum amount of work, placing the burden on his fellows. This is the way it worked: "Yaller Tom was seized by six strong men, who were apparently as ravenous as wolves and as ferocious as tigers; a rope was fastened securely around his ankles, firmly binding his feet together; the other end was thrown over the branch of a tree, and Yaller Tom was suspended head downward. His hands were tied to two stakes in the ground about four feet apart, and he looked like an inverted cross, stretched taut and immobile."

The strongest of the laborers took a board four feet long, four inches wide and an inch thick of hard wood and Yaller Tom's rear end was exposed to the air. A marker counted the blows and after 20 brutal whacks, with the flesh bruised, blistered and bleeding, the punishment was concluded. The negro wielding it then took a knife from his pocket and "cut a small notch in the board at the end of a row of other notches, yawned, and returned the board to the niche between the poles of the Commissary. Negro justice had been most thoroughly vindicated."

The second story, "Awful Shadows" (July 19, 1879), in its savage brutality, foreshadowed the style that was to make Morrow respected among members of his craft. It was a daring story. It opened like a thunderclap as did most of Morrow's tales: "A crime had been committed in Mississippi. One lovely evening in May, as a rosy twilight was stealing on, a little girl dragged herself to her mother's door.' The child has been raped and dies from the effects that night. "A chilling horror fell like a pall upon the people for miles around," Morrow wrote. "Women, pale and frightened, left their homes to find better security in a neighbor's house, and they huddled together like sheep that know a wolf is near. Mounted men, and men on foot, were scouring the forests all night, and toward morning they brought in a negro. He was the criminal."

Morrow makes clear that in the South there is no fouler crime than rape of a child and court trials are not held, but the lynch law takes over. However, in this case the whites thought lynching too kind. They turn their suspect over to Bony, a powerful negro engine fireman, noted for his extraordinary imagination. Ascertaining the nature of the crime, Bony starts in an almost ritualistic fashion to generate the hottest possible fire in the engine box. The suspect is tied to a flat board. The procedure has taken so long that night has fallen. The fire door has been thrown open: "It seemed to Angel that the gate of hell was open and that the shadows he saw were made by demons dancing before the sulpherous flames and reveling in a saturnalia of blood. One demon, larger and more frightful than the others, ten times as ferocious, a thousand times as hideous, with short legs and gigantic body, with a round head and neck like a bull's, with arms as long as the wings of a wind-mill; this monster, this king among demons, seemed to have just returned from earth, for he bore in his arms what might have been a human soul, lashed to a board. It seemed from the shadows that he laid his helpless victim at the edge of the opening through which issued the blinding rays from the unquenchable fire, and that he raised his arms in wild exultation, as though invoking the blessing of Satan for having performed his work so faithfully."

The blazing fire-door light is temporarily blotted out, then suddenly flares brighter than before. Then, "the demon bending over, his great, naked arm stretched across the opening, as if reaching to close the gate."

The story ends as "all was darkness again."

In "Old Aunt Rachel," Morrow turns from "bad niggers" to "good niggers," and with a vengeance. Black Aunt Rachel is the epitome of everything that can be fine in a working woman. It was slavery time but "Old Aunt Rachel" was beloved of the whites and the slaves alike. She knew every herbicidal remedy in existence. "She was the best nurse in time of sickness in the whole country. In her youth she could pick three hundred pounds of cotton a day.

She was a superb cook. She spoiled her mistresses rotten. She liked and tried to help everyone, even the trouble-prone Jake who was the perennial whipping boy for anything that went wrong.

One day Jake, sitting on top of a young bull, taunted it so that as a result of its commotion the cattle became frightened and began goring everything in sight, including Aunt Rachel. Her last thoughts are an admonition to whip that Jake within an inch of his life, but she does not live to again see that all-too-common occurrence.

In "The Burning of the College," Morrow turns from honoring a black woman to nostalgically mourning over a beloved black man. The locale is a college, evidently Howard College, and instead of Aunt Rachel there is Uncle Edmund. That old gentleman is the janitor of the college and his cabin is the retreat from study cares for a good many of the young students. Its walls are lined with the most incredible pictures taken from a wide variety of sources, serving almost as a gallery. Uncle Edmund makes a special mild beer and bakes an extra special hot gingerbread, both of which he sells to the students. In exchange for their patronage, they are permitted to sit around and chat with him about history, his past, their problems, special events and his patiently involved philosophy of life. On the conclusion of examinations, after he has treated some of his favorites to free beer, gingerbread and philosophy, a fire breaks out in the upper storys of the school. Uncle Edmund discovers it and in his efforts to prevent injury to any of the boys dies in the flames.

Both of the foregoing are superbly etched character sketches, written richly and with a fine ear for dialect, containing a great deal of humor, but in both of them, Morrow had been unable to dispense with the note of horror that was to be his trademark no matter what he wrote. Aunt Rachel is fatally gored, all the while delivering punch lines, and Uncle Edmund is burned to death, a hero in a fire.

There is no pretense at humor in "Among the Moonshiners" (October 4, 1879). The scene is in northern Alabama the winter of 1875. A group of young detectives go in to round up a gang of moonshiners operating a still in one of the most inaccessible rocky parts of the region. Taking losses, they finally fling a bomb hung on the end of a petard into the cave of their target. After the explosion: "A thing crawled to the opening. A few seconds ago it was a man. It carried something in its left arm — a shattered leg. It held a knife between its teeth and glared at its enemies. It only half glared. A ball was dangling against one cheek, which annoyed it, and it feebly struck at the ball once. Still the ball dangled, and it grasped the offending object, jerked it from the slender thread that held it, and threw it over the precipice. It was an eye. The thing continued to glare at its murderers."

Morrow extended no quarter to his readers. You got it, guts and all!

"A Night in New Orleans" (November 15, 1879), has Morrow evoking a new type of horror. A girl is walking a tightrope at *night* between two tall buildings in New Orleans for an audience of hundreds below. Flares on either side light the rope. But she is not feeling well and moves too slowly. When it comes time to make the return the flares flicker out and she is left in complete darkness and inevitably slips. First to one knee, then she loses her balancing pole, then dangles by her hand from the rope. Morrow builds from crisis to crisis, and finally lets the reader off the hook by effecting a thrilling and ingenious rescue.

Even more savage than anything that has preceded it is "The Bloodhounds," subtitled "A Sombre Incident of the Civil War." A deserter from the Confederate Army who has gone home to feed his family is tracked to his home four months later. He flees into the swamp, but bloodhounds are released after him. One of them is Old Tige who never moves in for the kill until all the younger dogs have given their best efforts. Cornered, the fleeing soldier, in a gruesome two-hour conflict, kills eleven of the dogs with ingenuity and his bare hands. He staggers to a stream and takes a drink of water. As he gets to his feet the shock, the loss of blood and exhaustion cause him to faint, and at that moment Old Tige romps out of hiding and tears his throat out.

"The Three Hundred" (January 10, 1880) is a story that though it apparently has never been reprinted, must reflect a true happening, because stories based on the same theme have appeared in print and on television. The end of the Civil War is drawing near. The South is approaching the point of capitulation. Advancing Union soldiers expect very little resistance. Five thousand foot soldiers following a lead salient of 70 cavalrymen rub their eyes with amazement. Near a University, lined up behind embankments, are three hundred midget-size Confederate soldiers with shiny new uniforms. They are the 12 and 13 year old cadets of a military college, too young to be sent into battle.

The cavalry sweeps forward and is cut down by accurate shooting, but the old instructor directing the boys is hit and his "troops" panic. At that moment one youngster steps forth, puts on the instructor's hat and rallies the boys. Eventually 900 men overwhelm the children. The boy leader refuses to surrender to a Union Captain because in his command he has assumed the rank of Colonel. The end comes with devastating impact as the revelation is drawn from him that the dead instructor was his father!

This story is certainly as good as the best that Ambrose Bierce did in his TALES OF SOLDIERS AND CIVILIANS and is a short story masterpiece. Yet, even here, as he delineates the feelings of the boys with the overwhelming odds assembled before them, and the repeated attacks and final loss, Morrow, in communicating their feelings tells a tale of peculiar horror.

Of unquestioned naive horror is "After the Hanging" (March 2, 1880). Five boys, four white and one black named Tony, watch a public hanging in Mississippi. The whites are a bit frightened but the black boy says "I wouldn't mind it!" They go into the woods to test him out, have him climb up a tree, tie a rope around his neck and jump. The rope is too slack and he hits the ground. He is ready to try again. They tighten the rope and he jumps. This time the rope breaks, but he is hurt so he wants no more of it. They insist he's got to do it and force him to try once more. This time he slowly strangles at great length and in immense agony while the other boys watch curiously. When they cut him down and he lays still with his eyes rolled back, they are puzzled that he doesn't get up. "They felt something awful had happened but were ignorant of its nature."

In his last story for 1880, "A Struggle With Fate" in the September 18th issue, Morrow tells of a well-bred young man who has met with ill fortune. He is advised by a San Jose drunk, Tarantula Joe, to try to marry a girl from a rich family. With considerable adroitness he convinces an attractive young girl from a suitable family to permit him to escort her home. On a bridge they are attacked by five men, one of whom fells Our Hero with a club. The others gag the young woman and strip her of her valuables. Our Hero comes off the ground and in a desperate battle in which knives are used as well as clubs, routs the three. Covered with blood he refuses the help of the girl after he has seen her home. They are married and live very happily. Two years later he reveals to her that it was all a put-up job inspired by Tarantula Joe and he is now confessing because Joe is trying to blackmail him. The story ends happily, which is unusual for Morrow. What is most significant is that the story is the first one by Morrow to take place outside the South. He had become a San Francisco writer in content as well as spirit.

XIV. HART COMES TO THE ARGONAUT

As the *Argonaut* moved towards 1880, it had become the most literary journal on the West Coast. Ambrose Bierce was contributing editorials, epigrams, poems, and his column "Prattle," though the longest thing he did of consequence was "That Ghost of Mine" that appeared in the April 6, 1878 issue and told of an incident that allegedly occurred to him while living in England, involving the shade of Thomas Hood, the son of the famed poet of the same name, who was a close friend of his. On his deathbed, Hood told Bierce that he had revised his beliefs positively toward the possibility of a spiritual world and a life in the hereafter. As Bierce tells it, while he was walking on the outskirts of Leamington, with his mind on anything but Tom Hood: "A tall dark man met me on the walk, his eyes fixed on mine with a familiar look of friendly recognition. It was Tom! It did not occur to me at the moment that he was dead, nor did I feel the faintest surprise in meeting him there, a hundred miles from London. All seemed perfectly natural, and it was only when he had passed me without salutation, or even so much as seeing my outstretched hand, that I felt a sense of surprise. And it was only when in my surprise I turned around to recall him, and found myself utterly alone — the sole occupant of the street as far as I could see in either direction — it was only then that I remembered."

Bierce claimed to have gone back again and again to the same spot to try to determine what set of physical conditions — because he still did not believe in the spiritual — could have conjured up the momentary vision of his friend. The closest to it he was ever able to come was a plant growing nearby that also flourished in Hood's garden, with a very distinctive odor that would have reminded him of his friend.

Bierce's contributions were *far* outclassed at that stage in his career by several of the magnificent occult works of Emma Frances Dawson, the brilliantly savage horrors of W. C. Morrow and the unbelievably believable science fiction of Robert Duncan Milne. When Ambrose Bierce decided to resign in November to chase gold in the Black Hills of North Dakota, the publisher, Pixley, did not regard it as a serious loss to his magazine, and he was right.

However, there was a much more pressing internal problem. His partner, Fred Somers, wanted to expand and do bigger and better things but Pixley felt there was a large enough job just making the *Argonaut* click on a weekly basis without starting a publishing empire. With Pixley not interested in new projects, Somers announced that he was going to start a monthly magazine to take the place of the defunct *Overland Monthly*. He had in mind something that would be the Western counterpart of *Harper's* magazine. This would have created an impossible problem with neither Ambrose Bierce or Fred Somers on hand to direct the editorial side of the magazine. Pixley had the foresight to anticipate the problem.

When he was planning the *Argonaut*, he was looking for a knowledgeable person to advise him on type styles. He was told that there was a young man named Jerome Alfred Hart, working for the Sumner Whitney Printing Company, one of the largest on the West Coast and printers of many notable magazines, books and weekly newspapers, who was outstanding for his ability in that line. He consulted with Hart and upon his counsel, selected a typesize so small that it strained the eyes even with the use of a magnifying glass. Despite this he was very impressed by Hart, who had a number of men working under him at the Sumner Whitney plant (which did *not* get the contract for printing the *Argonaut*).

Hart was not interested in switching to as speculative an enterprise as a new weekly, but he had been getting instruction in foreign languages and asked Pixley if he might be in the market for translations from foreign publications as fillers. Pixley said he was and Hart's first contribution was the translation of the birth certificate of Louis Adolphe Thiers, first president of the Third Republic of France 1871 to 1873, with appropriate introductory comments. This appeared on the front page of the October 6, 1877 issue of the *Argonaut*. From that time on, he supplied on a regular basis, filler material, research data and translations of stories from the French, beginning with the works of Gustave Droz, then a prominent author and painter. Hart was a frequent visitor at the *Argonaut* offices, on friendly terms with Fred Somers, Ambrose Bierce, as well as Pixley. He also had been assisting in slush-pile reading of freelance manuscripts, so he knew all of the magazine's best contributors.

Pixley suggested that Hart take over the editorial duties of Somers and Bierce and, if necessary, get himself an assistant. The *Argonaut* was then in its third year and it very much appeared to have a future. Hart, who had saved some money, bought part of Somers' shares in the magazine (after Somers had fruitlessly attempted to convince him to invest in his new publication, which he was to call *The Californian*). For the next 27 years, Jerome B. Hart was to be the editorial heart of the *Argonaut*, though his name was not listed on the masthead as editor of the magazine, until after Pixley's death in 1895. Hart's official title from 1880 to 1891 was Associate Editor.

Hart was born in San Francisco on September 6, 1854, son of James Hart and Sarah Marion Burke. His only formal education was in the public schools of his city. Mining losses (he was never quite clear whether it was his father's or his own) prevented him from going to college. He hoped to enter the United States Naval Academy through the influence of a United States Senator, but found out that politicians promise easier than they deliver.

He had a deep love of books and carried on an intensive process of self-education. He obtained a minor position with the Sumner Whitney & Company and showed such ability and diligence that he gained rapid promotion. In appearance he was a trim, well-featured man, with a full head of hair. He later cultivated a handsomely groomed beard and mustache. He wore pinc nez glasses and looked most distinguished. Reading his commentaries, one gains the impression of an individual extremely stable, sound in his viewpoints and conservative. Bierce summarized him as a man who "learned to write poetry, paint on velvet and smile, and became known as the Magnetic Clam." Hart's view of Bierce was much more sympathetic and highly complimentary, though realistic.

There was one thing that Hart was not conservative in and

that was his predeliction for short stories of the weird, horrific, supernatural and scientific. There is no denying that Somers and Bierce were no less favorably inclined toward such tales and the fact that Pixley never stopped their publication the entire time he was alive would indicate that he was more prejudiced for than against them. However, Hart, through the next twenty years of his editorial life, would maintain and increase the annual quantities of such stories and reserve his most glowing compliments for the authors who wrote them.

As a beginning editor, just 26 years of age, he found himself in a difficult political as well as editorial situation. Fred Somers had sold him only part of the stock he owned in the *Argonaut*, so Somers was still very much one of the bosses of the publication. This same Somers had launched *The Californian* and in its first, January, 1880, issue came off the presses with local talent Emma Frances Dawson, Robert Duncan Milne, E. H. Clough, W. C. Morrow and, via long distance, Ambrose Bierce! In addition he wrote a story of his own.

XV. THE CALIFORNIAN

Technically *The Californian* was not in direct competition with the *Argonaut.* It was a literary monthly, printed on good book paper, 10 inches high by 6½ inches wide, and containing 196 pages. It was to do for the West what *Harper's Monthly* and *Atlantic* did for the East. Somers, as one of the owners of the *Argonaut,* wasn't exactly stealing its best authors if he asked them to contribute to *The Californian,* too. But only a fool would have taken lightly the fact that the lead-off story in the first issue, "The Dramatic in My Destiny" by Emma Frances Dawson, writing at the very peak of her form, would certainly have graced the pages of the *Argonaut* but for Somers.

"'Alcohol is for the brutish body, opium for the divine spirit,' said Tong-ko-lin-sing, as he lighted the lamp. 'The bliss from wine grows and wanes as the body has its time of growth and loss, but that from opium stays at one height, as the soul knows no youth or age.'" So opened "The Dramatic in My Destiny." Yorke Rys is in the quarters of his Chinese friend. He samples a pipe of opium and terminates a kalaidoscope of visions with a descent down a long, dark flight of steps to be confronted by "a huge white form that tried to tell me something, some strange fact linked with my fate," then he is awakened. The story takes place in San Francisco's Chinatown. Rys, while with a girl he greatly admires, Elinor, goes berserk when he sees a Chinaman, Si-ki, bestow an unsolicited caress on her. He beats Si-ki with a fury that betokens no conciliation, thrusting aside any interference with warnings of "Between us two!"

Si-ki vengefully delivers poisoned candy to the girl and disappears. Rys sees the ghost of the girl after she has died, but no one else does, and he kills his friend who is trying to restrain him from reaching her.

Mentally unsettled for months, he employs his Chinese friend Tong-ko-lin-sing to locate Si-ki. After an interminable search, he finds himself led down a long dark stairway and a "ghastly figure crosses the rotten, slimy floor . . . "

" 'My dream! My dream!' " he barely utters, clinging to his Chinese friend, then: "An awful voice, discordant as a Chinese gong, the hollow voice of a leper, a voice unearthly as if we had been shades met in another world, cried: 'Between us two! *Between us two!*' "

Dawson wrote with a stylistic richness previously invoked in this country only by Fitz-James O'Brien and with tight control not only of her description, but of her plotting. The style that *appears* flowery leaves no room for distraction, a missed line or nuance and a later sequence in the story does not make sense.

That talented woman had been writing brilliantly. She had done a translation from the German for the May 8, 1880 *Argonaut* titled "At a Dizzy Height" (the name of the author was not given). This was not a free translation or a literal translation as was obvious from the complete change in the style of the story from the rich manner in which Dawson usually wrote, but a faithful interpretation into English of another's nuances. A young man in German, shortly to be married, is asked to pick up some cord and chloroform by the mother of his fiancee. He meets a former native returned from America who lures him to a high point of construction and frustrates any hope of descent. The young man learns he is to be killed because his powerful captor was also in love with the same girl before leaving for America. The wait will be prolonged so the young man may suffer in anticipation of his fate. The villagers stand around in horror as they realize what is to occur. During the night the "executioner" dozes off. The young man drops a cloth with chloroform over his nose, ties him up with the rope, and signals for help in descending. The elements of drama are competently handled and the means of succor are planted so early in the story that they come as an ingenious surprise at the end.

Dawson's command of languages was most particularly impressive when she translated in the same, August 14, 1880 issue, four poems from the German, French, Spanish and Persian respectively! They all read extremely well.

"Singed Moths" in the *Argonaut* of August 28, 1880 was her own work and it was an adroit handling of the entry into the lives of three sisters of a boarder. She tells the story from three viewpoints, since each of the girls cultivates an infatuation for the boarder, who at times appears the personification of Mephistopheles. The man touches the lives of each of them in a significant way and all of them have a portrait of him (no two alike) as well as a necklace he has given them. One morning he is gone and all the portraits have crumbled and in place of the necklaces there are little pebbles and leaves.

"Singed Moths" is undoubtedly autobiographical. In it, one of the sisters says: "Our past in the East is gone like a dream; folks treat us as though with our lost money went our brains."

Elsewhere Dawson wrote: "Our only caller, the landlady for her rent. Neither time nor money for books or papers. Theatre, concert, sail and drive, joys for us no more than if we were ghosts."

Another sister replies, "Shunned, except for insult, by those in our old rank of life, as if with our money went our culture, wit, sense, and purity. . . . A steady grind of small economies that are both comic and cruel — a struggle for ten cents' worth of flour, one candle, five cents' worth of sugar, seventy-five-cent boots, and twenty-five-cent gloves."

One of the sisters plays the piano at occasional parties and hopes that she will be fed and also be able to bring some leftovers home. When one states: "The water boils; come, we will play it is tea — but we must sweeten it with smiles, as we have no sugar," it leads up to a reference to "Duke Humphrey's Dinner." "Duke Humphries Dinner" was the title of one of Fitz-James O'Brien's more popular non-fantasies. This story originally appeared in *Harper's New Monthly Magazine* for August, 1855, then was produced as a play February 4, 5, 6 and 7, 1856 at Wallack's Theatre, New York. While it was not a commercial success in New York it may have been produced in San Francisco, which was a great theatre town. The play deals with a young couple in a barren apartment in New York who have no heat and no food, imagining various courses in a fabulous feast. It establishes Dawson's familiarity with O'Brien's works.

"Singed Moths" also displays a superb ear for the Irish dialect, which is handled with skill and authenticity.

The October 7, 1880 issue ran "Are the Dead Dead?" It tells of the Ghost Club, whose members spend nights in haunted dwellings. A young woman joins them in a San Francisco house where an artist married to and supported by a woman he didn't love winds up a suicide. She is now dead, too. No ghosts are seen but between sessions the young woman is strongly attracted to a personable man who also seems involved with The Ghost Club. She catches sight of him again and again but he is drawn away by a jealous woman who is sometimes with him. Then, one night, alone in the haunted room with her little dog, that other woman tries to kill her and is thwarted by the man she is so attracted to. The story ends with the realization that he is the ghost of the man who committed suicide and the would-be murderess is the shade of the unloved woman who was married to him.

As if this was not enough, William C. Morrow's story "The Man From Georgia," in the same issue, was hailed as a masterpiece by the literary of the West Coast. It deals with an ex-convict, released from prison, whose mind has been turned simple by his ordeal. He obtains a job as a handyman at a resort, but insists that the invisible ball and chain be unlocked every night before going to bed. He answers as readily to "Hunder'n One" as any other name. The man proves an extraordinary worker, never complaining, loyal and honest, but Morrow produces a unique sense of horror in the agony experienced by this individual in attempting to adjust to *kindness*. He dies heroically tending the victims of cholera. Though the story has a hooker, in which it is revealed that "Hundred'n One" was pardoned for a crime he never committed after serving 15 years of mind-breaking hell, the brilliance of the story lies in the character-delineation of the protagonist. This story was later collected as "Hero of the Plague."

The second issue of *The Californian*, February, 1880, had a signed contribution by Robert Duncan Milne, "Hoodlums on a Hop Ranch." (At least one of the unsigned fillers in the previous issue in a long section called "Outcroppings," containing fiction, essays, poems, criticism, anecdotes and humor, titled "Reveries of a Sheepherder," was undoubtedly Milne's.) Milne had taken a job on a hop ranch at harvest time, enrolling as a cook. These ranches employed the cheapest labor at harvest, this time experimenting with boys 16 years of age or under plus some older riff-raff. They were an unruly group and when one had beaten up two of the cooks, Milne reports that he personally, "casting scruples to the wind and sacrificing nice punctilios to expediency, 'launched myself,' as the French say . . . and 'fired' him across a bank of fire-wood where he lay for a moment stunned and discomfitted." The culprit got a gun, pointed it at Milne and pulled the trigger twice, but it did not discharge either time and he took off into the brush and was seen no more. Taking what seemed an incredibly dull subject — hop harvesting — Milne did a lively and entertaining account of just how it was carried out.

While this was a long way from science fiction, a 2,700 word work of science fiction, *not listed on the contents page*, printed in microscopic type, was crammed into the "Outcroppings" section in back of the magazine. Titled "Professor Stückenholtz," it was credited to "J. A. A.," which initials fitted no one then writing on the West Coast. It is an extremely important story, because in dealing with the creation of artificial life it discards the *Frankenstein* concept of taking parts from humans and animals, sewing them together and then shocking them into life with electricity. Instead, the author states that a single cell from any given organ in the body carries the ability to regenerate that organ. By obtaining living cells from all the human parts and providing them with the protoplasmic elements, Professor Stückenholtz literally produces a live human being. The drama of the story rests in his accidental death while working on getting some brain cells from a hapless victim. The next day in his laboratory is found "the body of a microphalus, or brainless idiot, which was elegantly formed, and from which life had apparently just departed."

The writing, technique, science, drama is compressed into a flawless masterpiece. A similar basic idea, that the cells of the body have codes that permit its reconstruction, appears in a Robert Duncan Milne story a few years later. Milne seemed the only one on the *West Coast* capable of writing so impressive a work of science fiction, but on the East Coast, working for *The Sun* in New York City, a man named Edward Page Mitchell had proved one of the nation's most adroit masters of science fiction and the German setting, the American student doctor (Mitchell had attended medical school) and the adroitness of style were all typical of him. Possibly it was neither man and another Western science fiction master remains to be discovered behind the cryptic initials J. A. A., but the suggestion makes it appropriate to introduce Mitchell.

Edward Page Mitchell first attracted literary attention when his short story "The Tachypomp" appeared anonymously in the March, 1874 issue of *Scribner's Monthly,* presenting in its context a theoretical method for moving faster than the speed of light. Other contributions both science fiction and supernatural to the nation's leading newspaper, *The Sun* of New York City, led to an offer of a permanent job by the editor, Charles A. Dana. Mitchell started work on *The Sun* on October 1, 1875, moving to New York from Maine where he had received his journalistic baptism. During the next 50 years, he would rise to the top editorial spot of that world-renowned paper and during the first 10 years on the staff would write an occasional story for them, which would always be published anonymously. The stories mark him as one of the great science fiction writers of history and one of the nation's most brilliant 19th century stylists. The story of his life and a collection of all his known stories was compiled by the author and published as THE CRYSTAL MAN by Edward Page Mitchell by Doubleday in 1973. Though anonymous, the stories were widely reprinted here and abroad, a situation aided by the fact that *The Sun* established the *first* fiction syndicate, selling rights to reprint its stories internationally.

Since Mitchell wrote some of the earliest stories so far discovered on themes as important as faster than light, a time travel machine, an invisible man, a friendly alien, electronic matter transmitters, thinking machines, suspended animation through deep freezing, and child mutants, he is obviously a major figure in the history of science fiction. Reprints of several of his stories in England are known and, while researching Milne, the appearance of three stories of Mitchell's in San Francisco newspapers was verified. Additionally, the *Argonaut* was the first newspaper in America to buy syndicated stories from *The Sun* and three of his stories appeared there. These appearances are of major importance to solidify the status of Mitchell as a shaper of science fiction and fantasy, though published anonymously. The stories were "An Uncommon Sort of Spectre" *(The Sun,* March 30, 1879), published under the title of "A Queer Spectre" in *The San Francisco Chronicle,* April 13, 1879 (also called "Old Twenty Flasks"), which tells of a ghost from the future who returns to haunt the past and, for the brief time he is about it his baby self disappears from the nurse's arms; "The Facts in the Ratcliff Case" *(The Sun,* March 7, 1879) published in *The San Francisco Chronicle* as "Mrs. Borgier's Eyes," December 7, 1879, telling of a woman whose eyes have a deadening narcotic effect on people, gradually killing the men she is married to, and has the power to put medical patients to sleep as though they had taken anesthesia; and "The Crystal Man" *(The Sun,* January 30, 1881) a story of invisibility that employs the same scientific methods and several of the situations of H. G. Wells' THE INVISIBLE MAN 16 years earlier, was reprinted in the *San Francisco Chronicle* for February 20, 1881.

The stories by Edward Page Mitchell that were reprinted in the *Argonaut* were "The Devilish Rat" *(The Sun,* January 27, 1878), an utterly diabolical tale of a man who in a metaphysical experiment succeeds through killing a giant old rat in accepting the wandering soul of Judas Iscariot which inhabited it into his own body, appeared in the *Argonaut* for March 9, 1878. It was, peculiarly, signed with the initials of "R.M.D." which were those of Rollin Mallory Daggett, formerly editor of California's *Golden Era* and then a resident of Los Angeles. The second story, "The Last Cruise of the Judas Iscariot" *(The Sun,* April 16, 1882), appeared in the *Argonaut* for April 29, 1882, is in an oblique sense almost a sequel to "The Devilish Rat," for it is about a ship that is believed to be "possessed" by the soul of Judas Iscariot and brings itself and its crew and passengers to continuous grief. The final story by Mitchell appeared in the *Argonaut* for March 10, 1883, and was titled "The Balloon Tree" *(The Sun,* February 25, 1883). It is one of the science fiction and American short masterpieces of the 19th century, relating with poignancy, beauty and imagination, the rescue of an explorer from sure death on the desert by a highly intelligent feminine balloon-shaped *flying plant,* which restores him to his companions.

It is quite likely that there were more of Mitchell's stories reprinted in *The San Francisco Chronicle* and other newspapers in the Bay area, but complete files of most of the papers do not exist and those on microfilm are frequently literally undecipherable, added to the fact that there were often title changes. The discovery of as many as six makes it quite reasonable to assume that not only were there more, but that they were read by writers like Bierce, Milne, Morrow, Dawson and others, and that because of their originality of subject and excellent literary value, had some influence.

If Mitchell should prove to have been the author of "Professor Stückenholtz" and "J.A.A." a meaningless disguise, it would link him, without question, with Robert Duncan Milne and strengthen further his already considerable status and influence. If it were Milne — not possible, because Milne had an article under his own name and a short piece under the pen name of "A Literary Tramp" in the same issue, February, 1880 — it was a masterly exhibition of superlative science, awesome originality and superb execution in the compass of a couple of thousand words.

The same issue of *The Californian*, immediately preceding "Professor Stückenholtz" in the "Outcroppings" section, carried another fantastic story, unlisted on the contents page, titled "Is Happiness a Myth?" attributed to "T.F.R." In this case, the initials are not cryptic, because they belong to T. F. Robertson, who would later write more science fiction for the *Argonaut.* At a reunion of four friends in Canada, one tells a strange story. While traveling in Northern California, he meets on a stage a man he has bumped into on literally a dozen occasions previously, from the time he was very young, and in locales as widely scattered as China, Paris and Washington, D.C., and whom he cannot mistake because of his peculiar complexion. The man does not seem to have aged in all those years. Confronting the person with these facts, he learns that the stranger is 116 years old, and when examined at the age of 50, it was found that he was born without a liver and that other organs had adjusted in some inexplicable fashion to assume its essential functions. Possessed of investments, he has an adequate income and has spent his life traveling about the world, but is an unhappy man because his friends die and there is then a human gap that is difficult to replace. He cannot marry because eventually his condition will be revealed. He has even tried enlisting in the armed forces and attempted to get himself killed, but never succeeding. "... Doomed like the Wandering Jew, to 'move on' for years, centuries, cycles, perhaps for eternity, but without his satisfaction of knowing that I suffered a just punishment for sins committed."

Milne did not seem to be writing science fiction for *The Californian*, not at least under his own name. He fell back on his considerable experience as a sheepherder, contributing a long and leisurely two-part article titled "Shepherds and Sheepherding" to the March and April, 1880 issues. The piece is interesting, not just frm the standpoint of Milne's considerable and obvious knowledge of the sheep business, but clearly indicates how he got into it. At lambing season, the big sheep "ranchers" require four and five times their normal complement of men. In order to get them they raid the cheap boarding houses, bars and hangouts of the nearby towns and pick up itinerant workers, tramps, drunks, or whatever is available. Pay was $25 to $40 a month depending upon experience, plus food. Lodgings, at best, would be a windowless wooden shack, with bunks built against the wall with a stove in the middle. At worst it could be merely a tent. Food consisted of lamb, bacon, beans, bread, coffee and chicory. Water usually had to be brought in, so its use was for drinking and cooking only. Washing in any form, even of the hands, was frowned upon.

Milne also makes some observations upon predators that are not commonly found in books on the subject. He disposes of the myth that wild animals usually kill only what they need and nothing more, and tend to weed out the weaklings. Only the grizzly bear singled out its prey and carried away just what it could eat, he observed. The panther or mountain lion, at that time called the California lion, he characterized as a fiend incarnate, killing for the sadistic pleasure of listening to the dying bleats and screams of the ripped sheep. He cites a personal incident where hearing a frantic movement on the part of a band, he moved in with a shotgun and dispatched a mountain lion and "found no less than nine muttons which had been slain in less than the same number of seconds by the murderous panther." Almost as bad was the coyote, which did not eat the flesh, but moved in at night to select a victim and gorge itself like a vampire on its blood. The sheep or lamb is found the next morning with only two marks on its throat. The coyote will return night after night to perform the same act until caught and killed.

The author who would really dominate *The Californian* during its early period was W. C. Morrow. His second story for them, "A Glimpse of the Unusual," which appeared in the April, 1880 issue, was bizarrely typical of him. A young newspaper reporter is assigned to make an ascent in a balloon. Before, after and during the trip he is asked the at first innocent-seeming and finally, through repetition, almost sinister question of "How do you feel?" Preceding and following a series of trips in the balloon, during most of his waking hours at work or at leisure, person after person puts this question to him until its utterance is enough to strangely alter his behavior patterns. When he warns a detective who is following him because of complaints of his erraticism, that he will beat him up if he continues, he is taken into custody and examined by a group of doctors to determine whether he should be institutionalized. Realizing that he is now literally fighting for his freedom, the protagonist engages in a grim and horrifying duel between himself and his examiners. Again and again he is tricked into giving answers that will commit him, with the detective the architect of his impending disaster. Finally, when all seems lost, he wins his release through convincing his interrogators that his strange actions and puzzling answers to their questions have been part of an extraordinary assignment by his newspaper, to get the inside story of what a deranged person is subjected to by authorities before being placed in an asylum. As he leaves the building, he says to the detective: "You are a fool." The detective replies: "And you are the devil!" The impression distinctly remains that *a truly insane man* has cleverly outwitted the authorities.

That very issue Frederic Somers severed his connection with the publication. The printer of the magazine, a publisher in his own right, had been Anton Roman, and Somers sold out to him. Roman put into the editorial seat Charles Henry Phelps, a 27-year-old, born in Stockton, California; a graduate of Harvard Law School, who was a practicing lawyer at the time he assumed control of the magazine and who would eventually leave for a New York clientele following the discontinuance of the title in December, 1882.

Robert Duncan Milne, Emma Frances Dawson and E. H. Clough did not appear again in *The Californian* after Somers left. Morrow not only continued, first with a sentimental characterization of a junkman ("Rags, Sacks and Bottles," August, 1880), but produced what is undoubtedly one of the purest detective novels of the 19th century written by an American, in the format that later became classic because of the popularity of A. Conan Doyle's Sherlock Holmes. Titled "A Strange Confession," it was serialized in *The Californian* beginning in the September, 1880 issue, and ran for seven installments through to the March, 1881 number. For a West Coast magazine to run a serial of this length, roughly 60,000 words, at any time, was extraordinary.

A shot is heard by a man and wife in a San Jose street and reported to the police. While the police are investigating the matter, a young man, John Howard, gives himself up as a murderer. The police return to report that a young girl had died of a small calibre gunshot wound to the heart at St. James Street. The young man says the woman is his victim. Present at the time of the incident were the confessor's mother and teen-age niece. The Chief of Police, Casserly, decides to investigate the matter himself. Despite it seemingly being an open-and-shut affair, he has doubts. To assuage them, he visits the home of his astute and philosophic friend, an 80-year-old retired Jewish Judge Simon, who counsels him on difficult cases. Simon analyzes and interprets not only the clues of the case but the meaning of the actions of the individuals involved. In a classic mold, the suspicion shifts from the man to his niece and then to his mother. A lynching is thwarted by Casserly, who is a prodigiously strong and level-headed officer. Deeply involved in the case is Garrett, a practical but overzealous coroner, who scientifically conducts an autopsy and scrapes up clues, accumulating considerable circumstantial evidence from the results that point to the mother of the accused. Retired Judge Simon has begun an investigation to prove that the woman is innocent and has gained her complete confidence. Garrett forges a letter to the woman from Simon, asking her to tell all. The case finally reaches an impasse where all three, John Howard, his mother and niece, claim they are guilty. The solution is that the "victim" was a suicide.

Not for its entire length does the novel cease to be a "Whodunit." It is the form of detective story handed down by Poe, and builds inexorably toward the final revelation which clears *all three* suspects and solves the riddle. It was Morrow's misfortune to have it appear in a short-lived magazine with limited regional circulation and to never succeed in getting it into hard covers.

While Morrow displayed one of the most gruesome, original and horrifying imaginations in 19th century fiction — so much so that his readers thought of him as primarily a writer of the supernatural — though actually a small minority of his tales were such, his greatest weakness was in his attitude toward love interest. It was Victorian, which was not surprising since he was writing in Victorian times, but the contrast with his otherwise remarkable insight into human motivation greatly flawed almost all such tales in which love interest was an integral part.

This was unfortunately true of his short stories in *The Californian,* possibly because the new editor preferred such elements to Morrow's customary brutally direct method of relation. "The King of the Carnival" (June, 1881) of two men, friends, who fall out over a woman and duel to the death in costume at the Mobile, Alabama Mardigras, is a story just about ruined by this element. "The Music Teacher's Sweetheart," which commences with elements reminiscent of Fitz-James O'Brien's "The Wondersmith," of a man who makes his living by teaching mockingbirds to sing and then selling them for a good price, is ruined by a conclusion where a prostitute who rejected the protagonist's love 15 years earlier is brought in to save him and they live happily ever after (with the most accomplished of the feathered singers) in a vine-covered cottage. This tale also has a Mobile setting and was published in the December 1882 issue of *The Californian,* its last before it was revived as a new incarnation of *The Overland Monthly.*

Contributions to the *Argonaut* by Morrow contained none of the romantic sentimentality that shattered his *Californian* short stories. To the contrary, "A Night With Death" (February 5, 1881) is an uunbearably grim narration, telling of a man who for four days and four nights has kept a vigil by the bed of his dying friend, truly believing that he can prevent death by sheer force of his will. To keep awake he writes the story of another horrifying vigil, when the bursting of a steam locomotive had literally cooked his friend Tom Burkett alive. He tells of the eyes blinded white by the steam, the skin of Burkett coming away in his hands as he attempts to guide him from the scene of the accident. The ligaments and bones exposed and then the gradual wearing off of the anesthesia, followed by the shock and the minute description of the infinite agony that Burkett experiences as the nerves carry the fearful messages of the condition of his body to the brain. The story ends with the narrator learning that death has defeated him again.

Morrow's final contribution to the *Argonaut* in this period was "The Three Friends" (May 7, 1881), which is not really a story at all, but might conceivably have been a vignette taken from Morrow's youth. It tells of his dearest friends, two oxen Buck and Brandy, the impending death of Brandy, and his writing a poem which he then reads to that beast to comfort its dying moments.

For one shining moment with the completion and hardcover publication of another novel, BLOOD-MONEY, issued by T. J. Walker & Co., San Francisco in 1882, Morrow dared hope for wider recognition. It was a grim narrative wherein Henry Webster murders his own father, with the full knowledge of his brother, in order to rob him of money which they bury under the Lone Tree. Each is too cowardly to dig it up, so finally Henry Webster hires a man to kill his brother so that he will not be betrayed. The book is filled with a number of scenes of gruesome horror, particularly grisly is the prolonged description of a man trying to cut off his own leg. Ambrose Bierce later extravagantly praised the tales of William Morrow and singled out the sequence of the man severing his leg at the knee with a pocket knife for special commendation.

The magazine to which Morrow had given his major output during the years 1880, 1881 and 1882, the *Californian,* changed its name to *Overland Monthly* (Second Series) with the January, 1883 issue and fell into the hands of Millicent Washburn Shinn. A University of California graduate, she created an "intellectual" magazine slanted at women. In her opening editorial, she announced eight outstanding writers to contribute to forthcoming issues and seven were women. Her assistant editor was a man named Charles S. Greene, who became "noted" for such inspiring epics of investigative reporting as "Parks of San Francisco," "Dairying in California," "The Fruit-Canning Industry," "Rabbit Driving in the San Joaquin" and "The Restaurants of San Francisco," *after* he got into his stride. The cordons of new women writers admitted to the ranks of the magazine wrote pieces that were referred to by the unenchanted as "Those icicle drippings of the intellect." The magazine survived, but either did not pay contributors at all or paid them little and late. Possibly the magazine's openness to women was partially because it did not have to pay them.

Morrow's "Blood-Money" received only a few lines of mention in the February, 1883 issue and they were not favorable. They read: "Mr. Morrow's new novel, 'Blood-Money,' deals with the Mussel Slough Affair, and is a very bitter indictment of the railroad company. Regarded as a novel with a purpose, it overshoots its mark, by making out a case too bad to win credence; from a literary point of view, it is not equal to the author's average." The review told it all. The magazine wasn't going to antagonize the powerful California railroads that, in addition to buying advertizing, *literally* mailed a monthly cash contribution to magazines and newspapers which presented their viewpoint. This practice continued at least up until the outbreak of World War I.

Morrow, who had come to California and taken up reporting on Oakland papers (briefly living in Fresno the first six months of 1881), who had contributed so auspiciously to the *Argonaut* and the *Californian;* had graduated to full-length novels and succeeded in getting his first hardcover published within three years, threw it all up. He had secured a reporting position with the *San Jose Mercury* in late 1881, living at the Lick House Hotel in that city. By 1884 he had left the paper and was working as deputy county clerk at the San Jose Court House. He had met Lydia E. Houghton, who would later also become a journalist and writer. They were married in a small ceremony October 5, 1881 by Minister C. C. Stratton in San Jose.

XVI. HART REBUILDS THE ARGONAUT

Lacking Somers' aid on the *Argonaut,* Jerome Hart was permitted by Pixley to hire an assistant editor. Hart had received a story laid in France, with what he felt exuded the essence of that country. He wrote to the author, Harry D. Bigelow, and asked him to call at the office. When he found out that the very young author was looking for a steady job with an opportunity to write, and particularly when he found that his eager prospect disdained alcohol, he hired him. Their tastes in fiction and poetry were similar, so Bigelow while he was an employee made many of the reprint selections from foreign publications. The new employee proved so deft and talented that for fear of losing him the *Argonaut* actually paid him what he was worth.

Fred Somers made one more effort to carry on publishing in San Francisco, producing a *daily* "newspaper" with the issue dated Saturday, December 4, 1880, which carried *no news whatsoever.* There was precedent for such policy in France, in *Gil Blas* and later *Figaro,* both renowned for the contributions of Guy de Maupassant. Titled the *Epigram,* "A Political, Satirical and Society Journal," the majority of its items were one paragraph long, despite the fact that the paper was full-sized. The front page featured "By Telephone," which took up a full two columns daily, was headed by a line drawing of a man speaking on an old-fashioned wall telephone, and consisted of imaginary phone calls relating to local politics, other publications and "humor." A typical entry: *Hyde Street*

"*Epigram.*"

"Yes."

"We are discussing the Schroeder case. Give us the best definition of emotional insanity."

"Whiskey and jealousy."

Almost three columns on the front page dealt with the theatre and quips relating to the stage under the title of "Plays and Players," and another column titled "Bric-A-Brac" consisted of humorous tid bits from papers across the country. Most of the material was jokes and entertainment, though there were reviews, columns, society squibs, short stories and poems. It was a daily of light entertainment, for those who preferred the departments and fillers in a newspaper to the news. All reports indicate that the *Epigram* lasted one week, but many of the journalists in San Francisco contributed, including Frank Pixley, Jerome Hart, Dan O'Connell, Robert Duncan Milne and Thomas E. Flynn, a *San Francisco Chronicle* man. Following its failure Somers went abroad, returning in August 1881 to sell all of his remaining shares in the *Argonaut* to Hart, who then became Pixley's junior partner in a real sense. Somers left California for New York, and according to Gertrude Atherton made a substantial sum on the stock market, traveled constantly abroad, returning to New York in 1888, and on her advice decided to start a new magazine.

Hart found himself at the beginning of 1881 minus his crack team of fantasy and horror fiction writers. With Robert Duncan Milne, you didn't find him, he found you. All the years Milne wrote for the *Argonaut*, Hart never knew his address. That was because Milne never stayed long enough at one address to make it certain that mail would reach him. From 1880 through to his death, Milne was usually listed in the San Francisco city directory, but never two years running at the same place. In 1880 his address was given at 812 California Street; in 1881 it was 225 Minna Street, but in 1882 it was 68 Minna Street. Hart could have consulted the city directory, but by the time he did Milne was off to another location. Emma Frances Dawson was a recluse and she had seemed to stop writing altogether. Possibly she was giving music lessons, but no one could be sure where. Morrow, after a few desultory efforts, had moved to San Jose and most of his considerable output during 1881 was going to *The Californian*.

The major fantasy that the *Argonaut* featured during the first half of the year was a three-part story, "A Study in Psychology" (March 26, 1881 to April 9, 1881), from a renowned figure in Western literary history, Joseph Thompson Goodman. Samuel Clemens worked on Goodman's newspaper, the *Territorial Enterprise* in Virginia City, Nevada in 1862, and in that paper first used his famous pen name Mark Twain. He became San Francisco correspondent for Goodman's paper and was so devastatingly effective with his brand of investigative reporting that he had to leave town to escape the corrupt *police*, and while living with a miner wrote the short story "The Celebrated Jumping Frog of Calaveras County" *(The San Francisco Sunday Press,* November 18, 1865), which pointed him in the direction of fiction and literary immortality. Goodman was already setting himself up for a life of comfortable ranching in Alameda, but there was still printer's ink in his veins.

More than that, there was in Goodman a completely unsuspected love of the bizarre and fantastic tale as Hart, with his unerring instinct for such things, had ferreted out. Goodman in the opening segments of his story makes some very perceptive remarks upon Edgar Allan Poe:

> My mentor in philosophy was Edgar A. Poe. The confession only excites a smile at myself now; yet, if I was to live my life over, I feel that I should no more be able to resist — as what boy has ever resisted? — his wonderful fascination than I was when I first experienced the spell of his magical creations... I am certain it is to him, more than to all causes besides, that I am indebted for my total disbelief in unearthly manifestations of whatever kind. This statement may seem incredible to those but imperfectly acquainted with his works, who share the common notion that they deal principally with ghostly subjects and agencies. But the fact is, while Poe made use of all the preternatural machines which a wild imagination and mind curiously learned could furnish him, in no instance that I can recall did he have recourse to the supernatural as a foundation for his weird superstructures. His most marvelous incidents and ca-

tastrophes turn upon actual or plausible scientific principles, real or suppositious, intellectual and moral influences, and established or assumed psychological laws. The coinage of his fancy may be counterfeit, but it always bears the stamp of the natural upon its face; he never sought to impose supernatural currency upon his readers.

The foregoing was by way of Goodman convincing his readers that fictional events which normally would be closeted with the supernatural might have a natural basis.

At Montgomery and Second Streets, San Francisco, the hero of Goodman's story sees two men, so alike in appearance and manner that they might be the same. They are seen often, but never together.

He relates this observation to Rachel Claghorne, a girl he knows, who has claimed to have seen apparitions on several occasions and appears to have the faculty of seeing and hearing *through walls*. He is shaken to find that one of the "twins" he has observed downtown is a frequent visitor to the house, a Mr. Overton, a dealer in real estate. Overton, when spoken to, possesses no knowledge or interest in his "doppelganger."

One day Rachel professes to see Overton in the room — but invisible to our protagonist — warning that under no circumstances should he venture downtown. Disregarding this warning, our unnamed narrator does go to a downtown restaurant where he meets Overton's double, who tells him that he has an unusual book bearing on an article by a German scientist, presenting evidence that certain minds can communicate by thought. This is but a trap to lure him to a room where he is drugged and may possibly be killed. He is rescued by Rachel who has experienced another premonition concerning him and with the help of the real Mr. Overton, who has spotted and recognized his companion as a criminal. Goodman set up a series of unusual events, maintained reader interest throughout, but his ending proved to be a letdown.

Hart had gently lured Emma Frances Dawson back to the pages of the *Argonaut* with the May 28, 1881 issue by agreeing to publish a long poem titled "Decoration Day." This was an unusual experiment in which Dawson wrote certain stanzas in the same sense that Poe wrote "The Bells," to express with repetition and arrangement of consonants, the cadence of a variety of musical instruments. She attempted the bassoon, drum, tambourine, clarinet, horn, cymbals, trumpets, bugles, flute, crescent and trombone, and in between the stanzas of each instrument were the refrains of the ghosts of the dead. Hart's instinct was good, Dawson would work for him again, but tragically nearly all of her future work would be translations, predominantly of tales of supernatural and horror, but not her own work. Like the late Russian novelist and poet Boris Pasternak, who lamented in his published letters that literally half of his total production had been translations, which he performed to keep himself alive (he estimated that he had given 12 full years of his life to nothing but translations), she would sacrifice her own creativity to bring to the public translations that could not compare with her own special genius.

That was to be Dawson's situation for the rest of her active writing years. She imagined herself a poet and she was — let us say it — a most artificial one. She had a vocabulary that rivaled Clark Ashton Smith (though she was never in his class as a poet), her mastery of difficult forms was accomplished, but the effect of her verse does not compare with even a popular jingle, because her style lacked the quality of song or the lyric quality. It is probable that she wrote fiction as an excuse or a frame to get her poetry into print, because she sprinkled it throughout her prose. It marred her fiction for she was one of the finest women prose stylists this country ever produced. All her poetry should mercilessly be cut out of her fiction including connective lines, and the woman's fine works be restored to literature.

XVII. MILNE MAKES IT

There was now a clear field for the remarkable science fiction of Robert Duncan Milne, if Hart could find him, and find him he did. Milne had made contact with William W. Randall, a man obsessed with the theatre, but working as a bookkeeper for E. W. Scott & Co. San Francisco was one of the great centers of theatre of the world, not just for traveling companies but for locally produced plays. There were also playhouses in nearby Stockton, Sacramento, Fresno, Oakland and San Jose. Milne had spent a good part of 1881 writing the dialogue for stories suggested to him by Randall and was paid a flat rate for each play, relinquishing all rights to future royalties. Among the plays they wrote in "collaboration" were "Yosemite," "The Voodoo Doctor," "Lone Jack" and "One Summer's Fun," but none of these apparently survive nor has any data been located to determine whether they were actually produced, though they may have been.

A completely unpredicted comet had appeared in late June, 1881, visible in both Europe and the United States. As all such impressive bodies it aroused speculation as to a possible collision and the resultant "end of the world." Milne was the ideal man to present the facts about such "heavenly" spectaculars and Hart commissioned him to write "Our Celestial Visitant," subtitled "Theories and Facts Respecting the Orbit of the Comet of 1881," and published it in the July 2, 1881 issue of the *Argonaut.* Though more scholarly than popular in tone, Milne's piece delineating the known facts and conjectures about comets in general and this comet in particular, together with a diagram of his own showing its course relative to the earth, was an impressive document. Milne, the tongue-in-cheek hoax-maker, was masterly at putting out pseudo-scientific fires and quieting any doubts of the populace.

The fact that astronomy was in the news gave Hart the idea of having Milne write a series of fictionalized astronomical excursions and quite deliberately launched Milne into his most productive and effective period of science fiction writing.

The first of his new series, "The Aërial Cone Reflector" *(Argonaut,* August 6, 1881) was a return to the old newspaper hoax school of writing, where the entire emphasis was on making the public believe a startling new advance had been accomplished and no consideration was given to a story line. In this story, Milne had the invention of a telescopic device, intended to be used for observation of planets, which also catches the reflection of images from the upper atmosphere anywheres in the world and can magnify them so the viewer would seem to be a short distance away. Milne heralded this as an invention comparable to the telephone or the telegraph, which would make instantly visible (on a clear day) almost any part of the earth's surface. Milne's excuse for writing the account was because "As the facts which I am about to relate have somehow leaked out, and are being spoken of in a form garbled and calculated to mislead, I take the present opportunity of furnishing the public with the only authentic version of the remarkable affair."

"A Dip Into Space" (August 27, 1881) was a sequel to "The Aërial Cone Reflector," but only in the sense that Milne claims to have been stopped in the street by a man who said he had an invention far superior. Taking him at his word, Milne agrees to dinner at the man's home and is regaled with an elaborate lecture on the science of optics. What he will be permitted to witness is a device that will give him close-ups of the planets, through a combination of chemical and optical means. At no point is Milne obscure about how the entire apparatus works, even including a very clear diagram with the story. The high point is a close-up of Saturn showing its surface to be an unending barren waste of ice, but the rings also prove to be almost entirely of ice, the pieces that compose it colliding with one another in their circular transit. As the inventor is about to focus on Jupiter, the apparatus goes akilter and Milne is invited back some other time.

"Good as his word, the inventor has Milne back in "A Peep at the Planets" (September 10, 1881). To lend credibility, Milne includes the exact date, August 27th, and his host, Major Titus, has dinner with him, plays some billiards and then at 12 midnight, mixes the proper chemicals for the new try at the planets. Milne is informed that despite its distance from the sun, due to the actinic action of the sun's rays on its atmosphere, Uranus is warm enough to support life. Titus has also deduced that Uranus does not revolve on its axis, it rolls, wheel-like. As a consequence, one side is eternal summer and the other eternal winter and there are no seasons. Vegetation is detected as well as living creatures of such vast size that our prehistoric dinosaurs were tiny by comparison, but his apparatus is not capable of more sharply defining them.

They focus on Jupiter and though they view it very closely, impenetrable masses of whirling gases, with incredible Jovian "hurricanes" make it impossible to see the surface. When momentarily the storm causes a rift in the surface cover, there seems to be a sea as smooth and calm as glass. No land mass is detectable and with a density that of water, none is expected, though the possibility of some sort of aquatic life is not ruled out. In a stroke of luck, a gigantic, saurian-type creature is discovered swimming in the "ocean" of Jupiter, but now it seems certain the substance is probably not water at all, but something else.

The device is next turned on Mars and it is determined that there are seas filled with apparently real water, the surface is covered with red vegetation which gives the planet its distinctive hue, there are rivers of immense size "bounding over awful precipices," forests and great plains. Then, the ruins of masonry appear, blocks of stone, hundreds of cubic feet in measurement strewn over areas of hundreds of miles. There were many such ruins and no sign of animal life and the conclusion is that once there was intelligent life on Mars, but it is now a dying planet.

The next part of this story, titled "Venus and the Comet," appeared in the September 17, 1881 *Argonaut* and continues from where the first had broken off, this time with observations of Venus. Their instrument shows them a previously unknown satellite of Venus, half the size of our moon and just as barren. On Venus proper they really hit "pay dirt." There are green meadows and flowers, beautiful alabaster structures, through which move people clad in shining garments. There are extensive towns and calm seas sailed by definite ships. It is concluded that Venus is a Utopian world. That session ends with the observation of a comet, and an excellent, highly technical theory of the composition of such a body is offered. That the entire series of stories may have been inspired by the introduction of the comet into the newspapers of June, 1881 seems entirely probable. The first story in the series dealt only with observations on earth, but all the others, which followed Milne's dissertation on the nature of "The Comet of 1881" were interplanetary in scope. That they were popular and appreciated was obvious, otherwise they would not have been permitted to continue for four issues.

Hart decided that Milne was good for the magazine and he would suggest ideas that might help circulation. "He was one of the few writers I have had to deal with who would take a suggested plot or idea and work it up into a finished story," said Hart. "The invasion of San Francisco was suggested to him, to be modeled on 'The Battle of Dorking.'" *Blackwood's Magazine*, a British publication with an American edition, had printed in its issue for May, 1871 a story titled "The Battle of Dorking" which was attributed to George Chesney. It told of an unprepared England, invaded and conquered by Germany, her days of glory over and her people emigrating to other shores to find a future. This was reprinted in brochure form by William Black and Sons, Edinburgh and London, the same year and became a bestseller inspiring many sequels. It is credited with alerting England to the need for preparedness.

Blackwood's Magazine had an American edition and was distributed here. "The Battle of Dorking" appeared in hardcovers from Porter & Coates, Philadelphia, as THE GERMAN CONQUEST OF ENGLAND IN 1875 (1871). What probably proved Hart's inspiration for the suggestion of a similar story about the invasion of San Francisco was the interest shown in the book THE LAST DAYS OF THE REPUBLIC by Pierton W. Dooner, published in San Francisco by the Alta California Publishing House in 1880. The Chinese imported to the West Coast to help build the railroads and to provide cheap labor for the mines and the fields had been a source of much discussion and concern. Dooner projected the condition to the turn of the century, where six giant Chinese companies have made great economic inroads into the United States and are a cover to bring in more orientals and plot the conquest of the nation. This is brought about through arming of the Chinese already in the country and supplemented by a direct invasion from China. The Chinese arrange a war to distract the Europeans and then proceed to the conquest of the United States. The book ends with the lines: "Thus passed away the glory of the Union of States, at the dawn of the Twentieth Century."

Milne's story, "The Bombardment of San Francisco," printed under the cognomen of "Told by an Eye-Witness" appeared in the October 8, 1881 issue of the *Argonaut.* The writing was extremely good and this time Milne actually told a story. A ship flying the Chilean flag, named the *Huascar,* steams into San Francisco, lowers its colors and hauls up the black flag of piracy. She fires several shells over the city from a spot behind an island where shore batteries cannot reach her and then, through an emissary, demands $10 million in gold, or she will devastate San Francisco. The *Huascar* is completely ironclad with a very effective long gun in the fore, which can outdistance anything the Americans can bring up.

There is no stupidity or foolishness on the part of the San Franciscans, to the contrary they act with great coolness. Word is sent to all the fortifications in the immediate vicinity. Messages go out to three nearby American warships, though none of them are ironclads or a match for the Chilean vessel. A local expert begins to rig up mines and improvised torpedoes and the $10 million is raised and turned over as slowly as possible so as to gain time for action.

Nothing prevails. The gold is delivered. The American warships are unable to stop the invader. The shore batteries fail to make any effective hits, and in the second installment titled "How San Francisco Was Ramsomed" (October 15, 1881), a local synagogue and the Palace Hotel are hit by fire from the invader and she departs, struck twice but undamaged.

It is learned that the ship and its crew are in the employ of the Japanese, though manned by Chileans, for the Japanese are engaged in a war with China. However, the ironclad never returns to

Japan but disappears forever. The payoff occurs when the Captain of the *Huascar* is recognized by one of those who delivered the gold, living in fabulous luxury in Mexico.

The circulation-raising qualities of the story were pronounced enough to arouse the envy of the local press. In recording the incident Hart recalls: "But one of the San Francisco dailies solemnly accused Milne of stealing his story from 'The Battle of Dorking.'

"Poor Milne showed me this paragraph and remarked: 'Hard lines Mr. Hart. A man who has more ideas than he can use, yet is accused of stealing the ideas of others.' "

"The Palaeoscopic Camera" by Milne in the December 24, 1881 issue of the *Argonaut* displayed that Milne was well on his way towards mastering his unique form of science fiction. The story deals with a special camera and a method of photo developing which, affected by the radiated heat of old walls, successfully takes photos of *past* events. The "story" takes place in an old mission near Tucson, but with Milne the concept, and a plausible explanation of it, *is* the story. Writing superbly and richly, in nothing more than an exchange of dialogue between the narrator and the inventor of the marvelous camera, Milne fascinatingly constructs the theories that point to the plausibility of such a camera. He explores the possible negative factors and mounts evidence to dispute them. The reader becomes so absorbed in the ingenuity and resourcefulness of Milne's arguments that the theories not only become the focus of the story but are accepted as the story.

XVIII. MILNE TURNS TO DRAMA

Then, just as Hart seemed to have Milne pinned down, his services were temporarily detoured again by W. W. Randall, for whom Milne was fleshing out the dialogue for play outlines. Theatre was big in San Francisco, and through the years a number of theatrical papers had been established, several of them attained a certain degree of success, such as *Figaro*, which was a daily paper concerned with the theatre (no connection with European publications of the same name), which was widely read during the 1870's in San Francisco. Another, *The Dramatic Chronicle*, which started in 1866, was so successful that under the management of two teenagers, Charles and M. H. De Young, it metamorphisized into *The San Francisco Chronicle*, still published today. Randall was associated with another such publication, a weekly titled *Dramatic Brevities*, which began publication November 20, 1881, owned and edited by Francis L. Fisher, a printer and engraver located at 518 Sacramento Street, but Robert Duncan Milne secured the post of co-editor (probably because of the plays he had written for Randall). The weekly covered drama, music and art and included portraits of notables.

On November 15, 1881, a play written in collaboration by Randall and Milne had opened at the Stockton Theatre, Stockton, Calif., and was so favorably received that it was shown in nearby towns and then in San Francisco in January, 1882. The play was called "Senator Silverbags; or, The Power of Money," and was billed as "An Entirely New and Original Comedy; A Humorous Satire on American Society and Politics, Founded on Events of the Present Day," starring the noted comedian M. A. Kennedy. It was a play of pretenders jockeying for money, power and position. Fraudulent titleholders from abroad, looking for a wealthy woman;

a newly-rich but ignorant miner elected to the Senate; educated but economically deprived women seeking wealth and rich women on the scent of titles.

Randall, anticipating the success of the play, and aware of Milne's chronic need for drinking money, had Milne sign an official document dated November 3, 1881, waiving all rights to his half of the play for $10.00 in cash. On December 10, 1881, Milne signed another strange statement *verifying* that he had *indeed* turned all rights over to Randall on November 3rd. These statements were published in *Dramatic Brevities*, listing Randall as "Sole Proprietor and Manager."

When the play opened in San Francisco, the local correspondent of *The New York Dramatic News* claimed that Milne had plagarized the idea for his play from one produced in Germany titled "Moneybags." Evidence of that fact, he suggested, was the pittance Milne had accepted for all rights.

A furious Milne replied in *Dramatic Brevities* with a communication dated January 5, 1882 to the effect: "Now, the fact is that the German comedy of "Gelt Saecke," by Dr. Bendix was produced in Vienna, three months after "Senator Silverbags" was copyrighted by Mr. Randall in Washington, and that simple fact disposes of *that* line of argument." The Randall and Milne collaboration had indeed been copyrighted June 20, 1881. Milne suggested that the German play had been adapted from his, not the other way around: "*Facts* are stubborn things and *dates* are hard to get around," he said.

The fact that he had disposed of his interest for $10 Milne felt was his own business "and the attempt to disparage a work of *art* in such a shabby and contemptible manner, as reducing it to ordinary monetary values *ought* to be beneath the notice of any honorable journalist or dramatic manager."

Milne also took umbrage at the statement that he was "clever at adaptation," which he interpreted as meaning that he had no ideas of his own. He shafted the critic with the retort: "I thank Heaven that my faculty of *adaptation* still runs in the grooves of education and human experience, and these are the only preserves that I never mean to poach upon," underscoring his own superior academic credentials.

Dramatic Brevities' publishing longevity is unknown. Randall worked as manager of *The City Argus*, a weekly, through 1880, became an advertising agent for *The Daily Exchange* at least through 1882, and some time after 1884 left for New York City, where, with the issue dated August 30, 1893 he launched a new weekly theatre magazine titled *The Amusement Globe*. This paper was tabloid size, 28 pages, printed on good stock, selling for 10 cents a copy. It was well edited and entertaining, with reports of casting openings in all major cities of the nation. It only survived about 18 months, but the October 4, 1893 issue is of interest to science fiction readers for its well-done story "The Season of 2093" by Charles H. Day. In describing preparations by one "A. Swift, A Circus Manager," for the forthcoming season, a number of inventions are noted. They include the "Under-ground Oceanic Electric Railroad" to Europe, which will transport the entire company for the circus to the U.S. on 24 hours' notice. There is the "Pneumatic Tubular Train" from San Francisco to New York, which makes it at the incredible time of one hour. Illustrations and photographs for the Circus Program are wired from Paris.

The circus owner's prospective son-in-law is working on a rainmaker that appears to be a "sure thing." With this rainmaker the circus owner plans to keep drenching his leading competitor everywhere he shows, so that he will be bankrupted. Type is set for printing by talking into a microphone. Paper and ink are manufactured as needed for publishing. The circus owner's daughter Electra is visited by her suitor in a flying machine that can hover outside her window. The young man sells rain machines to both competitors, forces them to come to a truce, marries the daughter, sets out to make a fortune with his rainmaker in California and begins plans for organizing air passenger lines to put the railroads out of business.

As late as 1917 William W. Randall would register copyright for a play "Where There's a Will There's a Way," a farce in three acts, so his theatrical activities continued for many years. Beyond that, his record fades into obscurity.

XIX. THE BRIEF, BIZARRE CAREER OF NATHAN KOUNS

The preoccupation with the theatre and *Dramatic Brevities* had limited Milne's production, but Hart was after him and he was promising a new good one. The only thing to tide the readership over in the way of the strange and supernatural was an anonymously published tale in the March 11, 1882 issue of the *Argonaut* titled "Janet and the Devil." A story of a young Scottish minister who hires a slightly addled housekeeper, who develops to be a cadaver inhabited and animated by the Devil, was actually Robert Louis Stevenson's famous short story "Thrawn Janet." There was a difference, however. Stevenson had written his story in the Scottish dialect and the *Argonaut* published a version rewritten into standard English, with no acknowledgement of source or author. The story had been written in May, 1881 and published by the *Cornhill Magazine* in England for October, 1881. Obviously, Hart had spotted it there and had rewritten the story. Ironically, the *Argonaut* had unquestionably been one of the publications that Stevenson had desperately tried to sell to while sick and starving in San Francisco. Hart later *reprinted* his version in the January 1, 1900 issue of the *Argonaut*, still, evidently unaware that it was by Stevenson, because he gave no credit.

Even Hart's assistant editor Harry D. Bigelow was thrown into the breach to contribute supernatural stories, for he had a short signed bit titled "The Spectre Priest" in the March 18, 1882 issue. Presumed to be a "true" story of a British ghost in the year 1752, it told of a young bride awakened by a wailing noise in a manor in which she was staying. Following the noise she sees a priest standing before a picture. He strangles a baby and throws its body into a concealed cavity behind the picture. Screaming, the girl arouses the household and a skeleton of a baby is indeed found behind the frame.

When Milne's new story appeared as a two-part serial in the *Argonaut* for April 1 and 8th, 1882, it proved well worth waiting for. This time, Milne placed his imaginative concept into a carefully knit, well-organized, narrative form. Titled "The Iguandon's Egg," the story told of the shipwreck of three sailors on an unexplored portion of the coast of Papua. They are treated kindly by the natives, who apparently have never even seen a white man before. There seems little hope of rescue, so one of the sailors, Ben, "marries" a native girl. There is a mysterious grove which they are kept from entering. One day, in a religious frenzy, the priests drive twelve young girls into the grove and kill them. Under cover of the night, the sailors venture into the grove, where there they find a mound covered by skeletons. They dig all night and uncover what appears to be a gigantic, wrinkled ball, 15 tons or more in weight. Discovered by the natives, they are saved when they light wet mangrove roots soaked in tar, arousing superstitious awe in their powers.

The strange ball is rolled into an opening, where day after day it is subjected to the tropic heat. One afternoon, with Ben seated atop it, a crack appears and a 12-ton dinosaur with a vicious horn on the end of its snout breaks out and lumbers to the swamps. It grows month by month until it is somewheres between 80 and 100 feet in length, but since it is primarily a vegetable eater, harms no one, except inadvertently.

The story is narrated by the one surviving sailor who gets back to San Francisco, in a sort of lingo, replete with speech mannerisms, which is a difficult narrative method, but Milne pulls it off with great success and readability. There have been many stories of the type written since, so the novelty of the plot is non-existent, but the story has suspense — even a cliffhanger at the end of the first chapter — and is a very creditable effort.

"The 'Judas Escariot,' " Edward Page Mitchell's tale of a ship that had a will and luck of its own — all bad — appeared in the April 29, 1882 issue. It had originally been titled "The Last Cruise of the Judas Iscariot" when it appeared in *The Sun* out of New York for April 16, 1882, only 11 days before. Since it took at least 10 days for a transcontinental trip by train, the cold figures reveal with what speed the story was rushed into print.

Similarly, the reprint of "The Diamond Lens" by Fitz-James O'Brien in the July 8, 1882 issue of the *Argonaut*, a story which had originally been published in the *Atlantic Monthly* for January, 1858, indicated not the dredging up of an old story for a filler, but timeliness, because the first collection of O'Brien's works, titled THE POEMS AND STORIES OF FITZ-JAMES O'BRIEN, edited by William Winter, had appeared in 1881 and had evidently been sent ahead for review. The interesting thing was that in his story of a world in a drop of water revealed by a super-microscope, O'Brien's character had discovered a beautiful feminine creature which he named "Animula." In the *Argonaut*, the name had been changed to "Gracilia" throughout!

The *Argonaut* was the constant scene of development of new talent and one of the most promising was an author said to have been a veteran of the Confederate army, named Nathan C. Kouns. All of his stories were about the South and the Civil War period and there was about them a richness of style and authenticity of background that branded him a man of exceptional talent. His first story for the *Argonaut* had been "Alabam," published in the February 19th and 26th, 1881 issues. It dealt with a strange aide to a Confederate officer, who follows him with extraordinary devotion and attempting to save his life is shot, who turns out to be a vagrant girl deeply in love with him.

His other stories all combined the elements of rich background, fine writing and surprise endings, but except in mood did not strike the chord of the unusual or bizarre until "The Wraith of Stephen Arnold" which appeared in three installments in the August 12th, 19th and 26th issues of the *Argonaut*. A Confederate soldier travelling home on a furlough is passing across a battlefield littered with the paraphernalia of battle when he is gripped by an arm extending out of the ground. By a system of signals involving tightening and releasing of pressure he establishes communication and then the arm of the dead man, supplied with a paper and pencil, writes out a message. He wishes to take possession of the body of the soldier long enough to ease the problems of his 17-year-old widow who is pregnant but whom no one will believe is actually married to him, and then will voluntarily withdraw. The soldier agrees and becomes a subordinate center of awareness in his own body dominated by another's will. The resemblance between him and the dead man, by coincidence, turns out to be striking, and people assume the differences are due to the years he has been away at war. All the wrongs are righted and the spirit of the dead man leaves the body of his host as promised, but the living man returns to marry the sister of the dead man Stephen Arnold. The story is impregnated with a morality and a code of ethics that belonged to a recent past, but it is effective, rich and imaginative nonetheless.

Highly unusual is "The Man-Dog" by Nathan Kouns from the September 30, 1882 issue of the *Argonaut*. The murder of a plantation owner's wife by his young mulatto slave girl is solved by a man who has the ability, superior to that of a dog, of following scent, since he can follow one right up a tree. Utilizing his exceptional talent he locates the cabin of a runaway slave who has killed the plantation owner's wife, and as a friend raises a rifle to kill the mulatto girl who has masterminded the scheme, he is stopped by the grief-stricken husband with the words: "No! No! Let the girl go! She is my daughter!"

Kouns would disappear from the pages of the *Argonaut* and reappear with a novel-length exhortation for Catholicism, thinly disguised as fiction in ARIUS THE LIBYAN published by D. Appleton and Company in 1882. This nearly 400-page sermon would be reprinted as a one dollar hardcover book in 1928.

XX. SAN FRANCISCO'S GREATEST SCIENCE FICTION WRITER

A new comet had appeared in the skies during the middle of October, 1882 and elicited considerable wonder. Milne was now the resident authority on comets so he came up with an article illustrated by four diagrams in the October 21, 1882 *Argonaut*, quite appropriately titled "The Comet." His knowledge and scientific command of the facts would be impressive even by today's standards, and engenders a healthy respect for Milne's background research. Most fascinating were his conjectures at the close of the article on what might happen in the event of a collision of the comet with the earth. "It is perfectly admissible," he said, "to conceive of a comet whose principle element was hydrogen, combining with the oxygen of our atmosphere, and precipitating upon our surface such devastating floods of water as it would be impossible for the higher forms of animal and vegetable life to withstand; or of one composed of nitrogen, whose contact would destroy all life from the face of the planet; or, say, a carbonic acid, which would have an equivalent effect; or still larger proportion of hydrogen, which would refuse to combine with our atmosphere in the proportions HO^2, but would doom us to a fiery death. In short, the possibilities for injury are as boundless as the chances for any such casualty are infinitesimal."

The comet had given Milne an idea for a story which appeared the following month in the November 18, 1882 issue as "Into the Sun." The scene was set in San Francisco and the time was 1883.

It was the same comet he was writing about in October, which has been retarded by passing too closely to the sun. Milne handles his science brilliantly, and the story is the prototype of many that have appeared since. Messages began to pour into San Francisco from New York, Chicago, Memphis and New Orleans telling of unusual lights in the sky like a gigantic fire burning in the distance, and rising temperatures. London reports that the temperature has risen to 113 and people are dropping dead in the streets. Abruptly, the messages from London stop. The only theory is that the comet has fallen into the sun and excited a tremendous outburst of heat.

It is night in San Francisco and people are out in the streets, watching the appearance of a great fire in the sky. Fear spreads and looting begins. Religious fanatics are everywhere preaching the end of the world. At the newspaper office, ice wagons arrive to help counter the rising temperature for the working press.

It is 6:00 A.M. in New York City and the wires report that the sun has risen, with thousands already dead from sunstroke, thousands more bathing off the docks. A repetition of London is seen and San Francisco realizes it has but three hours to prepare for the inevitable. At the suggestion of a doctor friend, the reporter accompanies him to make a balloon ascension on the knowledge that heat is generated by action of the sun's rays on the air and the thinner the air, the less the heat. As they launch the partially inflated balloon, the temperature is already 133 and the sun has not risen. It is deduced that the great heat will make the gas in the balloon expand more than normal and that a fully inflated bag would burst. Through a telescope they see almost nude bodies of thousands of people immersing themselves in the waters of the bay. Their thermometer reaches 147 degrees at an altitude of 11,000 feet, so they can contemplate what is happening below. At 25,000 feet the heat seems to stabilize.

The doctor predicts that evaporation of water because of the heat will cause torrential rains and great mists which will protect the earth from continuous temperature rises, but most life will not survive. A strange sound anticipates convection currents in the upper atmosphere caused by the heat. They alternately are whirled about and becalmed. Then a vicious downdraft drives them beneath the cloud cover and while they can clearly make out the outlines of the peninsula and the bay there is no longer any city visible. Not even flame exists any longer. Everything is ashes. A violent gust throws the doctor from the balloon and the reporter is now alone. The ballon begins falling. The story ends: "I am nearing

HISTORY OF THE MOVEMENT 146

the molten surface. My feeling has changed. I am conscious that it has ceased to seem to rise. I feel that I am falling now — falling into the fiery depths below. Nearer — nearer yet; scorched and blackened by the awful heat as I approach — I fall — down — down — down — "

The story is a masterpiece of science fiction, undoubtedly one of the best end-of-the-world short stories ever written. Milne's complete command of the science at every point, his justification, logically, for every event, could scarcely have been surpassed by any living man at the time the story was published. This story justifiably "made" him reputationwise. He was more than a brilliantly logical hoaxer, he was a masterful storyteller who could imbue heavy science with all the suspense of an action thriller. Years later, outstanding California authors like Gertrude Atherton and Geraldine Bonner both claimed he was their inspiration. Bonner's first story several years later would be an out-and-out rewrite of "Into the Sun."

The demands on the *Argonaut* to provide a sequel were irresistable. Everyone in San Francisco wanted to know what had happened after the frightful conflagration. Had anyone survived? Was the earth even habitable? Milne obliged with "Plucked From the Burning," appropriately subtitled "A Picture of the Earth's Condition after the Fiery Cataclysm of 1883" in the December 16, 1882 issue of the *Argonaut.* Our reporter recovers consciousness high in the Himalayas, tended by some Tibetan monks. His ballon had been caught in tremendous currents and whirled around the earth to come to rest in Tibet. Apparently not all of the earth's surface had been struck with the same intensity by the blast from the sun.

An exploration party is organized and as they descend, utter devastation and death is everywhere. Almost all of China is gone. In a harbor in Macao, they find a ship that can be put in shape to steam back to California. As they traverse the Pacific, they note that there are strange pockets that have been hit less hard than others. Luxuriant plant life is rapidly covering seared fields. San Francisco, however, is just one charred heap. Only the broad expanse of Market Street is definable and there are slag piles where some of the prominent structures once rose.

They find two men in San Francisco, miners who were underground during the worst of it and are digging in the basement of the Nevada bank for gold, the realization not having struck them that it will be useless. The story ends 10 years after the inferno, with a world without arts or sciences — and no need for them — rebuilding a simpler civilization. The sequel is more of a summing up than a story but it is very effective, its mood appropriate to the situation and its science explaining away the survival of the remnants quite adequately. It was satisfying with its final lines: "Utopia 1893."

Milne was now not only a regional writer of great popularity, he had become an influential force in two fashions. First, there would be gradually increasing demand and awareness of the appeal of science fiction. Second, when he later began to taper off, the need to fill the demand for science fiction would encourage Hart and others to develop a school of science fiction writers on the West Coast.

Milne had one more story in the *Argonaut* before the year ended, a lost race yarn in the December 23, 1882 issue titled "The Lost Ship Marigold," telling of an uncharted island in the Pacific, where descendants of shipwrecked Englishmen have lived for over 300 years. He secured his plot from LIVES AND VOYAGES OF DRAKE, CAVENDISH AND DAMPIER, which told of the mystery of the ship *Marigold*, with a complement of men and women, which was separated from two companion ships by a gale in September, 1578 and never seen again. A group of Americans discover the island on which they were cast ashore, and a community still exists speaking Elizabethan English. The centuries-old clothes have been stored away in trunks and are still in excellent repair. One of the Americans falls in love with an island girl and has a shooting contest with another suitor, the winner to get the girl. The islander uses a bow and arrow and the American, with a gun, wins handily. Enraged, the "native" shoots him in the back with an arrow. In a sense, the snake has been introduced into the Garden of Eden. The story ends on a note of great sympathy for the island people, whom Milne deduces will never survive the contact with modern civilization.

During the year there had been a well done story reprinted from UNDER THE SUN by Philip Robinson titled "The Man-Eating Tree." Stories with this theme were almost standard fare during the last quarter of the nineteenth century, enough being available to fill a fair-sized anthology, and this one was exceptionally grisly. This tree grew in Nubia. A boy chasing a doe, together with the animal, is swept up by it. Each leaf was instinct with life and exhibited a hunger for flesh. When they touched one another, there was a sucking sound and one would droop dead. The tree is attacked by a man with a gun, and at each shot a limb, a leaf, a bole demonstrably dies, while the tree writhes in agony and tries to tear itself from the ground to grasp its tormentor. The job is finally finished with a knife, but the boy is dead. The next day a great bird with a mighty beak appears and begins to feed on the decaying fruit.

Hart's predeliction for the supernatural with a tinge of the scientific frequently resulted in real services to literature. Theophile Gautier's great vampire story, "La Morte Amoureuse" or in English as "Clarimonde" or "The Beautiful Vampire," since its initial publication in *Chronique de Paris* for June 23rd and 26th, 1836, had become an acknowledged classic of the Western world, with its poignant detail of the love of a priest for a female vampire. Gautier had been dead since 1872, yet most of his works had not been translated into English. Just the previous year, two of his novels, ONE OF CLEOPATRA'S NIGHTS and THE ROMANCE OF A MUMMY, had appeared in the United States for the first time. Perhaps this evoked the initial translation and printing of "The Avatar" by Gautier in the *Argonaut's* issues of January 27th and February 3rd, 1883, under the title of "Metempsychosis." This novella had originally appeared in France in 1856. The translator was Philip Shirley, a pen name for Annie Lake Townsend. She had a minor reputation in San Francisco literary circles because in 1879, when she was only 20, A. L. Bancroft, the leading book publisher in San Francisco, issued her skillfully written novel of manners, ON THE VERGE. That was the era when outstanding writers might labor their entire lives, gain popularity among the readers of the weeklies and the newspapers, and never succeed in getting any of their material into hardcovers. Knowledge of both French and German were flaunted in ON THE VERGE and since Miss Townsend was now translating the work of a writer whose style was frequently referred to as "prose poetry," just how well did she do? "The Avatar" did not receive another translation in the United States until Myndart Verelst translated it for Brentano's, where it lead off a two-story collection published in 1887 titled TALES BEFORE SUPPER. A comparison between the two translations and between the standard translation found in COLLECTED WORKS OF THEOPHILE GAUTIER (Walter J. Black, 1928), reveals the young woman was every bit as competent as those who followed her, the only difference being that when Gautier would get carried away in poetic description, she would sometimes omit a few passages.

Actually, "Metempsychosis" or "The Avatar" is scarcely as well-written as "Clarimonde," but it tells an interesting story. Octave de Saville is impetuously in love with the wife of the Polish Count Labinski, whom he can never have. An old doctor, Cherbonneau, wise in both science and the secrets of India, succeeds in transferring their personalities. Sensing that something is wrong, the Countess will now have nothing to do with her husband. When it comes time to reverse the transfer, the soul of de Saville refuses to return to its own body and disappears into limbo. The doctor quickly writes a note willing most of his estate to de Saville, leaves his 70-year-old worn-out shell for the body of the young man, and with his "inheritance" starts a new life.

Milne was back in the *Argonaut* with a minor effort, "Seen in a Trance," the issue of January 27, 1883. A man who claims to have clairvoyant powers permits himself to be mesmerized, and uses this device to witness a drama of a man who, having lost the hand of his cousin to another, finds he will receive no inheritance unless both of them die childless. He first is responsible for wrecking a train on which his cousin and her husband have left on their honeymoon in which 50 are killed but they are unhurt. He sets fire to the hotel they are staying at and taunts them as he proceeds to escape through a window using a long wire. He becomes entangled in it, the firemen rescue the couple, but the building collapses before they can save the villain.

Because of his insatiable love of alcohol, the full extent of Milne's general knowledge was never utilized, but it was known and reported in the San Francisco press at the time of his death that he occasionally wrote and sold articles on banking to Eastern magazines. Some credence is lent to this facet of his interests by the story "A Theft of Seventy Millions" in the February 10, 1883 issue. The story is very carefully told in the form of statements from five concerned parties: Amos Quigley, valet of Dr. Basil Thorndyke; William H. Vanderbilt, one of the leading U.S. financiers; the United States Counsel of Halifax, Nova Scotia; the superintendent of the New York Safe Deposit Company; and the Assistant Treasurer of the United States at Washington, D.C.

Vanderbilt is suing the safe deposit company for negligence for permitting $70 million in 4% bonds to be removed from his vault by Dr. Thorndyke, and the U.S. Government for reregistering the bonds in Dr. Thorndyke's name in what appears to be one of the greatest crimes of the centry. Dr. Thorndyke has disappeared and cannot be located.

From these statements we learn that Dr. Thorndyke was a scientist who was master of the use of electricity, protecting his laboratory with charged locks as well as being adroit at mesmerism. The Doctor has his steam-yacht, capable of making 16 knots an hour, outfitted with scientific apparatus, including a comfortable chair with the legs set in glass and an electrical conduit running to it. He pursues Vanderbilt's yacht, overtakes it and delivers a forged message to the effect that business enemies have aligned themselves to scuttle some of his best enterprises while he is overseas. He offers to take Vanderbilt back on his fast yacht to a place where he can quickly return to New York. As his guest, Vanderbilt is seated in the special chair, an electrical current paralyzes him, making it impossible for him to move or speak. Thorndyke then hypnotizes him.

The next time Vanderbilt is seen is at the office of the U.S. Counsel in Halifax, who witnesses a statement turning over to Thorndyke $70 million in bonds and Power of Attorney to do anything he wishes with them. Vanderbilt then is returned to his yacht and continues to Europe.

Thorndyke shows up at the safe deposit company with the Power of Attorney and the combination to the special locks of the vaults. Assisted by the safe deposit company, he removes three boxes with the $70 million in bonds. He then proceeds to Washington, D.C., shows the assistant Treasurer of the United States his Power of Attorney and receives assistance in converting the bonds to his name.

Clearly no crime has been committed by anyone but Thorndyke, and it now appears that his name was assumed and that since the bonds were transferred to him, they have been reregistered many times in many names and will be almost impossible to find.

The scientific aspect of the story is minor but Milne exercised considerable skill in both the manner of telling and the actual writing. What happened is revealed to the reader in the opening paragraphs. How it was done is the point of the story and accepting the hypnotic aspects, Milne proceeds with high interest to delineate the facts.

This year also saw the printing of Edward Page Mitchell's "The Balloon Tree" (March 10, 1883) and a number of translations by Emma Frances Dawson. These translations were all from the German, but always of something outre, offbeat or horrifying. "An Aerial Voyage" (February 24, 1883) relates the experience of three balloonists forced to take off at night and being carried so high they fainted from loss of air and then almost drowned in the ocean; "The White Death" (March 17, 1883) was a story of pioneer life on a Paraguayan plantation where there are a series of battles against invading ants, seemingly endless snakes and a man-killing jaguar; "A Mysterious Disappearance" (March 31, 1883) tells of a woman who falls into a cataleptic trance and is placed in a locked room to recuperate by a doctor and is forgotten while he takes a 36-day trip to tend to an important man; "The Severed Head" (May 5, 1883) is a grim story of a doctor asked to cut the head from a deceased woman's body and as he slashes the neck finds he has killed a living woman; "The Enchanted Ship" (July 21, 1883) is an unusual story of a pirate Captain and crew who have killed one another in a mutiny and are doomed to relive the events every night until their heads touch the soil — for fifty years this ship has sailed the seas with corpses that revive nightly to replay their own brutal passion play; "Why She Killed Him" (August 11, 1883) is a story of an Italian girl who has murdered her husband and will not reveal why, until the final moment when she confides to her mother he had sold her services to two passing Englishmen. All of Dawson's stories were translated from the German, and all were anonymous, but it was obvious that the stories were originally French, Turkish, Persian, Italian and Spanish in origin and had been translated by the German papers that Dawson had picked them up from.

During 1883, the San Francisco City Directory listed Milne as residing at 255 Stevenson Street, but Editor Hart again averred that he never knew Milne's address. Periodically Milne would send a *friend* and ask for an advance against his next story. Despite Milne's weakness, Hart said he *always* complied because the author kept a scrupulous record of his debts and when he was paid or a remittance came from abroad he honored them. While Milne could not be depended upon for work reliability, what he did produce was received with great enthusiasm by the readership. Even the hardheaded businessman Frank Pixley had nothing but kind things to say about Milne, which would indicate he was good for the financial side of the magazine. Pixley stated and believed that Milne was probably the greatest scholar living on the West Coast. Despite his drunkenness, he studied incessantly and kept up with all the latest scientific, economic, literary and political events.

Hart's financial advances and Pixley's praise paid off constantly. In their July 7th and 14th, 1883 issues, they ran a two-part story by Milne titled "A New Palingenesis." This remarkable story found Milne scientifically fielding the beliefs of the spiritualists and theologians in a manner to anticipate the theory of DNA, altering the message of the cells to produce a healthy individual from one legally dead. The wife of a doctor is dying from tuberculosis. Through scientific experimentation he devises a scientific method of chemically and electrically reducing her body to individual cells, then reforming those cells into protoplasm and then having the electrical life force of the woman participate in stimulating the protoplasm so as to reform her body with the disease eliminated.

A final step in the creation of a revised human being is the consumption and absorption of food as a cell binder. When the experiment fails before this cannot be adequately done the doctor's wife is saved by a shot of alcohol which is justified because it is more swiftly absorbed by the body than any other food!

Despite all the embroidery Milne has decorated his story with, what it implicitly states is that if it were possible to break the cells down into basic living matter, it might also be possible to substitute in the unhealthy cells the code that will mean the development of healthy cells without disease. He is talking about what we today call DNA. There is a relationship of theme between this story and "Professor Stückenholtz" by "J.A.A." previously reviewed. Both concern building a human body from protoplasmic cells, both imply cells must have the right signals to form the proper tissues, both involve a scientist with electrical chemical tanks who has as an observer and narrator a man who is forced to participate against his will. Milne who had material in the same issue in which the earlier story appeared as the leading writer of science fiction on the West Coast would certainly have read it — if he did not indeed write it — and might very well have been influenced by it. Both stories are of major importance in tracing the evolution of the concept of genetic manipulation in science fiction.

Milne did not appear again until the Christmas number, but the persistence with which the *Argonaut* continued to produce fantastic tales — particularly stories of the supernatural — was undeniable evidence of a hard, fast policy. The *Argonaut* introduced writers who would make an outstanding reputation later on for well-written and well-plotted regional stories through the door of the supernatural. Yda H. Addis, whose married name was Storke, had come to California as a child. She was a rich stylist, ingenious in plotting, with a driving thrust to her stories that belied her personal modesty. Her earliest story, "Over the Cliff," which ran in the issues of September 15th and 22nd, 1883, dealt with a girl whose fiancee has left for Argentina and who sees his apparition beckoning her to a dangerous mountain road. She travels to South America, and with the aid of his ghost discovers he has been murdered, finds his body and assists in the death of his murderer. T. F. Robertson, who had contributed "Is Happiness a Myth?" the tale of an immortal man, to *The Californian*, produced "A Dissipated Ghost" (October 20, 1883), about a bank teller who cashes a check for $1,500 for a war comrade he thought killed in battle, spends a wild night roaming the hot spots with him, and then the next morning is dismissed from the bank for forgery when all evidence concludes that his former companion was *indeed* killed during the war.

An outstanding discovery proved to be Adelaide J. Holmes, married to a wealthy mining man and regarded as one of the prettiest women in San Francisco, who turned to writing under the initials of "A.J.H." with "The East Wing" (August 25, 1883). A girl finds that the man she has married has a walled-off room on the east side of his house and through dreams in which her mother appears discovers that this man has murdered her mother and buried her body beneath the floor of the sealed room.

A second story by her, "A Fatal Freak" (November 10, 1883), showed considerable promise with its picturization of a woman opium addict who in a drug-induced dream watches the death throes of another woman addict across the city, which turns out to be accurate. That drugs and liquor were as much a problem then as now is evidenced by the revealing paragraph: "We did what a thousand other girls did, do now, and probably will do again. And we did more. Each one of us, five Diablesses Noires had an unconquerable curiosity to know how it seemed to be under the influence of chloroform; to experience the excitement which absinthe gives; to realize the fascination that lurks under the sparkle of intoxicating drinks; to experience the dreams of the hashish-eaters; and to travel in the famed heaven of the opium-smokers."

Then with her third story, which appeared in the December 22, 1883 Christmas number of the *Argonaut*, Holmes produced a short masterpiece which understandably won her stature on the West Coast. The story was "A Ship on the Desert," in which a writer for the *Atlantic* visits another literary man on a remote Nevada ranch. The man has a young daughter, Ysbel, who had designed a wagon powered by a sail which her father built for her. She has never ridden in it out of fear. One night, her father, who is paralyzed from two previous strokes, has a third and she sets off for the doctor in the strange wagon accompanied by the writer, with winds driving them at 60 miles an hour. A boulder which rolls across their path causes an accident and Ysbel is killed, but the writer who has fallen in love with her carries the memories of that night. It is unique of its kind, atmospheric with the mood sustained throughout.

The *Argonaut* reprinted another of Fitz-James O'Brien's most memorable stories, "The Lost Room" (November 7, 1883), of a man who leaves his room for a moment, returns to find it filled with men and women in a wild orgy of merriment, with garish furnishings, a great organ and a gourmet's repast. After losing a toss of dice, he is thrust from the room and turns to find there is no longer a door but a blank wall and is never again able to find his former room.

The highlight issue of the year seemed to be the Christmas number which had carried Adelaide Holmes' remarkable story. The woman who wrote the drama reviews under the name of "Betsy B" was in actuality Jerome Hart's sister, who was married to a Dr. Joseph Austin. She had written for this special number, which ran 48 pages instead of the usual 16 (16 of them advertising) and featured a handsome black and white cover of a girl looking out over San Francisco bay with a giant bear curled at her feet, a light piece of fiction titled "A Tale of Modern Improvements." The widow of a rancher who has put quite a bit away, decides to build a house that has everything the ranch never had. She builds a house in San Francisco with hot and cold running water, sprinklers for the lawn, gas and electric lights, a steam furnace, supplemented by a fireplace in every room, a battery-powered burglar alarm, a telephone with an automatic switch for the most commonly used numbers, combination locks on the doors, and flush toilets. The adventures of her and her friends testing them reads like science fiction and makes one realize that all the things we take for granted today were the science fiction of yesterday.

Dan O'Connell, friend of William Henry Rhodes, who had edited CAXTON'S BOOK, contributed to the Christmas issue "The Duke's Daughter, A Christmas Tale of Some Centuries Hence," which opened in the San Francisco of 2002, and promised much but did not deliver. It was a tale of how the people of the future would celebrate Christmas in an era when there were in America Barons, Counts, Dukes and other titled privileged classes, when people looked to the past as the Golden Age. As satire and humor it was a failure, though there may have been some inside jokes that have not carried over to the present, and even though the story takes place in the year 2002, it would be overly generous to term it science fiction.

Robert Duncan Milne was represented in the December 22nd issue, too, and this time combined his two strong talents, science fiction and detective fiction. "A Dead Man's Ring" is a scientific detective story wherein a man is stabbed to death with a stilletto in a hotel room. A photograph taken of the outside of the hotel includes the window of the room in which the victim was murdered, but under a microscope it is discovered to be out of focus and no details can be seen.

A friend of the detective is a master photographer who has invented a device for rephotographing out-of-focus photographs and bringing them into focus. The immense detail with which Milne describes the equipment is so believable that it probably could prevent a patent and seems to indicate an in-depth knowledge of the photographic process. When the picture is developed, it shows the arm of a woman with two rings on it identical to the one found on the body of the murdered man.

He knows his *wife* wears those rings and it seems the murderess has been found, until in a resimulation of the event a creole woman, wearing identical rings, goes berserk and it develops that she formerly had an affair with the murdered man and never forgave him for ditching her and marrying another woman. Though only peripherally classifiable as science fiction, it is an extremely well-done story.

The fifth story in the issue that classified in the realm of the fantastic and unusual was by the assistant editor, Henry D. Bigelow, titled "The Blot on the Scutcheon." The Vicomte Saint Hubert on a visit to the estate of his friend Marquiss de Merillac finds himself falling in love with the daughter Yolande. Lost on a hunting trip they take refuge in an abandoned Chateau to rest before continuing back. In the Chateau, Saint Hubert enters a giant hall which is suddenly thronged with men and women of the past and one woman, incredibly like Yolande, is to be duped into running off with a man who will transfer her to the king's "harem." He tries to stop it but is killed and awakens to the real Yolande. He resists her love because he feels there is bad blood in her ancestry. His attitude he believes justified when he later learns she has joined the "harem" of Louis XIV. The story showed skill and richness in writing but a vagueness in meaning and organization. It was the last Bigelow would write as an employee of the *Argonaut*, because he had decided to go into his own business with a new publication, the *Ingleside*. He went into partnership with Harry McDowell, a Texan educated in San Francisco and the East, who had acted as a correspondent of the *Argonaut* under the nom de plume of "Viveer," specializing in things regarding the Chinese, of whom he had considerable knowledge.

XXI. THE INGLESIDE AND CITY ARGUS

The original concept was to publish a magazine strong on sensational serials and not quite as highbrow as the *Argonaut.* The weekly *Ingleside* was launched with the issue of November 25, 1883.

The editors proved masters of what is today called "The New Journalism," probably proving that little is actually new. While the weekly did run recipes, this was the maximum concession they made to the "masses," because the publication was extraordinarily strong on theatre, books and music. Its editorials were nothing if not candid, and the fiction strove for quality. The publication particularly cultivated the works of women writers and there were periods of economic stress when Minnie Buchanan Unger claimed to have written literally entire issues: fiction, articles, columns, reviews, and what have you.

Among the *Argonaut* authors who had signed contributions in the *Ingleside* was Robert Duncan Milne, but since his first such contribution did not appear until the magazine was more than six months old it is probable he did other unsigned work for them right along. The reason for suspecting this is that for the first nine months of 1884 no contribution by Milne appeared in the *Argonaut.* His first in the *Ingleside* was in the issue dated November 1, 1884, "The Great Goat Island Bonanza," concerned with a clever and legal fraud in financing a non-existent gold mine. A Mexican who has "salted" the mine obtains a $100,000 *loan* from San Francisco businessmen at the low interest rate of one percent to develop the mine to which he has a legal inheritance. In exchange for the low interest loan, the investors own 50% of the mine. Instead of working the mine, the Mexican invests the money at a higher rate of interest and lives comfortably ever after on the difference. There is no law against securing a legitimate loan freely given, even for the development of a worthless project.

A San Francisco weekly that had succeeded in a less highbrow approach with its readers was the *City Argus*. This paper ran an occasional piece of fiction, both original and reprint, as well as poetry, but its main thrust was local politics and problems. Founded with the issue of December 14, 1878 by Robert E. Culbreth, it is believed to have continued publication through to 1905, though no complete set is known to exist to verify this. For reasons that seem inexplicable, no reference to the publication is ever made in books or articles that review the history of San Francisco publishing, though even one-issue magazines and foreign language newspapers are sometimes covered. Perhaps the reason was the front-page feature topped by a cut of a bathrobed man holding a receiver of an ancient telephone to his head and subtitled merely "By Telephone." This column was taken over from the *Epigram*. The telephone was still a unique device and the content of this regular feature consisted of questions and answers to political figures, city officials, socialites, entertainment celebrities, and particularly *other publishers*. For example, from the issue of December 27, 1884:

"Hello, Deacon Pickering!

"Hello, Argus!

"A. 'Is it true that Supervisor Shirley is a stockholder in the *Daily Report* and therefore interested in making that journal the official organ of the city?'

"P. 'It is true that at one time he held a large amount of the stock of that paper, and no one has ever heard of its transfer to other hands. It is also true that the Supervisor always votes to give the city printing to the *Report*. The public can think as it pleases about the matter.' "

Robert Duncan Milne off and on worked for that magazine for 20 years, writing many of the "By Telephone" sections and much internal material which was usually very local in nature, heavy on politics, social matters, though there was a great deal of "boiler plate" pick-ups from papers across the country, yet the magazine survived.

At no time during the 20 years he worked for the *City Argus* did Milne's name ever appear on the masthead, though in the City Directory for 1885, while living at 526 Kearney Street, Milne's occupation was given as "City Editor, Argus." Again in the 1891 directory, while resident at "The Washington," his profession was given as "Literary Editor, City Argus." In the issue of *City Argus* for December 27, 1890, a statement appeared as an introduction to a poem in *Latin* by Milne, the *same* poem for which he won the Knox Prize at Trinity College at the age of 16, that he had "been connected with this journal for the past twelve years as literary editor and a member of the editorial staff."

The evidence is incontrovertible that Milne had a long-standing association with this paper, a publication of generally second-rate quality, and gained some sort of income from this association. Strangely, only a very few pieces signed by him appeared in the history of this magazine and none at all between 1879 and 1890. Such contacts as those with *Dramatic Brevities, City Argus* and *Ingleside* helped explain — not forgetting the "remittances" — the occasionally long lapses between stories.

XXII. FANTASY AND MILNE CONTINUE IN THE ARGONAUT

How integral the publishing of science fiction, fantasy, supernatural, occult and off-trail material was to the fiction policy of the *Argonaut* can be underscored by listings of its offerings in that vein as 1884 progressed: "The Blood Seedling" by John Hay (January 1) was a reprint from *Lippincott's* of 12 years past, involving a horror visualized by a medium; "The Witches Ring" by "F. R. H." (January 12) told of a midnight adventure in a New England graveyard: "The Sheik's Vision" was a translation from the Arabian by "J. H. S." (January 12) of a man, who with a kiss, awakens Marie de Rohan, dead for 200 years and is consigned to hell because of it; "The Haunted Flat" by A. E. P. Searing (January 19) tells of workers frightened from the site of their camp by nocturnal cries of "Help! Help!" emanating from no discoverable source; "The Magical Cards," a translation from the French of Prosper Merimée (February 9) is a fantastic comedy of a gambler whose skill wins 12 men out of Hell; "The Last Revel" by E. A. Wolcott (March 15) was a grim tale of 13 men — one of them a warlock — in a black room with a skeleton, uttering incantations that drive all of them but one out into the night as the building is consumed by fire and strange shapes move through the holocaust: "The Pot of Tulips" by Fitz-James O'Brien was reprinted from his 1881 collection as a two-part serial in the May 24th and 31st issues, a tale of ghostly visitations to apprise heirs of a hidden fortune, it has since become an acknowledged classic; "The Mysterious Clock" (May 31), an anonymous reprint from *Macmillan's* magazine, centered on a strange electro-magnetic-chemical clock that foretold death; "The Requiem of a Roman" was a fantastic story by the Frenchmen Erckmann-Chatrian (June 14), translated by Sallie Ritchie Heath; "The Missing Locket," a frightening story of mesmerism and murder (June 28) was also from the French; and "The Priest's Ghost" was an unusual story from the German of Max Schlagel printed in the July 12th and 19th issues and translated by Helen Lake.

Certainly the purest bit of science fiction the first eight months of 1884 and one which had undertones of criticism for some elements of "progress" was "The Artificial Man," subtitled "A Semi-Scientific Story," the work of a little-known San Franciscan author Don Quichotte, which appeared in the August 16th number. The narrator in the home of a chemist friend, finds seated there a sickly-looking "being" with "a waxy, bloodless skin, and, to crown all, scanty, silky, sickly hair, whose dull red color reminded me of German dolls' wigs."

He learns that this "being" has literally been created in a test tube, with no mother or father. He was one of three, the other two being disposed of to concentrate on him. Conversation discloses that the "being" is not, by any circumstances, human, though he has all the appearances and speech of one. He is incapable of absorbing natural foods and consumes nothing but synthetics. His body does not manufacture the requisite acids to digest foods and every eight days the gastric juice of a newly-killed calf is poured into his stomach through a covered metal tube in his side. Even his brain is a component, his skull can be opened and its contents temporarily removed without killing him. The "being" can be repaired, just like a mechanical device. The constituents of his blood are not the same as those of a human being and his creator is still at work making improvements in him.

The message the being imparts — already old at 18 — is that he is the prototype of future man. "This senile appearance I owe to the chemical methods of which you and your children will realize the dangerous benefits. Constitutional debility will be the heritage of your posterity, and in a few centuries these miserable but highly perfected races will walk the earth with their families reduced to the lowest degradation, incapable of exertion, of industry, of reproduction. In that mechanical age individuality and free-will can exist no longer." The story ends with the lines: "So spake in my startled ears the Artificial Man."

"An Unborn Ghost" was a highly original and unusual ghost

story contributed by Leonard Kip to the September 16th and 23rd issues of the *Argonaut*. The title relates to the Pettengal family, whose spirits and ghosts are created several generations in advance of their physical bodies and though unable to influence the paternity of their hosts, do work very hard to influence the choice of their mothers, since they want to be the ghosts of the very best type of person. The only other ghost story with a remotely similar theme was Edward Page Mitchell's "An Uncommon Sort of a Spectre," originally published in the New York *Sun* for March 30, 1879 and widely reprinted. In that story a ghost from the *future* returns to the past.

Showing some influence of the increasing modern desire to explain the supernatural rationally was Helen Lake's tale "If a Woman Die" (October 25). The spirit of a dead woman whom a man deeply loved takes possession at intervals of the body of another girl he is now seeing. Despite its emotion-charged elements, there is an almost clinical manner in which the struggle for the control of the girl's body which results in her death is related and sympathy is projected for the spirit of the dead girl rather than for that of the living person whose life has been taken.

Milne's first signed science fiction of 1884 was "A Modern Magic Mirror" in the September 20th *Argonaut*. It begins with a slow, philosophic essay on the relationship between mind and matter. The narrator then meets a friend who is very worried because his wife has gone to visit relatives in Poughkeepsie, N.Y. and has not telegraphed him. He has a feeling that something is wrong, but can't put his finger on it. They pay a visit on a professor at the Palace Hotel who claims to have had some success at reading thoughts over a distance, but there is nothing occult about his methods. He seats all of them on chairs insulated by glass and mounts on their heads flexible platinum helmets wired to what appears to be a large mirror. Then the three of them concentrate their thoughts on the wife of the worried friend and gradually, clearly shown on the mirror, the figure of the sleeping wife is seen in the home of his brother, with her pocketbook and money on the table and the children sleeping nearby. Then, to their horror, a burglar enters with a bludgeon, and seeing the woman stir, moves towards her to strike. At the urging of the professor, they all concentrate on sending a message to the brother sleeping in a nearby room. He awakens, and without realizing what he is doing, dashes into the room of the threatened woman and tackles the burglar. The noise brings others running and suddenly the connection is broken.

A reply to a telegram reassures them that everyone is safe, the burglar was overpowered. The relieved husband states: "I'll be blessed if I can see into that magic mirror business yet."

And his friend replies: "Why, my dear boy, there are electricians in London and New York who say that they can not only make Patti or Langtry appear upon a dozen stages at once, but also guarantee that the various audiences shall hear them sing — and all done by one little wire. Professor V--- has done pretty much the same for us tonight, with the single exception that the wire was left out."

The next three contributions from his pen were extremely well-written but almost trivial pieces involving the Mexicans and Indians of California. "A California Lochinvar" (October 4, 1884) tells of a Mexican senorita near Salinas who is saved from marriage to a middle-aged and penurious ranchero by her dashing young lover and forty of his caballero friends. "The Squaw's Rock" (October 25, 1884) purports to be the true story of the legend of the rock in which a half-white, half-Mexican youth is thrown from a 500-foot precipice to his death by the Indians who object to his attentions to one of their maidens and how she leaps to her death after him. "A Forest Fire" (November 22, 1884) relates the story of an Indian woman and her baby trapped in a forest fire and the discovery by the ranger who attempts to rescue her that she has permitted herself to be burned to death to save her child by throwing her body over it.

"The Loves of Sense and Spirit" by Milne in the December 13, 1884 issue was not science fiction either, it was occult, but it dealt with a very current movement of that time, theosophy, introduced to the United States in 1875 by Madame H. P. Blavatsky and codified in her immense half-million word, two-volume masterwork ISIS UNVEILED: A MASTER-KEY TO THE MYSTERIES OF ANCIENT AND MODERN, published by J. W. Bouton, New

York, in 1877. Theosophy purported to be a belief that combined science and religion. Madame Blavatsky claimed that the "adepts" of Tibet had been the custodians of ancient sciences of past civilizations that had been swallowed up by upheavals of the past. They were the repository of all wisdom and had strange powers, including the ability to appear and disappear anywheres upon the earth at any time. There was nothing strange about these powers, they were simply advanced science that had been achieved in the past and had not been rediscovered by modern man.

"The Loves of Sense and Spirit" mentions that Madame Blavatsky, when passing through San Francisco to India in 1880, had helped form a branch of the theosophical society there. The unnamed hero of the story, having expressed his interest in the society, is invited to an exhibition of some of their secrets. He finds a pentacle in the center of the floor of an apartment and while he watches it flaming letters form the name "Agatha" who steps from the observers into the pentacle, grabs a slip of paper that has appeared in the air and reads it. The event ends with a bouquet of flowers materializing from out of nothing.

Returning to the apartment on a pretext, our protagonist finds it empty, but an adept appears before him from out of the air, stating he is from Tibet. When asking the adept how the feat was accomplished, Milne almost pulls away from the occult by offering the explanation: "It is simply the working of the same law in the case of organic as of inorganic matter. The current is formed, the body disintegrated at one end, and re-integrated at the other. It is simply the law of the telephone or the telegraph applied to a higher purpose and extended to a wider field. We have heard of the tour of the world in eighty days, and of Puck putting a girdle around the earth in forty minutes. Once our currents are formed — or, to speak to your comprehension, our invisible rails laid or wires set — our speed is only bounded by the possibilities of thought."

The narrator is transported to Egypt by the adept and returned to San Francisco in time to watch one of the girl theosophists who has lost her heart throb to another utilize the ancient powers for her own ends, but her efforts to draw upon them produce a horror *a la* Lovecraft, which destroys her sanity and is described as: "It

HISTORY OF THE MOVEMENT 166

was not however, the whitish semi-transparent mist I had seen before, but a black, murky cloud which completely obscured the glass beyond it, and even the moonlight from the figure of Miriam. The cloud seemed to roll sluggishly and convolute upon itself like a mass of slimy, crawling serpents. Was it fancy, or was it fact, what I then saw in broken configuration through and between the flower-stems that partially obscured by field of vision? Was it merely the effect of moonlight and shadow projecting a vision upon a strained and heated imagination, or did I actually see a portion of a face so lurid and terrible, so hideous in its awful deformity, with eyes of such piercing and devilish malignity that I instinctively closed my own, powerless as I was to avert my head from the fearful spectacle: I fervently trust that I will never know."

The theosophical society decides not to pursue their researches further and disbands.

The fascinating thing about the story was that the flaming letters, the sudden appearance of flowers from nowhere and even the snatching of messages on little pieces of paper were among the "inexplicable" phenomena attributed to Madame Blavatsky, the last having been observed by Edward Page Mitchell when she invited him to tea after having read his occult story of a double materialization in the *Sun* (New York) for January 6, 1878, "An Extraordinary Wedding."

In his essay "Modern Mythological Fiction," Robert Butman underscored how many of the ideas from ISIS REVEALED and other books by Madame Blavatsky showed up in authors of supernatural and science fiction, including figures as notable as H. G. Wells and H. P. Lovecraft. The author of that excellent and convincing piece published in three parts beginning in the October, 1945 *Reader and Collector* (H. C. Koenig), can now add to his list, if it is ever revised, Robert Duncan Milne.

The Christmas, 1884 issue of the *Argonaut* (a 27th issue in a volume normally 26), led off with Robert Duncan Milne's "A Christmas Wedding at Guadalajara." This strange story of Mexico, which was set on Christmas day, 1853, is a special mixture of old-fashioned South-of-the-Border color and hard science. It is not science fiction because the science accomplished *was* possible with the technology of 1853. There is to be a marriage but two male relatives of the girl, one in priest's garments and the other a doctor, conspire to kill her for they are the next in line for the inheritance if she is gone. They are assisted by Conteras, a losing suitor for the girl's hand, who thinks only the groom will die. Their method of accomplishing this is quite ingenious. The doctor has a large plate-glass electrical generator from his college days, a dozen Leyden jars with a fresh coating of tin foil, which were placed in a tray and connected so as to form a battery. When the Leyden jars are fully charged with electricity from manually turning a glass handle which rubs two pieces of silk together, they will contain enough voltage to kill several people. This bulky apparatus, seven feet long by two feet wide, is hidden in the altar where the marriage is to be performed. Copper wires are attached to the batteries and strung under the carpet to the spot where the bride and groom must stand, pulled through the carpet and bent back three feet buried in the silk. When the groom is about to put the ring on the bride's finger, the current would be sent coursing through the wires, the ring would complete contact, and both would be killed.

Instead of placing the ring on the girl's finger, the bridegroom embraces her. Conteras, mistaking this for the moment, applies the wire to the battery terminal to complete the circuit and in so doing trips against the fake padre and the charge passes through him paralyzing him for life and killing the other man.

The story is extremely well written and Milne's description of the period-piece generators and batteries makes it sound like a new invention.

XXIII. J. ESTEN COOK AND JULES VERNE

If Milne's piece was merely an adroit yarn, the story "Dr. Magnus's Great Discovery" by J. Esten Cooke, published in the issue immediately preceeding the Christmas Number, December 20, 1884, was something else again. The editor announced in a blurb: "It is a most ingenious story of the Vernesque school, with threads of a love story interwoven, and will suggest to many the style of our California writer, Robert Duncan Milne." Despite the fact that the story carried the legend "Written for the 'Argonaut'," it was quite obviously one of a series of stories obtained through *Argonaut's* new special syndication arrangement with S. S. McClure, New York, where they supplied a story a week for $8.00 exclusive only in that area. The story may have appeared eventually in a dozen newspapers. Future stories were announced by such luminaries of the day as Julian Hawthorne, Frank R. Stockton, William Dean Howells, Thomas A. Janvier, Sarah Orne Jewett, J. S. of Dale, and others of similar ranking, all handled by McClure.

Cooke is still highly regarded as a writer by literary historians of 19th century American fiction and non-fiction. He wrote novels in the manner of James Fennimore Cooper and his fiction of Southern life previous to the Civil War is credited with contributing to the "Poetic idealization" of the period. His biographies of men as prominent as Thomas Jefferson, Stonewall Jackson, Robert E. Lee, and Samuel J. Tilden are solid works for the time, and because they were written close to the events have a feel of authenticity to them. There may be a number of uncollected works of science fiction of his, at least one other short story, "A Magnetizer," appeared in *American Homes* for December, 1874. In that story hypnotism is used for painless surgery and for inducing clairvoyance. The tale is highly scientific.

"Dr. Magnus's Great Discovery" is of historical importance because it describes an explosive and resultant "fallout" that is as close as one can come to predicting the effects of an atomic bomb before the discovery of radium. It can only be set off by high-voltage electricity, it can be harnessed "to make aerial navigation possible, to drive the largest ocean steamer without fuel at the rate of a mile a minute, to move machinery of every description, and, if used as an explosive, the mountain barrier of Nicaragua in the way of an inter-oceanic canal would disappear in an instant."

The inventor is reluctant to give it to the world for "apart from its immense power, the gas arising from this substance is deadly and extends to an incredible distance. It would be possible to destroy whole armies by it or the inhabitants of entire cities. From the moment when it fell into bad hands there would be no safety for human life. Great capitals, with their swarming populations, their public buildings, and works of art, would be at the mercy of a few wretches, and it is scarcely an exaggeration to say that the result might be the ruin of civilization, if not the complete destruction of society."

Unlike other explosives, "In the case of this substance, I hold the effect continues, and the force exerted is practically irresistible." The narrator gives credence to the story because the inventor has previously invented a method of making artificial diamonds from pure carbon that are so perfect he has become rich from their sale. In a test he blows up a mountain with an ounce of the substance and "The white smoke from the explosion had risen to an immense height, and had assumed the exact form of a girl upon her knees, looking up with clasped hands and apparently praying."

The story ends when the inventor, his daughter, and the narrator are in a mountain retreat built like a Swiss chalet, when out of a storm a lightning bolt strikes the home and laboratory they have left and an incredible explosion "and the great mansion resembled the crater of a raging volcano."

The role of the *Argonaut* as one of America's greatest exponents of science fiction, fantastic and supernatural literature of the 19th century continued unabated when in the January 3, 1885 issue it heralded "Jules Verne's Latest Fantasy" and translated it under the title of "The Midnight Visit of Dr. Trifulgas" from the December,

1884 issue of the Paris *Le Figaro Illustré*. The story may be familiar to many American and English readers of the past 25 years because it was translated by Willis J. Bradley for the July, 1957 issue of *Saturn* under the title of "The Ordeal of Dr. Trifulgus"; and translated again for *The Magazine of Fantasy and Science Fiction,* November, 1959, as "Frritt-Flacc" (its original title) by I. O. Evans, who included it in his British collection of Verne's short stories titled "Yesterday and Tomorrow" (Arco, 1965) also as "Frritt-Flacc." The *Argonaut's* publication was unquestionably its first in the United States, and there is very considerable difference in the three translations, though all are effective.

It is the story of a doctor in some familiar but impossible-to-positively identify European land, who is implored first by a daughter, then by the wife, to attend to a dying man on a bitter winter night. Twice he refuses because the fee, to be paid in advance, is not high enough. The third time he agrees and follows the aged wife behind his dog who carries the lantern in his teeth. They reach their destination and the woman points to the house. Suddenly there is an earth-shaking blast from a distant volcano and the woman is gone. The doctor proceeds into the house to find he is back at his own home and he is in bed dying from a massive stroke. He has been called out to save himself! He desperately tries to accomplish that but to no avail. He is found dead in bed the next day and his dog "may still be seen, with his lantern relighted, scouring the hearth and howling for his lost master."

It is an effective supernatural story, sardonic, atmospheric and moralistic. Obviously it is something Verne wrote for a Christmas assignment as so many other famous authors did in the heyday of Christmas annual issues.

XXIV. MILNE THE MAGNIFICENT

As a prelude to warming up for a new spate of science fiction, the California champion of the genre, Milne, had "A River Tragedy" in the January 17, 1885 issue of the *Argonaut*, about two loggers moving across the floating logs on a stormy night to get medicine for a girl sick with pneumonia, and the sacrifice of the life of one of them. The story indicated that Milne had considerable familiarity with the Redwood logging region of California.

"Prof. Vehr's Electrical Experiment" by Milne in the January 24, 1885 issue was an important story on several counts. It was a sequel to "A Modern Magic Mirror," bringing back the brilliant Prof. Vehr. It also underscored Milne's inability to leave a fantastic situation *without* a scientific explanation as he had tried for the first time in the occult "The Loves of Sense and Spirit." The Professor avers that he can duplicate the transmission of a person from place to place *scientifically* in the same way the Theosophists claim they can accomplish it by control of "occult" means. With an elaborately described special apparatus he breaks a man down into raw energy and transmits him by telephone wires from San Francisco to New Orleans and brings him back with his girl the same way. The method of transmission is convincing, but there is a gap in explaining its control. Nevertheless this was an important early story of its type, preceded most prominently by Edward Page Mitchell's "The Man Without a Body" (The *Sun*, March 25, 1877), where telephone wires are utilized for the same purpose.

The following, January 31, 1885, issue began a two-part story by Milne, "The Awful Cataclysm in Ireland," which told of half of Ireland blasted into the sea by a man-provoked volcanic explosion. The Irish revolutionaries have set off devastating explosions in the Tower of London, the Houses of Parliament, demolished the

Washington Monument, and culminated their acts of terrorism by blowing to pieces Pope Pius the Tenth along with a dozen Cardinals, by hollowing out the sacred tiara, charging it with a nitro compound set to go off during the ceremony of coronation and enthronement.

A millionaire, who has suffered the loss of one son and the crippling of another in the Tower of London blast, is privy to the meeting of two engineers, one of whom claims he has a compressed air drill which can penetrate to almost any depth at speeds of a foot a minute with minimal wear, and the other who has a controlled nitro engine capable of supplying the kind of power required to keep such a drill operating efficiently. The millionaire agrees to finance the drilling as a test, offering to pay a prize wager to the men if it works and a consolation sum if it does not. The drilling is begun off of Shannon through a caisson sunk in the floor of the waters, but when it reaches a depth of over 10 miles it releases volcanic pressure which half destroys Ireland, creates a new island, and leaves only the Captain of the drilling ship with two of his men to tell the story.

From a narrative standpoint it is one of the best of Milne's efforts, starting with high interest and maintaining it throughout. Though it is a descendant of the newspaper hoax style of science fiction, it is not intended to fool since none of the events described in the opening had occurred previous to the printing of the story. It substantiates the influence of William Henry Rhodes on Milne, because the plot is close to that of "Earth's Hot Center," first published in 1872, where a similar major drilling operation unleashes a lava flow that it is predicted will cause an eventual landbridge between England and the continent, with incalculable damage.

In "The Russian Invasion of India" published in the *Argonaut* for April 11th and 18th, 1885, Milne again perpetrated a little political science fiction. Two men conceive a scheme to splice into the telegraph cable lines that carry messages from India to London, and since in the recent past there had been a patched-up threat of Russian invasion of India, send fake messages through to the effect that the Russians are already storming the passes of India, then carefully monitor all messages, letting none go through that might expose their plan. By the time their location has been discovered, they have cleaned upon on the stock market and returned to respectability without a trace. Milne shows excellent knowledge of the scientific nature of the telegraphic system and the type of coded messages that are sent by business and governments.

"The Man Who Could Not Die," which appeared in the May 30, 1885 issue of the *Argonaut* was published anonymously, but there is a literary reason for that since a note precedes the story saying it is a copy of a manuscript found in a secret drawer of "an old escritoire by a gentleman who obtained the latter from a second-hand furniture store on California Street." It is the seemingly standard story of the elixir of immortality, but with a number of fascinating differences. The man who penned the manuscript claimed to be 200 years old at the time, born of a titled British family, who near death as a youth is given a tiny vial of liquid by a man dressed like an Eastern Sage, which restores him to health.

Once more dying of illness at the age of 56, he is visited by this man again and given the secret of the manufacture of the elixir. It is at this point where the story incontestably appears to be a work of Milne. No simple compound of chemicals, this drug, but water, subjected to bombardment of electricity under tremendous pressure, so that it separated into gas and the gases reformed into a different weight (possibly anticipation of heavy water). More than that, there is an elaborate description of old age being attributed to clotting and hardening of the arteries and the effect of this water is to keep the arteries clean and supple: "If these are kept soft, to their minutest capillaries, each organ and tissue of the body will be properly nourished, and can not itself harden or decay, for is not every portion of the system renewed every seven years?" The real indelible trademark of Milne is the statement: "Even alcohol, the most spiritual essence of which your western civilization knows aught, and fast as it causes the vital fluid to bound within the veins, and potent as are its virtues to arrest molecular change within the tissues, has no power to renew them."

As the years pass the man finds that the atomic density of his body is changing and he has reached the point where he can walk through walls. One of the more believable aspects of the story is that the elixir of life is as habit forming as opium and the craving for it increases, requiring daily impotation. The message ends as the "immortal" has become so tenuous that he can no longer direct a pen and will soon dissipate entirely, creating the strange mystery of the San Francisco man who disappeared from a closed room and was never seen again.

The theme of the Fourth Dimension was once a distinctive gambit in science fiction, particularly in the twenties and the thirties. Some stories and series gained considerable favor, including "Into the Fourth Dimension" by Ray Cummings *(Science and Invention,* September, 1926 to March, 1927); a related group of stories by Bob Olsen in *Amazing Stories,* starting with "Four-Dimensional Surgery" (February, 1928) and ending with the "Four-Dimensional Auto Parker" (July, 1934); "The Fourth Dimensional Space Penetrator" by Julian Kendig, Jr. *(Amazing Stories,* January, 1930); and "The Fourth Dimensional Demonstrator" by Murray Leinster *(Astounding Stories,* December, 1935). The theme has survived in scores of stories and has been treated in many ways: an extension of the three dimensions, length, breadth and thickness, that would permit people to put two objects in the same space (Bob Olsen); another plane of existence, superimposed, alongside or parallel with our own with a different people and civilization (Ray Cummings); that the fourth dimension is time or duration and you can pick up any number of people or things by going back a few seconds further each time (Murray Leinster); to shrink in size until the atoms are relatively as big as suns and planets (Julian Kendig, Jr.); or in more recent times Rod Steiger's television series "The Twilight Zone" found it endlessly useful to explain any number of fascinating hypotheses. Where the theme really became clearly defined in science fiction has not been established, but certainly "A Mysterious Twilight" by Robert Duncan Milne in the *Argonaut* for June 27, 1885, very specifically subtitled "Being a Dip into the Doings of the Four-Dimensional World," deserves a place in its development.

Milne credited the idea for his story to philosophers Emanuel Kant and Karl Friedrich Gauss, but it is quite possible he also read a little pamphlet titled *What Is the Fourth Dimension?* by C. Howard Hinton, issued in England in 1884 and later collected as part of a volume titled SCIENTIFIC ROMANCES published by George Allen & Unwin Ltd., London, in 1886, which delightfully presented the various theories of the fourth dimension that science fiction writers have been using ever since. If Hinton were the seminal source of the "modern" fourth dimension theme, then Milne may very well have been the first writer to incorporate it into fiction.

"In "A Mysterious Twilight," Milne tells of a man named Rayburn who has begun to see apparitions in his apartment that appear to take no notice of him and walk through objects. He confides in a friend, who brings in a third party named Heywood. The three of them, when conditions are right, observe the juxtaposition of a ballroom scene at which a youthful Heywood is present with a girl. In a kalaidescopic effect Heywood's marriage, its breakup and events following are viewed as though they were contemporaneous. The final scene is a hospital ward with a dying woman struggling upright in bed and the nurse striding right out of the "vision" toward Heywood, demanding that he follow her. He does, completely out of the room into the hospital ward to the sick woman. There is a flash and an explosion and the hospital ward disappears from sight. In the next room Heywood is found electrocuted near an electrical apparatus which Rayburn had built for special experiments. The strange astral visitations have only started since two wires had been strung up the side of the house five weeks earlier. There are indications that the electrical machine had in some way been motivated at the time of Heywood's death. A gold locket is found on his neck containing a photo of the woman in the "vision" (who was his wife). Two days later a St. Louis paper carries a story of the death of a woman in a hospital who owned a gold locket carrying a photo of Paul Heywood, and her last words were testified to by the nurses as: "Oh, Paul, Paul, at last you have come. All is forgiven." Dr. Rayburn, in whose apartment the event occurred, is never again troubled by four-dimensional beings.

Milne's "A Family Skeleton" in the July 25 and August 6, 1885 *Argonaut* was a superbly polished, bizarre masterpiece. Though the story is told by a French innkeeper in Alemeda, California, its locale is the home of a French nobleman. His wife had died in childbirth and the delivery of the child by Caesarean finds the father grief-stricken and shocked by a baby born with *two faces, one on each side of its head.* As the child grows, the two faces, though possessed of two necks, two throats and two brains, are lodged in one skull and develop as separate personalities trapped in a single body. Most of their lives are spent on the grounds of the French Count's estate, and they adopt the device of pretending to be twins, covering one face at a time and appearing as a normal person. Milne is magnificent in his delineation of the accomodations these two personalities must make to get by and sustains his narrative on a very high level. By tacit agreement each personality controls one arm. Everything goes well until, when, at the age of 18, they both fall in love with the same girl. The story ends unexpectedly and tragically when in a fit of jealousy and passion, the two personalities choke one another to death, each using his exclusive arm!

It is often difficult for an author or a publisher to determine why a particular story, which seems no more meritorious and sometimes even less so than the average of the others, strikes the public fancy, but it happens all the time and Milne was no exception. Many years later, an anonymous obiturary writer for *The San Francisco Bulletin* detailed from memory and at some length the plot of "Baron Von Steinbach's Soul" from the October 3rd and 10th, 1885 issues of the *Argonaut.* Again, Milne brought back the brilliant Professor Vehr, who has invented an elaborate electrical device that will free the "soul" or the "mind" from the body and transfer it in a corporeal state anywhere in the world. Baron Von Steinbach, who happens to be in San Francisco, has Prof. Vehr transfer his consciousness to Germany and return it safely to his body again. The entire experience is so exhilarating that Von Steinbach enters the laboratory when Prof. Vehr is not around and tries the experiment on himself. This time he carries with him the arboreal essence of the professor's dog, who happened to be curled up at the seat of the apparatus. When returning, his intelligence enters the body of the dog and vice versa. His harrowing adventures as a dog and his near destruction at the dog pound, do provide entertaining and even philosophical reading.

Milne was not new with the idea even then, for Britain's *Belgravia Magazine* for July, 1885 had anonymously carried "The Great

Keinplatz Experiment" by A. Conan Doyle, in which, through the use of hypnotism, a professor switches bodies with a student. That *Belgravia* circulated in San Francisco was undeniable because the publications there frequently reprinted from it. However, Doyle, who quite often appropriated ideas, had unquestionably picked it up from VICE VERSA by T. Anstey (Thomas Anstey Guthrie), which had scored a bestselling success in 1882 (even reprinted in America the same year). In the plot of VICE VERSA, Anstey utilized the supernatural powers of a talisman; Doyle had employed hypnotism; but true to his quirk Milne had an entire room of buzzing and crackling equipment. Perhaps he was the earliest to transfer human intelligence into an animal *scientifically*, perhaps not, but he impressed the San Francisco natives. Where Anstey got it we do not know, but no deep bow was in order since the theme had been used by Edward Page Mitchell in "Exchanging Their Souls" in the New York *Sun* for April 27, 1877. There was a touch of humor and morality in "Baron Von Steinbach's Soul" and, despite the scientific explanations, fine movement and plot interest.

Milne showed astonishing versatility in writing for the Christmas, December, 1885 issue of the *Argonaut*, the novelette "The Subterranean Secret of the Sierras." This proved a light, imaginative, ingenious narrative of a man who falls into an underground stream while exploring Calaveras Cave in the Sierra mountains. After being carried underground for many miles, he emerges at what seems to be an hour between twilight and night, in an area illuminated by a great fire in the distance. Making his way to it, he is attacked by a 200-pound bat, which he kills with a six-shooter whose powder had remained dry. The only plants are giant white mushrooms and a white moss which carpets the ground. A small village is reached inhabited by a hairy, Indian-looking race who live in huts and are possessed of tails. He wins their respect by killing a bat that is carrying off a child.

Exploring this world, he realizes he is in a limited cave, lighted by a perpetually-burning lake 200 to 300 feet wide. He is attacked by a bear-sized, hairy, crab-like spider, from which he is rescued by the natives. The ecology is perfectly balanced. The natives kill the bats and use their fur for clothing. The bats prey on the giant spider crabs. The crabs live off the fish and the natives eat the legs of the crabs, the fish, and use the mushrooms in place of bread. The food is cooked by immersion in the boiling waters of the lake. Since the caverns can support only a limited number of people, which our narrator estimates at roughly 350, those children considered excess are tossed into the boiling lake. When a male native dies, our hero learns he must mate with his horrendous widow or be killed. He dashes for an opening where the stream that had conveyed him into the cavern flows out into a dark, swift channel. Pursued by the widow, the natives, and creatures that resemble half-dogs, half-pigs, with bristles in place of hair, that they keep as pets, he dives into the swift current and reaches the outside world where he tells Milne his incredible story. Again, as in "The Iguandon's Egg," Milne makes excellent use of the vernacular of the West to lend a note of authenticity to an extremely well thought-out entertainment.

The year 1885 had been spectacular for Milne and his reputation as the *Argonaut's*, and probably the San Francisco-Bay Area's, leading contemporary short story writer, was unquestioned. This did not except Bierce, then between jobs, having left *The Wasp*, a satirical weekly for which he had written some of his most barbed epigrams and his mercilessly scathing column, "Prattle."

Milne's considerable talents were further demonstrated in the December 26, 1885 issue of his friend Bigelow's *The Ingleside*, which carried his story "The Mystic Rosary." This narrative was based on the ultimate exercise of the discipline of transcendental meditation. The story is told by a Russian in San Francisco who first engages in a dialogue with the narrator — overly long for a work of fiction — on the theory that man once possessed expanded powers of the mind, whose techniques for application were lost through the parade of calamities and natural catastrophes that are the unrecorded history of our planet. The idea that the Great Flood was caused by the earth ceasing its rotation and then beginning to spin in the opposite direction is proposed.

The Russian Czar has been assassinated and the Russian had been friendly with a savant suspected of being implicated. He finds himself shipped off to Siberia for 10 years of hard labor but not before his scientist friend presses into his hand an old amber rosary, given him by a teacher who had been a master at transcendental meditation and who had claimed that having on your person an object previously owned by an individual adept at mental contact, assisted in establishing rapport.

Sick and miserable in a Siberian hut, the Russian, in mental despair, fondles the rosary and in so doing suddenly sees a vision of a great old white-bearded patriarch in a beautiful glen with a young Indian girl beside him. The old man seems to be urging him to counter all obstacles and come to him.

Escaping from the Siberian camp, the Russian makes his way across the northern landscape and boards a ship for Japan. A storm forces them into Sitka, Alaska and, moved by a compulsion, the Russian walks inland and comes upon the site of his vision. Sure enough the aged patriarch, well over 100, and the Indian girl are there. This is the same master of transcendental meditation that had given the rosary to his convicted friend and he has been transmitting impulses to guide others here, where he has discovered a vast deposit of gold, one large enough to finance a revolution against the government of Russia. He dies before he can pinpoint the spot of his discovery, but as the story ends the Russian is about to conduct an intensive search to uncover its location.

Milne thereby anticipates the Alaskan Gold Rush and the Russian Revolution, neither too difficult, but nonetheless indicating an open mind. Though his story starts slowly, the unfolding of events once the Siberian portion of the tale commences is superbly delineated. Unlike his other stories, Milne leaves the explanation of thought transference and mind control in the realm of the unknown, suggesting it as a lost and fugitive talent, surfacing under rare occasions.

XXV. FANTASY IN THE SAN FRANCISCAN

That issue was the dying gasp of *The Ingleside,* a paper highly regarded and a competitor of the *Argonaut.* Most of its fiction was not on Milne's level for the magazine was crammed full of love stories. Possibly the editors were misguided in setting their editorial sights on an intellectual level below that of the *Argonaut.* Another competing publication that set its level *above* that of the *Argonaut* and began publication concurrently with *The Ingleside* was *The San Franciscan.* Mentor of that publication was Joseph T. Goodman, previously mentioned contributor of tales of mysticism and the West to the *Argonaut* and publisher of Mark Twain in the Virginia City *Territorial Enterprise.* Twain did not forget Goodman's role in launching him on his writing career because he contributed an original piece of work to the first, February 16, 1884 issue of *The San Franciscan.* That first issue was outstanding, for it also contained articles, fiction or verse by Sam Davis, the brother of Robert Hobart Davis (the great fiction editor of *Munsey, Argosy, All-Story* and *Cavalier);* Rollin M. Daggett, who had a key role in the success of the *Golden Era,* the journal that was required reading in the camps during the gold rush days; Arthur McEwen, a contributor to the *Argonaut,* a co-editor of the publication and destined to become one of the most renowned newspaper editors in the nation; and Ina D. Coolbrith, the most popular of the early woman California writers.

The magazine, unlike the *Argonaut,* was printed handsomely in a type size that did not require a magnifying glass, even though of near-tabloid format. Goodman was not adverse to an occasional fantasy. Dan O'Connell's "The Magic Ottoman" (March 15) told of an ancient ottoman cover, once the possession of Indian philosopher Dschellaleddin Rami, which when placed properly on the suitable piece of furniture results in everyone telling the absolute truth and in such circumstances the results are always somewhat shocking and amusing. Nathan C. Kouns appeared in the April 19, 1884 issue with "Did the Colonel Go or Stay?," one of his unusual, richly constructed short stories. This title was an imitation of Frank R. Stockton's "The Lady or the Tiger?" which originally appeared in the November, 1882 *Century,* and was to be the title story of Stockton's short story collection in 1884. In Kouns' story, a Confederate officer who has lost an arm is taken to a Southern mansion to recuperate. The daughter of the family there, whose husband has been lost in the war, labors under the delusion he is her husband returned. She realizes her mistake but by the time the two are deeply in love. He has not heard from his wife in three years and she is probably dead, but he decides to do the honorable thing and quietly departs. She intercepts him and, throwing her arms around his neck, pleads: "Come back to me my love, my life, come back! The poor lady yonder in Missouri must have died, or else you would have heard of her. Come back and marry me, and I will run the risk!" The story concludes: "Did he go or did he stay? What would you have done under these strange circumstances?"

A phantasmagorical waking dream is experienced by a printer who is shocked into mental and physical collapse by a wife who is testing his love in "A Printer's Phantasy" by Ella Sterling Cummins in the June 4, 1884 issue of *The San Franciscan.* Cummins was later to prove the most assiduous historian of San Francisco literature and publishing the region ever produced.

Particularly interesting was a new translation of "Doctor Trafulgas" by Jules Verne in the April 11, 1885 issue of *The San Franciscan,* even though the story had appeared in the *Argonaut* for January 3, 1885, and it was literally impossible for the editors of *The San Franciscan* to have been unaware of it. This was picked up from the S. S. McClure Syndicate, which the *Argonaut* had dropped. Several weeks later, the April 25, 1885 issued carried Robert Duncan Milne's first signed contribution, "A Mountain Tragedy," though it unexpectedly was not science fiction or fantasy. A Californian, lost in the mountains, runs across a man who tells him the story of his life. His wife died on their wedding day. He left home and lived for years in the mountains. One day, mistaking a moving object in the underbrush for a deer or a bear, he shoots it. It turns out to be his brother who has tracked him down. The narrator barely escapes with his own life and, in returning with help to the scene, finds the disturbed man lying dead across the grave of his brother.

An Oakland writer, F. R. Porter, had "Dr. Coccyx's Skeleton," appropriately "A Weird Love Story," in the December 19, 1885 issue of *The San Franciscan.* Dr. Coccyx, telling the story of his life, relates his falling in love with a pragmatic and atheistic girl, who does not believe in God, religion, the soul or free will. The human races are automatons, she avers, whose every circumstance is dependent upon utter chance. This does not deter him, so a marriage is arranged, but before the date she is killed when a bolt of lightning fells a tree in the Orange Mountains west of Newark, N.J. Following her funeral he enrolls at a medical school and when taken into the dissecting room finds the body of his late betrothed floating in a tank of brine. Her skeleton now hangs in his office.

Milne's final story in *The San Franciscan* was "The Late Boom in the Silver Star" in the issue of January 16, 1886. The plot of this story was basically the same as that for "The Russian Invasion of India" the previous year, where intercepting and transmitting false messages from a remote point along the telegraph wires in a "secret" cipher permits a speculator to clear $2 million on the stock market.

If there was any doubt in anyone's mind that A. Conan Doyle's "The Great Keinplatz Experiment" from the British *Belgravia* magazine was readily available in San Francisco, it was reprinted anonymously *(Belgravia* usually did not append the author's name to a story) in the April 17, 1886 issue of *The San Franciscan.* It is one of the ironies of life that *San Franciscan* readers probably thought that some British author had lifted the idea from Milne's "Baron Von Steinbach's Soul."

The San Franciscan did not survive 1886 and thereby, within a short time, two outstanding competitive weeklies to the *Argonaut* disappeared.

XXVI. THE ARGONAUT OF 1886

The early part of 1886 found little of the literature of the fantastic in the *Argonaut*. The earliest thing of any note was "The Cities of the Dead," subtitled "A Legend of Another World," reprinted from *Macmillan's Magazine* in England. This is an allegorical fable allegedly set in another world or dimension. The protagonist is an "immortal," somewhat akin to our God, with his limitations explained. This man lives eternally, watching the race grow even more amoral and degenerate. He has the power to eliminate all life and he does so, rescuing only one baby girl. When she grows up, in a surrounding of dead and silent cities, an advanced "man" from another world appears and marries her. Her guardian permits it because he feels such an elevated race will have high ethical and moral standards, but after a period the alien disappears and she is left with her children. The children are cynical and quarrelsome and when she tries to break up a fight between them she is accidentally stabbed.

The race multiplies and the entire sorry mess begins again. The story ends with the Immortal stating: "I dared, with my infinite will, to meddle with issues that were infinite. How, then can there be any end to my sorrow, since there is no end to the misery I have made?"

Certainly the most fascinating bit was the reprint of a segment from THE LIFE AND ADVENTURES OF PETER WILKINS by Robert Paltock, one of the greatest science fiction adventures ever written, published in 1751 in England and reprinted frequently since then. It is a fine story of the shipwreck of an Englishborn gentleman on an island inhabited by a highly intelligent race of men and women. The *Argonaut* reprinted a sequence which they called "The Flying Princess" in their May 8, 1886 issue which they learned of "In a very pleasant book, 'The Seer,' by Leigh Hunt" (the famed British poet). There is a discourse in the novel by Hunt from which they quote.

The almost complete disappearance of Milne from the *Argonaut* during the first eleven months of 1886 appears to be due to his working on the weekly *City Argus*. At least, the San Francisco Directory for 1885 and 1886 has him living at 526 Kearney Avenue and listing his position as "City Editor" of that publication. His reappearance in the December 4, 1886 issue of the *Argonaut* with "The Telescopic Marvel," probably underscored the fact that his drinking habits had forced a severance of an in-office working status for him at that publication.

"The Telescopic Marvel" marked a return of Milne to an interplanetary theme. The early part of his story is taken up with the science of the manufacture of telescopic lenses and the problems attendant upon maximizing distance and clarity. This moves from his contemporary observatories to the experiments of Germans who have created a new substance suitable for lenses which has none of the imperfections of glass. These are made, built into a telescope at Lick Observatory, and focussed on Mars. An advanced civilization is viewed there, with humanlike creatures much larger than earthmen. One of the most unusual features is that they seem to have a method of rendering heavy objects weightless and moving them from place to place with ease. They also have vehicles run by no apparent mechanical means. Unexpectedly, giant letters form before their lense — the Martians are communicating with them. They learn that the Martians have watched eight great civilized epochs of mankind destroyed by catastrophes and they have been in communication with them in the past. They say the device of rendering objects weightless was once possessed by an earlier earth civilization and has been lost. The story ends with the earthmen grinding new lenses and putting their equipment in shape for further communication.

The last fantastic tale of 1886 in the *Argonaut* was "A Tale Told by a Skull" (December 18), reprinted from THE SENTIMENTAL CALENDAR published by Charles Scribners & Sons and attributed to J. S. of Dale, who enjoyed a literary vogue for some years. Dale was the pen name of Frederick J. Stimson, a Boston resident then 30 years of age, a graduate of Harvard, Class of 1876, as a lawyer. In this work, a skull, at a Philadelphia party, tells its story of an afterlife and retention of senses though unable to move of its own volition. The relation is a true fantasy and the doubt remains as to whether the skull actually spoke or a clever ventriloquist was the agency of its words.

That the *Argonaut* often reprinted by reader request and even had stories worthy of being reprinted called to its attention was affirmed by the blurb to "The Tale of Kosem Kesamin" (January 22, 1887), which stated: "Editor Argonaut — I have transcribed for you this weird and mystic legend from a little-known and unfinished work by Bulwer, written years before he gave us 'Zanoni' and 'The Strange Story.' For beauty of language and imagery, I believe it to be almost unequalled, and unlike the tale of 'The Solitary' which I sent you, this one terminates exquisitely. H.F.C." The story was a lengthy, biblically-cadenced parable of a young man of the days of Egyptian pride, who suddenly has following him around everywhere a bright, laughing flame. Though the flame claims to be "the living principle of the world," and though the young man lives a life of happiness and pleasure, his consuming desire is to gain "not knowledge by the *source* of knowledge." Entering death to find the ultimate, he learns with horror that all life, whether in the earth, the water or the air, germinates from corruption and decay. *"Such,"* said the voice, *"is Nature, if thou acceptest Nature as the First Cause — Such is the universe without a god!"*

"A Man Who Grew Young Again," which marked Milne's first effort of 1887, appearing in the February 19th issue of the *Argonaut*, was superficially ordinary, but upon close examination is actually one of the most extraordinary of his stories. In the year 1887, blood transfusion was a rare medical procedure. The narrator of the story is a doctor, and his friend, the well-to-do 45-year-old Wycherley accidentally receives a shot-gun load in the leg during a hunting and fishing trip. Almost certain to die because of loss of blood, his life is saved by the unique device of improvising a three-way hookup between him and two sturdy 20-year-old farm boys. Veins from a freshly-killed cow are used as conduits between the three and the trio are kept convalescent while their combined blood supply makes a traverse of the bodies. Even after the sick man is well, the medical arrangement is continued, and when the men are finally separated the 45-year-old wounded man seems to have gotten younger and the farm boys older, all three now looking to be about 28 years of age.

The death of the wounded man's son, Stephen, finds the father actually marrying his son's fiancee. Few believe that the man is actually not the son. The farm hands are handsomely rewarded for their services and a signal episode has been added to the history of medicine. In truth, given the knowledge of the times, it is a marvelous story, extremely well told, and must certainly have had considerable impact on the readership of the *Argonaut.*

As highly unusual was Milne's "A Challenge to Psychology" in the April 9, 1887 issue of the *Argonaut.* In this story a doctor has invented a minute diamond drill which can penetrate the skull of a human in a minute. By injecting chemicals into selected areas of the brain he can bring about a change in personality within days with no more harmful effects than a bad headache. Brain surgery to accomplish the same thing had been suggested in Edward Page Mitchell's short story "The Professor's Experiment" in the February 22, 1880 edition of the New York *Sun,* but Milne had carried it through in a very clever, highly advanced style. He had, notably, completely disallowed phrenology as having any real scientific basis.

XXVII. THE INFLUENCE OF MILNE

It is important to mention that following his story "The Shadow of the Fancher Twins," a tale of two brothers with one life spirit, in the January 17, 1886 issue of the New York *Sun*, Edward Page Mitchell had turned from fiction and devoted full time to his editorial duties. Mitchell had begun writing science fiction in 1874 when he contributed "The Tachypomp" to the March, 1874 issue of *Scribner's*. That remarkable story, presented a theoretical method of moving faster than the speed of light, with an android that can solve mathematical problems, a set of meters which can record the progress, weight and height of a visitor on the staircase, and a tunnel through the center of the earth thrown in for good measure!

Between 1874 and 1878 Mitchell had anonymously written some of the most promising science fiction in the country. Between 1879 and 1886, he was joined by Milne and the two were the leading proponents of science fiction in the nation. They were in every sense contemporaries. Following 1886, Milne continued writing at the top of his form, whereas Mitchell quit altogether. The wide reprinting of Mitchell's tales, despite their anonymity, undoubtedly influenced writers both here and in England, but subtly. Milne's influence was to prove more direct.

The Californian had changed its name to the *Overland Monthly* with its January, 1882 issue, but under the editorship of Millicent W. Shinn emphasized the work of women writers and printed a negligible amount of science fiction. An important exception was "In Favilla. A Phantasmagoria," a first story by Geraldine Bonner in its May, 1886 issue. Bonner was then 16 years old and one of the highlights of her reading background had been Milne's "Into the Sun" in the November 18, 1882 issue of the *Argonaut*, the year she had come to California from her Staten Island birthplace. It had an even greater impact on her than on Gertrude Atherton, who was to later single it out for special attention. "In Favilla" displayed considerable stylistic skill, utilizing the diary technique. It narrated the discovery of a comet approaching the earth, the reactions of the populace and, like Milne's work, civilization is destroyed as the young man who is recording the events tells of his girl's last kiss, "All at once there was a crash, and the earth reeled beneath us. The pond dried up instantly. The stars, as I seemed to see them, began to fall, in clusters, by the millions by the myriads. Thick rolls of black smoke darkened the lurid sky. The ground on which I stood kept slipping away from my feet.

"The end had come."

The story takes place in the year 1902 and is set in New York and not in San Francisco. The government has socialized the railroads, electric air yachts are playthings of the rich, there are steam velocipedes as well as electric duplex curricles. Thousands of dug-out shelters are built in anticipation of the comet and the son of Thomas Edison constructs a diving bell capable of holding several thousand people to wait out the crash at the bottom of New York bay. Her concept as to the source of comets was every bit as impressive as Milne's.

Despite its derivativeness, "In Favilla" was an outstanding story and instantly made Bonner's reputation. She would appear in the *Argonaut* with "The Sailing of the Boomerang" (August 6, 1887), but it was a love story of yachts and society life. She became the foreign and dramatic critic of the *Argonaut* in 1887 and worked in that capacity until 1891. Her father, John Bonner, had written short stories for the *Argonaut* and was an old newspaper man from *The New York Tribune* and a former editor of *Harper's Weekly*. Geraldine was to become a well-known detective-story writer, one of her best was "The Castlecourt Diamond." But her earliest reputation as a novelist came from books that built from her Western experience, HARD-PAN, A STORY OF "BONANZA" FORTUNE" (1900) and THE EMIGRANT TRAIL (1910). Her short stories of both society and working people appeared in many of the nation's leading magazines. Though no other tales of science fiction by her have yet been located, in summing up the writers of science fiction and fantasy on the West Coast, as late as 1899, *The Forum* magazine lumped her with Robert Duncan Milne, Ambrose Bierce, W. C. Morrow and Emma Frances Dawson as a practitioner of such fiction. When the Paul Elder Publishing Company of San Francisco decided in 1907 to include "The Case of Summerfield" by William Henry Rhodes as one of a series of Western Classics, they asked Bonner to write the introduction because of that single science fiction tale she had seen published!

Her inspiration, Milne, was still climbing toward the apex of his popularity, though "A Wireless Telegraph" in the June 25, 1887 issue of the *Argonaut* was not one of the most effective stories. It is one of the earliest works of science fiction to acknowledge the transition of the term *mesmerism* into *hypnotism*. It attempts to project the use of a crystal to amplify post-hypnotic directives so they will be obeyed over a distance by thought and not word command. Working demonstrations are given in a parlor scene in the story, leading up to the conclusion that this method has been utilized to get a lawyer to burn a client's will so that his estate will go intestate.

"A Base-Ball Mystery" by Milne in the September 10, 1887 issue of the *Argonaut*, if not the first science fiction sport story in history is certainly the first science fiction baseball story. Milne displays considerable knowledge of the game, which he asserts in the story was a new vogue sweeping the east. He is also familiar with the vernacular of the sport and inserts in his story the complete score card of both teams, showing times at bat, hits, walks, outs, errors and what not. What has happened was that Indianapolis, with a terrible losing team and a mediocre pitcher named Hurlbut has played an extraordinary game against Pittsburgh. No one on either team seems capable of hitting the ball. It slightly evades the bat every time. The one exception is Hurlbut, who connects for two home runs, winning his own game. After the game, the baseballs in Hurlbut's dressing room have the covers cut off and his bat, which he split on his last home run, develops to be hollow. A scientist, working for a gambling ring, has provided special balls and bats with positive and negative electrical charges so that they repel one another when in close proximity. These devices, which the inventor removed after the game, have scientifically distorted the outcome of the game. Other "peculiar" games have been reported and it is wondered if the future of the sport itself is now in danger.

It was E. H. Clough who had originally, nine years earlier, introduced W. C. Morrow to the *Argonaut*. Clough's appearance with a horror story, "The Kiss of Death," in the September 17, 1887 issue, a first-person report of a man who awakens to find himself buried alive, proved to be a portent of Morrow's return to the pages of the magazine where he had achieved his initial recognition. After his marriage, Morrow had secured a position as Deputy County Clerk at the Courthouse in San Jose and established a residence with his wife Lydia at 214 North 3rd St., where he would remain until 1890. His wife would become an operator for the new-fangled telephones, which position she still held in 1889. Morrow had gone back to work as a newspaperman with the *San Jose Herald*, holding the title of Editor as well as Secretary of the Herald Publishing Company.

It is quite probable that constant prodding by Clough had forced him back into the writing of fiction. Correspondence still exists between the two life-long friends, and up until the year of his death Clough never stopped urging Morrow to increase his fiction output and to take his work more seriously.

When Morrow did reappear with "The Surgeon's Experiment" in the October 15, 1887 issue of the *Argonaut*, that single story gained a reputation for him that far exceeded the renown accumulated by all of his past work combined. "The Surgeon's Experiment" was the original title of his famous short story, now better known as "The Monster Maker," which would be considerably rewritten for later book publication. This was to be Morrow's first pure work of science fiction. A surgeon has conducted experiments in cutting a man's head off and keeping the body not only alive, but active and growing. A round metal ball is set in the center of the shoulders and a silver tube descends toward the stomach for feeding. Some minute, instinctive intelligence is retained by the motor nerves of the body, which seems to increase in muscularity and physical energy day by day.

The subject was a young man who wished to die but was too cowardly to commit suicide. He paid the professor $5,000 to painlessly put him to death. The story ends when the now immensely powerful subject, years after the experiment, inadvertently and convulsively wraps his arms around the scientist, killing him. In the process a lamp is overturned, setting the house on fire and destroying all evidence of the experiment. "The Surgeon's Experiment" was science fiction used to create a mood of horror and it succeeded. Horror had been the major ingredient of Morrow's stories all along, but he focussed attention on his work when he employed science fiction as the medium through which to generate it. There seems little question that it was the example of Milne's continuous success and recognition through specializing in science fiction that convinced Morrow it was worth trying.

Meanwhile the *Argonaut* continued to publish the unusual and strange wherever it could find them. "A Worker of Wonders" by Arlo Bates in the October 1, 1887 issue was a reprint from the *Boston Courier* and a rather well-done job of describing an exhibition given by a masked man at The Psychical Club of increasingly occult phenomena, terminating in a demonstration of levitation. The show completed, the "Magician" whips off his mask and is recognized as a popular member of the club, but upon his leaving, the memory of who he was is wiped from the minds of all present.

A distinctly above-average yarn was "A Lost Astral Body," contributed by Arthur W. Pleace to the November 19, 1887 issue. The locale of the story was Mexico, and the author resided in El Cubo, Mexico. A wanderer caring for a Mexican ranch has afternoons to do as he wishes and he practices projection of his intelligence out of his body to London and succeeds. He creates two personalities, one the prime resident of the body in Mexico, and the other a fine young man, rapidly accumulating wealth and reputation in London and who is capable because of his insubstantiality of literally walking through walls. His alter ego is by far the better person and commences courting the girl he left behind in London. The Mexican original blows his brains out in a dangerous experiment to see what will become of his London self. That alternate then gains human substance, marries the girl, and both live happily ever after.

XXVIII.
WILLIAM RANDOLPH HEARST, JR. AND THE EXAMINER

The San Francisco Examiner in the early months of 1887 was a morning paper owned by William Randolph Hearst, Sr., one of the wealthiest men in America (reputed to be worth $20 million at the time, most of it made in silver and gold mining), and operated at a loss to promote his political aspirations. He had taken over the paper in October, 1880 in lieu of repayment of loans and used it as a base for Democratic Party ambitions. The paper only achieved a circulation of about 25,000 and lost money constantly, but the older Hearst kept it afloat.

William Randolph Heart, *Jr.* was born in San Francisco on April 29, 1863, the only child of a rich father and doting mother. Nothing was denied him. On entering Harvard in 1882, his allowance was ostentatiously the most generous of almost anyone there. He took over as business manager of *The Harvard Lampoon*, a paper that operated at a loss which was generally made up by the students who edited it. Hearst was obviously best qualified to make up such losses but he was so industriously astute in the securing of advertising and contributions that *The Harvard Lampoon* quickly showed an embarrassing profit.

That renowned college paper aroused his interest in a journalistic career and he began to study leading newspapers of the nation, particularly those in New York City. By the time graduation approached he was writing not only long letters of criticism of the *Examiner*, but asking his father to turn it over to him. An immense prankster, he got himself expelled in his Junior year at Harvard by sending each instructor a toilet seat with their names lettered on the inside bottom. He then insisted more than ever that he be given the *Examiner* as his own, but his father felt that even if successful there wasn't enough money to be made from it to warrant the boy's effort.

He tried to interest his son in running ranches or mines, but the boy was adament. William, Jr. got himself a job on *The New York World,* run by Joseph 'Pulitzer, which was the paper he admired most. This gave him enough background so that his father, a newly-elected Senator after a campaign which had cost him $500,000, not without some misgivings, told his son that if he left *The New York World,* the *San Francisco Examiner* was his. On March 4, 1887, the first issue under the boy's control was published.

The role of the *San Francisco Examiner* in the history of newspaper publishing has often been told. What is to appear here is its role in the history of science fiction.

Wanting to upgrade his staff, Hearst began looking about for crack newspapermen who were willing to relocate. One of the first he hired was Henry D. Bigelow, whose reputation for digging up fascinating tidbits while editor and publisher of the late lamented *The Ingleside* was still remembered. The dapper, slick, sophisticated, derbied Bigelow would more than justify his reputation as one of the nation's greatest reporters. Before even demonstrating his great ability he was made one of Hearst's chief advisors.

Hearst personally visited Ambrose Bierce, then unemployed and residing in Oakland, and made him an acceptable offer for the period of $35 a week for a column plus space rates for other material, which was immediately agreed upon. Bierce's first "Prattle" column for the *Examiner* appeared in the March 27, 1887 issue, containing among other items a defense of dueling as a much more civilized and humane method of settling disagreements than the Western habit of shooting a man on sight and without warning.

Hearst did not stop with Bigelow and Bierce. He proceeded to hire as many good reporters and writers as he could wean away from other papers through the offer of more cash and a chance for journalistic creativity. The exact dates and order in which he added these men either to his payroll or to his list of regular contributors has never been ascertained, but starting in 1887 Robert Duncan Milne received a high priority and was certainly working for *The San Francisco Examiner* by the end of the year. Both E. H. Clough and W. C. Morrow showed up as contributors of short stories, and within a few years Morrow's contributions were so frequent as to indicate that if he was not a regular employee he was at least on a retainer. Sam Davis, brother of Robert H. Davis, was an employee and Robert H. Davis was a contributor. Joseph T. Goodman, who everyone thought had retired to a farm, eventually popped up to finish a story by W. C. Morrow.

The picture is clear. *The San Francisco Examiner,* which often ran a daily serial and featured short fiction regularly in its Sunday edition, was in a position to pander to the demonstrable tastes of San Franciscans for science fiction, occult and horror. This it gradually began to do.

XXIX. THE EXAMINER TURNS TO SCIENCE FICTION

The *Argonaut* was running some very fine science fiction and occult tales on a regular basis, but even when serialized in two parts, as they sometimes were, it was unusual for them to use a story much longer than 7,000 words. Hearst came in with a blockbuster. What was the biggest name in science fiction in 1887? Why Jules Verne, of course! Daily serialization, including Sundays, began of Verne's now-famed novel "The Clipper of the Clouds" the week of May 22, 1887. This was no reprint, it was a roughly simultaneous serialization by 13 newspapers of that dauntless character Robur, who sought, unsuccessfully, to conquer the world through the use of his giant heavier-than-air craft, propelled by the helicopter principle. The story ended with the edition of Tuesday, June 14, 1887 and there was a notice informing latecomers that all back numbers containing previous installments were obtainable at the *Examiner* offices at 756 Market Street. There were dozens of well-done illustrations. (The *Argonaut* literally never illustrated any story or feature.)

The story was obtained from the S. S. McClure syndicate, and the translation was the one later used as standard in the 15-volume WORKS OF JULES VERNE, edited by Charles F. Horne in 1911. The newspaper serialization could not have been later and might even have been earlier than the first United States hardcover edition issued by G. Munro, New York in 1887 as ROBUR THE CONQUEROR. In France it had first been serialized by *Le Journal des Débats* in 1886.

The illustrations for the novel were also supplied by S. S. McClure, because it was his policy to do so, particularly with his famous adventure novelists such as Robert Louis Stevenson and H. Rider Haggard. Even if they had not been, *The San Francisco Examiner* had its own art staff, which in a few years would rate second to none in the newspaper business.

Only a few weeks after the conclusion of "The Clipper of the Clouds," the *Examiner* began the serialization of Jules Verne's novel of the American Civil War, "North and South" (the original title was "North Against the South"), this beginning on Sunday, July 10, 1887 and running every Sunday thereafter until November 13, 1887. On Thursday, July 14, 1887, the *Examiner* ran an interview titled "Jules Verne at Home," attributed to Henri Pene du Bois and credited to *The Boston Herald*. This interview may also have been supplied by the S. S. McClure Syndicate, which made it a point to send out publicity concerning their more outstanding authors, for it specifically discusses the origin of "North and South."

Leading into his interview, du Bois utilizes a remarkable passage from the diary of Edmond and Jules de Goncourt, the men who endowed the institution in France which annually awards the Prix Goncourt: "To the author of an imaginative prose work of high merit." They had written: "After reading Poe the revelation of something that critics do not appear to have found, Poe, a new literature, the literature of the Twentieth Century, the miraculous scientific; imagination by the dint of analysis; the making of fabulous tales by A and B, a literature at once monomaniac and scientific. Zadig, a judge; Cyrano de Bergerac, a pupil of Arago. And things taking a better part than beings, and love, love lessened in Balzac's works by money — love yielding its place to other wells of interest; the novel of the future to tell the story of things that are in the brain rather than in the heart and humanity."

Du Bois wrote: "I wondered what Jules Verne, whose first novel appeared in 1862, would think of that, and I went to Amiens."

Verne agreed completely with the Goncourts and stated that Poe was his inspirator for the science fiction format and Fenimore Cooper his model as to style. Verne was still ailing from having been shot in the leg by a close relative and it was not healing. At the time it appeared, the interview contained much information that must have been new.

XXX. MORROW COMES TO THE EXAMINER

The Verne stories were a harbinger of what the *Examiner* was to present, but they would not settle for imported talent alone. William C. Morrow had an original story, "The Gloomy Shadow," in that paper on October 16, 1887 and he was back in the groove. A boy child, whose father is a master of phrenology (the "science" of reading the bumps on one's head), paid special attention to applying his findings towards guiding his children's careers. He unerringly placed his many children into the right profession, but avoided giving any assistance whatsoever to one boy. Once the youth finally confronts his father with this neglect, he finds his progenitor literally trembling with fear, showering him with platitudes but offering no help.

Finally he seeks out another competent phrenologist who does not know him. A few seconds of examination and the man is consumed by terror. With considerable difficulty the boy forces from him the finding of the vocation he is best suited for.

"There is only one thing in life you are fitted to be," he finally said, "and it pains me infinitely to add that it is the only thing which Nature in her inscrutable wisdom has decided you cannot avoid being."

"And what is that?"

"A murderer."

Morrow followed this story with "The Jailer's Wife" in the January 15, 1888 issue of the *Examiner*. It is a typical ingenious Morrow story told by the Sheriff of a town who, accompanied by his deputy son, went to arrest a man for horse-stealing. The man kills the son and is convicted by a jury of murder and sentenced to be hanged. The killer asks that the Sheriff's wife write a letter for him. After she has talked to him alone she is taken physically ill.

She continues to act peculiarly and one night the Sheriff awakens to find her and the keys missing from under his pillow. Through the window he sees his wife and the prisoner saddling up horses to leave. He fires at the prisoner but his wife flings herself in front of him and is killed. The prisoner escapes, but in a note the wife has left the Sheriff learns that the man she protected was her brother. The story was illustrated, and since it was not syndicated it was an indication that *The Examiner* was going to do the right things by its own.

At the request of Hearst himself, Ambrose Bierce had inserted in his column of February 19, 1888 a list of words commonly misused, sparing none of the sarcasm. He followed this up in several more columns only to be definitively replied to in a long letter headed "Reporter's English" by Morrow in the February 26th issue. As it later developed, Morrow was a philologist of no mean capability and his posthumous book on the subject, THE LOGIC OF PUNCTUATION FOR ALL WHO HAVE TO DO WITH WRITTEN ENGLISH, would appear from H. Low, San Francisco, in 1926. A two-column reply by Bierce in the March 4th edition, took no digs at Morrow, who was a friend of his, but argued his case with considerable logic. If there was the least doubt about Bierce's partiality, it was in the edition of April 1st, in his "Prattle" column, where he made his famous statement regarding Morrow's old novel "Blood Money": "I know nothing in literature surpassing the ghastly realism of Mr. Morrow's manner in with minute particularity the progressive stages of this horrible surgical operation (amputating one's own leg).... It is really one of the most powerful studies in that kind of art ever executed in words." His comment was inspired by the fact that a similar true-to-life incident had only recently occurred.

It is a misconception all-too-common that Ambrose Bierce was, in the decades following the departure of Brete Hart from the city where he had won his literary reputation, the most highly regarded fiction writer in the West or at least the very best. The truth was that Bierce's desultory earlier fiction attempts were not very good and were recognized as not being very good not only by the editors and readers but by Bierce himself.

Robert Duncan Milne, W. C. Morrow and Emma Frances Dawson were writing stories far superior to anything Bierce had written up to that date and his publicly published praise for *all* of them was his acknowledgement of that fact. Additionally, many of the other regional writers were occasionally coming up with individual yarns of considerable merit. The period when Bierce developed into a truly distinguished short story writer began after his affiliation with *The San Francisco Examiner* and with the short story "One of the Missing" in the March 11, 1888 edition. If there was any model it was indeed W. C. Morrow, then writing vigorously in the columns of the same newspaper and superbly, brilliantly in the *Argonaut*. In "One of the Missing," Joseph Shearing, a scout for General Sherman's army during the Civil War, observing the Confederates from the top of a small, ruined building, cocks his rifle to take a pot shot at them before returning with his report. A random artillery shell fired by the Confederates strikes the structure and he is buried in the debris with the rifle's muzzle pointed straight at his forehead. He is trapped, pinned and fears movements to extricate himself will set off the hair-trigger of the rifle. Rats appear, waiting for him to weaken. After a long period of mounting horror, he gradually moves a board to the trigger guard of the rifle and then thrusts it at the trigger. The gun has been discharged in the fall, but Shearing dies of fright at the instant of the thrust.

The story is vague and unclear. Bierce rewrote the ending for later book publication but it did not help. One can interpret it to mean that the rifle shot had caught him when it initially went off, because he feels a continuous growing pain in his head while undergoing his ordeal. The Confederates who find him have apparently done so the same day, but they conclude that he has been "Dead for a week." That would make it a ghost story, of a type Bierce later executed masterfully.

The "Prattle" column of March 18, 1888 had Bierce reporting that he had just begun reading H. Rider Haggard's ALLAN QUARTERMAIN and has no intention of finishing it. His biggest objection seemed to be the quoted poem:

"In Kubla Khan a river ran,
    Through Caverns measureless to man
        Down to a sunless sea."

"Really," Bierce wrote, "Kubla must have been terribly inconvenienced by this sort of thing going on in his cavernous inside."

XXXI. AMBROSE BIERCE'S DYSTOPIAS

There has been little comment on Ambrose's Bierce's dystopian fiction, ostensibly told from the vantage point of the far future and intended as devastating satires. The first of these was titled "The Fall of the Republic, An Article from a 'Court Journal' of the Thirty-First century," of novelette length, published in the March 25, 1888 *San Francisco Examiner.* In Bierce's COLLECTED WORKS, the only other place it is known to have appeared, it has been *massively* rewritten, lengthened and retitled "Ashes of the Beacon, An Historical Monograph Written in 4930." In that later version Bierce pushed all the dates further back. The two versions are so different in facts and events that a special dissertation is needed to deal with them. In the original, the American Republic collapses in 1950 with the defeat of the Republican army near Smithfield in Northern California. In that year, the victorious Field Marshall Sir Henry Burnell established himself as the Emperor of the Occident. A dynasty that endured until the year 2781 when John XI "was compelled to abdicate."

Bierce utilized this dystopian format to dispense what he considered Swiftian satire, sarcastically objective observations on the government, the system, the nation's philosophy, hypocrisy and other matters. At junctures he would interrupt his pontifications with a brutal review of a few of the historical battles and revolutionary events that resulted in the dissolution of the United States. Neither in style, substance or story does "The Fall of the Republic" rank high, though it demonstrates Bierce's familiarity with this format of presenting opinion.

"The Fall of the Republic" was but the first of a series. The second, "The Kingdom of Tortirra" (April 22, 1888), "Some Account of the People of a Recently Discovered Country," concerns an unknown group of islands with several strange races, providing the basis of commentary on politics, public issues, courts and other matters. Again, this piece was extensively rewritten in the COLLECTED WORKS, though the title was not changed.

Bierce had a number of stories in *The San Francisco Examiner*, but with "A Tough Tussle" (September 30, 1888) he struck again a note of true horror with implications of the supernatural. A Federal officer, seated in an outpost, is made uneasy by the body of a Confederate soldier laying nearby. He imagines he sees a slight movement. When the sound of battle is heard, the tension breaks, and sword in hand he lunges forth to do battle. The day following the battle the Federals find him dead with his sword through his heart and the decaying corpse of a Confederate soldier alongside him who has been stabbed and ripped innumerable times.

Bierce returned to his Swiftian mood with "The Tamtonians, Some Account of Politics in the Uncanny Islands," in the edition of November 11, 1888. It was a satire of American politics, attributing its most salient characteristics to the people of an unknown island and strange civilization.

When Bierce's column "Prattle" had appeared in *The San Francisco News Letter*, he had also on rare occasions contributed bits of fiction. The most memorable of them was "An Inhabitant of Carcosa," which appeared in the December 25, 1886 issue. A man who last remembers resting on a sickbed, finds himself on a sunless, semi-barren plain, where even the sounds of the insects are not audible. A lynx passes by him without paying any notice. He continues forward towards where he hopes his city of Carcosa may be, when he comes almost face to face with a half-naked man in skins, carrying a torch. The man pays him no mind and continues on, and for the first time he notices that while it is not dark the stars are visible "and through a sudden rift in the clouds Aldebaran and the Hyades!" He notes the almost smoothed remains of an ancient graveyard and on one of the stones reads clearly the date of his birth and death and realizes, once and for all, that not only is he dead, but *long* dead is his home city of Carcosa.

It is a good story, written in the form of a biblical parable, but the idea of the spiritual essence of a man discovering that he is a lost soul and his body is dead is as old as legend. The more unusual element concering it was that it apparently influenced the writing of the lead story in Robert W. Chambers' book THE KING IN YELLOW (1895), which was titled "The Repairer of Reputations." A poem to lost Carcosa leads off that story and in the text one of Chambers' characters is reading the manuscript "The Imperial Dynasty of America" from the opening lines where it states: "When from Carcosa, the Hyades, Hastur, and Aldebaran." These are two of the same stars cited in Bierce's story, which appeared in hardcovers as TALES OF SOLDIERS AND CIVILIANS in 1891, accompanied by excellent reviews. Chambers returned from France to the United States in 1893 and there is no question of his familiarity with that Bierce story. A more fascinating speculation is the theme of "The Repairer of Reputations," dealing with the future of the United States, the overthrow of democracy and the establishment of a monarchy. This is, of course, the theme of Bierce's "The Fall of the Republic." It could be a coincidence for at the time of its appearance Chambers was in France and it would not be reprinted until 1909.

Just as Bierce was free to sell other of his works excepting the column "Prattle" elsewhere, apparently this also applied to Robert Duncan Milne. His work on the *Examiner* was in a straight reportorial and feature writer capacity and obviously did not proscribe his appearance elsewhere, for "A Modern Proteus" was published in the *Argonaut* in the issues of March 24 and April 14, 1888. This was another indication of the versatility and flexibility of Milne's imaginative concepts. Proteus was a marine god of the ancient Greeks, noted for his ability to change appearance at will. Milne comes up with a man who has this remarkable power, utilizing it to assume the forms of bank presidents and intimidating the clerks into letting him make off with substantial sums of money. The only way he can be identified from those he mimics is through an unusual black spot in one eye that persists even after the changes. Eventually caught and imprisoned because of this clue, the detectives never do determine whether his changes are actually physical or hypnotic, though the evidence appears to lean towards the former.

HISTORY OF THE MOVEMENT

In the May 23, 1888 issue of the *Argonaut*, Milne presented "Life on the Planet Mars," a continuation of the observations of the remarkable new Lick telescope as first reported in "A Telescopic Marvel" (December 4, 1886). The telescope confirms the theories of Schiaperelli that the lines of Mars actually do exist and are canals. There are five major canals, three to four miles in width, and they all converge on a central lake about 30 miles in width, in which churn prodigeous fans or screws, providing the force driving the water along the canals. The power source is not determinable. Reconfirmed is the ability that Martians have to render objects nearly weightless and move them with ease. There are flying machines, boats and vehicles with no obvious source of propulsion. There is no attempt at a story line, just an illusion of an insider's story, of new discoveries in progress and a great deal of basic and speculative astronomy.

XXXII. STEVENSON RETURNS TO SAN FRANCISCO

Then, for a period of less than a month, interests of all literary people in the greater San Francisco area were diverted from the science fiction of Robert Duncan Milne or any other localite for that matter by the news that Robert Louis Stevenson was returning to town. This was the same Stevenson who almost died of illness and starvation eight years earlier, but his reputation was considerably enhanced. Three years past, Stevenson had written and had published by Longman's, Green & Co., London, in January, 1886, THE STRANGE CASE OF DR. JEKYLL AND MR. HYDE. As the story goes, it was written in three intense days, was criticized by his wife Fanny and he threw it into the flames, closeting himself in his room for another three days and emerged with a new version. When the story first appeared it was just as much a sheer fantasy as "Beauty and the Beast." In recent times the obvious effects of LSD drugs in completely changing a person's character has converted it into science fiction. Such drugs did exist, could have been found, and could very well have had the effect Stevenson claimed for them.

So convinced were the publishers of the public acceptance of the story that instead of releasing it immediately in hard covers, they issued it *first* in a paperback edition of 25,000 copies selling for a shilling (then worth about 25 cents). The now-famous plot line of a chemist who could convert himself from a good and decent person to an evil and depraved individual by taking a chemical mixture created an international sensation. Stevenson's reputation was made with that short novel, not only in England but in the United States, where the lack of an international copyright law made pirating legal. When that work was followed in six months by the publication of KIDNAPPED, destined to become a classic for teenagers, the man could do no wrong. He had arrived.

The death of his father in Scotland in 1887 sparked his decision to return to America with his wife, her child by a previous marriage, and his mother. Here he found DR. JEKYLL AND MR. HYDE a Broadway play, and offers to him of fabulous prices for fiction, articles, essays and poems.

The breaking up of his friendship with the British poet William Ernest Henley over a failure in collaboration on plays and that person's dislike of his wife Fanny (which dislike was reciprocated by her), irrationally decided Stevenson to leave America and sojourn in the South Seas. He assembled his entourage and arrived in San Francisco on June 6, 1888.

This time the reception was different. Reporters thronged his hotel, among the most prominent and regular Henry D. Bigelow and Robert Duncan Milne, both working on *The San Francisco Examiner* at the time. Eleven years later in Milne's obituary *The San Francisco Examiner* for December 16, 1899 stated: "When Robert Louis Stevenson dropped into San Francisco about ten years ago he and Milne became very friendly. Milne used to say that he had tried to find a market for Stevenson's writings in the offices of the local weeklies, but none were so poor as to do the Great Scot reverence."

The *Examiner* was still serializing Stevenson's "The Outlaws of Turnstall," which they had obtained from the McClure Syndicate, when he arrived and this novel (originally published in 1886 by *Young Folks* magazine in England as the "Black Arrow") ran in the Sunday editions from March 25 to June 24, 1888, concluding two days before Stevenson's departure. It was in the contrast between Stevenson's first visit to San Francisco in 1880 and his second in 1888 that the legend of the abuse of genius first began to flower. The truth is that there is not the slightest evidence that Stevenson offered the San Francisco publications at any time anything that has ever been identified as having merit worthy of publication. Before arriving in San Francisco, no New York City publication that Stevenson visited would buy whatever it was he was offering, either. It was claimed that he had briefly worked for *The San Francisco Chronicle* in 1880, that the first story he wrote had to be completely rewritten by another reporter, and that he continued to write for their Sunday edition. Despite several searches, nothing has been discovered in the files of the *Chronicle* attributable by external or internal evidence to Stevenson. John P. Young, publisher of the *Chronicle* wrote (presumably with staff assistance) a history called "Journalism in California" for the January 16, 1915 Golden "Jubilee and Exposition Edition" of that paper. In that history he said: "If The Chronicle could have added the name of Robert Louis Stevenson to the long list of distinguished authors who contributed to its columns in the early days it would have done so cheerfully, but the records of the paper were carefully examined several years before the fire, and his name was not found on any pay roll during the period of his sojourn in California."

There is always the inference that if a genius is sick and has had a very difficult time, he is automatically a fine person with a spotless character. The truth is that many underdogs when they achieve success often prove to be anything but peerless personalities. Robert Louis Stevenson was no paragon as Peter Lyons found out when he researched for his book SUCCESS STORY, THE LIFE AND TIMES OF S. S. McCLURE (Scribner's, 1963). McClure, who paid Stevenson more than anyone else for American rights to his stories; who protected Stevenson's literary efforts by securing first publication in newspapers with American copyright, thereby preventing them from being pirated; who not only catered to him, but acted as his agent, errand boy, trouble shooter and bill collector; was treated with sadistic cruelty in person and in print by Stevenson, who proved himself a liar, an ingrate, a double-dealer, unscrupulous in business, untrustworthy, unethical and unreliable. When he was in a position to call the turn, Stevenson was ruthless, had no objection to being paid for the use of his name on works written by others, and his story "The Bottle Imp" *(The New York Herald,* February 8 to March 1, 1891) was proven (partially admitted by Stevenson) in precise plot, sequence-by-sequence, as well as the *very title,* to have been appropriated from a German translation first published in English as one of the stories in POPULAR TALES AND ROMANCES OF THE NORTHERN NATIONS (W. Simpkin, R. Marshall & J. H. Bohte, 1823).

Did Milne ever show Stevenson some samples of his fiction

while the now-famous author was in San Francisco? It would have seemed strange if either in 1880 or 1888 when the two were briefly close that Milne would not have mentioned and brought around his stories. No reference to Bigelow, Milne or any other San Franciscan reporter appears in any letter of Stevenson's that has been preserved.

Stevenson left San Francisco on Friday, June 16, 1888 for the first leg of his journey to the South Seas where he would spend most of what remained of his life. The June 27, 1888 issue of the *Argonaut* ran Milne's latest work of science fiction, "A New Theosophy." It is possible that advance copies were available before Stevenson left and that he saw it. If so, it was Milne returning to the philosophy of Madame Blavatsky and fascinated by the ability claimed for adepts to will themselves physically from place to place around the earth, presenting the concept of a machine which magnifies the power of the will. "Seven gentlemen, some in evening dress, representing widely different circles of society, sitting on an insulated circular platform, their chairs ranged with mathematical precision in a heptagon, in their centre, a vast glass bell, from which radiated a system of telegraphic wires, while from their heads rose a structure of metal rods, which towered above them in the centre, looking, with its curved sides and spherical apex, for all the world like a giant crown."

With total concentration, they will in unison the reincarnation of William Shakespeare. The effort and the tension is great, but slowly the features of the Great Bard begin to take unmistakable form, and incredibly, success is almost at hand. A tremendous banging at the door of the room destroys the concentration. The great glass bell explodes, the vision of Shakespeare fades from sight. A new glass bell is ordered and the experiment will be repeated.

"What Is Fate?" by Milne in the July 30, 1888 *Argonaut* was a story of clairvoyance that was frankly occult and offered no scientific explanation. "There never has existed a time in the annals of recorded history, nor does there exist a race, even to the most ignorant and degraded of the human family, that does not show traces of a belief in the possibility of penetrating the veil of the future, and gaining the cognizance of events about to happen, affecting races, places or individuals, as the case may be," starts Milne and then proceeds with a straight narrative. An astrologer, Asgard, who is also something of a sensitive, predicts for his subject the death of both his fiancee and his uncle, the latter by a knife held in his hand. He will not marry his current fiancee, he is told, but his cousin.

All this comes true when the subject is cleaning his nails at night with a knife while aboard ship with his uncle and fiancee. There is a collision in the dark. The uncle is thrown against his knife and impaled. His fiancee strikes her head and is killed. The cousin who has come to meet them nurses him back to health and they are married.

"The Shaft in the Amargosa" by Milne in the August 27, 1888 *Argonaut* involves a clairvoyant who tells two men of a map that will lead them to a rich gold mine. They find the map, and on the road pick up a young Mexican to assist them. The shaft of the mine is located and at the bottom the mummified body of a dead man. He is hoisted up, but the rope into the mine is cut by the Mexican, dooming one of the prospectors to death. The Mexican turns out to be a woman, the sister of the dead man in the mine, left there by the trapped prospector. She reveals she was also the "clairvoyant," buries the remains of her brother and leaves. The story is extremely well written and organized.

XXXIII. FRED SOMERS LAUNCHES CURRENT LITERATURE

While the dates are not clear, another celebrity of considerable importance to San Francisco writers had visited the city earlier than Robert Louis Stevenson, and that man was Fred Somers, co-founder of the *Argonaut,* and former publisher of *The Californian* and *The Epigram.* He had been travelling abroad, had cleaned up some money on the stock market, and was relatively well-heeled. He had been gone long enough for West Coast writers to realize what a great encouragement and benefactor he had been for local talent.

He left San Francisco and settled in New York, meeting with Gertrude Atherton, the San Francisco author who had scored her first success in the *Argonaut* a few years earlier with "The Randolphs of Redwood." Atherton was the granddaughter and protege of Stephen Franklin, a nephew of *the* Benjamin Franklin, who was in turn editor of one of the first California papers, the famed *Golden Era.* He was to die in 1889. She married into a well-to-do family and widowed young, inherited enough to permit her to travel and write. Her fiction and articles were published in leading magazines and her subjects were sometimes provocatively "racy" for the times.

In New York Somers reviewed plans for several publications and won encouragement from Atherton for the idea of a magazine that would emerge with the issue of July, 1888 as *Current Literature,* "A Magazine of Record and Review." Frank Luther Mott, in his fourth volume of A HISTORY OF AMERICAN MAGAZINES describes the magazine as "by far the most attractive and entertaining eclectic journal ever published in the English language." Reading through those issues one is not only forced to agree with him, but add the opinion that for the few years under Somers it was the best literary journal ever to appear in the United States, with no exceptions. Never before or since has there been such an incredible quantity of inside news, discussion, editorializing written in so entertaining a fashion about the literary world. The quality that made *Current Literature* so brilliantly unique was its utter lack of snobbishness. It covered *all* the literary world and did not single out what was "worth" discussing. The magazine intended to discuss works that had lost favor and "to keep a literary record and preserve the ephemeral." Beyond its general excellence, *Current Literature* revealed, past any doubt or cavil, who was responsible for the successful literary policy of the *Argonaut*. Every issue of *Current Literature* reprinted a minimum of two, and sometimes three or four, supernatural, horror, science fiction or wildly off-trail stories in its 92 almost tabloid size, handsomely printed pages. It also ran *every* issue a column called "The Unusual — Superstitions, Ghosts and Queer," and this rarely was under 4,000 words in length.

In its first issue it reprinted from the *Argonaut* "Awful Shadows" by W. C. Morrow, Jr. and "One of the Missing" by Ambrose Bierce from *The San Francisco Examiner*. This was the first appearance of both of these San Francisco writers in a truly nationally read and distributed publication. With its second issue it ran "Parasee Fables" by Ambrose Bierce from the first year of the *Argonaut* when Bierce was editor; "The Man-Eating Tree" by Edmund Spencer, whose title is self-explanatory, from *The New York World;* and Edward Page Mitchell's "The Devilish Rat" from the *Sun,* under the title of "Iscariot's Soul — a Weird and Wicked Soul," as well as "L Immortel" by Alphonse Daudet, about a man who would like to discover the secret of immortality.

In that second issue it inaugurated a list of the leading books of the month as well as articles, fiction and criticism of the month from all the major magazines of America. An idea that has developed in current times to fantastic lengths.

The third, September, 1888, issue started a series of "Wonder Stories," the first "The Celebrated Moon Hoax" by Richard Adams Locke, and a translation by Ballard Craig of "The May Bug" by J. H. Rosny from the French.

The fourth issue reprinted, in addition to "The Gold Bug" by Edgar Allan Poe, "Following the Sea," an anonymous tale from the London *Figaro*, involving the fantastic events that occurred as the aftermath of an earthquake; "Peter Rugg" by William Austin, a time travel story about a man and a child travelling eternally into their future to find the road back to their home in the past in Boston.

This policy continued until the April, 1890 issue, replaced then in favor of excerpts from novels, with the announcement a month earlier that the first issue of *Short Stories* — "A Magazine of Select Fiction" would be issued on April 10, 1890, dated June 1890, with a policy of "25 stories for 25 cents." This was the same *Short Stories* magazine which later became a men's adventure magazine, continuing publication through to the 1960's. In its early days it read much like *The Black Cat* magazine and probably was a partial inspiration for it.

The similarity of the *Argonaut's* fiction policy to that of *Current Literature* was apparent, the major difference was that Hart was using original fantasy as well as translations and even the translations were new ones, especially done for him, like "Titane" by Jules Lermina from the French (October 15, 1888). The theme must have been old even then, of a botanist creating in his own hothouse a flesh-eating plant which begins to absorb him. His last words to the young man who kills the plant trying to save him are prefaced by: "Assassin!"

XXXIV. AN UNWITTING HOAX

Appearing October 8, 1888, "The Capture of San Francisco" by someone signing only as "S.E.M." was the type of tale that Milne had twice done successfully, but this was not Milne but an old-time San Francisco writer named S. E. Moffitt. The Chinese, angered by a Congressional law that all their nationals would be denied permission to emigrate to the United States, send 12 armored battleships to San Francisco. The hastily assembled defensive fleet and shore batteries are quickly demolished. A ransom is exacted from the city and it is then destroyed. The entire West Coast is pillaged and the fleet returns to China, while the United States assembles a fleet of its own which will eventually exact retribution. The story is extremely well told, the battle of San Francisco thrillingly described, and there are elements of invention and novelty in the technical end of the war.

"A Murderous Mesmerist" by Julian Hawthorne, the son of Nathaniel Hawthorne, was reprinted from the *Cosmpolitan Magazine* in the December 3, 1888 issue. In that story a man attempts to accomplish a horrifying murderous revenge in a most melodramatic manner through the use of hypnotism, including mass hypnotism and post-hypnotic suggestion. He almost succeeds, but chance foils his plans and he is accidentally killed.

Every author of any merit always has the single story that makes the most impact. It may not be his best story. It may not even be a good story, but it resonatingly strikes the chord of public interest at just the right moment. With Arthur Machen it was "The Bowmen," which originally appeared in England in the *London Evening News* of September 29, 1914. England was at war and Machen had read of what he termed "the awful account of the retreat from Mons." He then wrote a series of stories inspired by that retreat, one of which, "The Bowmen," told of a group of medieval archers, led by St. George astride a horse, who killed 10,000 Germans without a wound upon them, and permitted the British Tommies to escape from almost certain annihilation.

Several church papers asked for permission to reprint, then for permission to issue it as a pamphlet. Letters began to pour in ecstatic in faith that such a miracle could have occurred. The *Occult Review* sought explanations. No amount of denial by Machen could in anywise convince people that the story was not true. Machen cites discussions of the topic in *Truth, Town Topics, The New Church Weekly, John Bull, The Church Times* and *Pall Mall*. Witnesses began to appear that had "seen" the miracle. Survivors of the retreat from Mons swore to its authenticity and thought details of the story changed. Sermons were preached from the pulpit concerning it. When Machen in a hardcover edition of the story published by Putnam's in 1915 ridiculed the idea that his story was anything but fiction, Harold Begbie had published from Hodder & Stoughton, London, a paperback book titled ON THE SIDE OF THE ANGELS, THE STORY OF THE ANGELS AT MONS, AN ANSWER TO "THE BOWMEN," the same year. Begbie felt that by denying the story, Machen was "committing what I feel to be a grievous sin in the region of taste if he had reflected long enough upon the moral teachings of Christ," because "Mr Machen's book as it stands must add to the bitterness of this present grief and lamentation. Hunger and thirst for consolation is treated to an Introduction ... which will certainly not medicine the agony of the human heart." He then goes on to retell the story the way it *really* happened and in considerable detail.

Robert Duncan Milne's story "Ten Thousand Years in Ice" received, through a peculiar set of circumstances, a similar, if less aggravated, reaction. The story appeared in the January 14, 1889 issue of the *Argonaut*. It told of a block of ice unloaded at the San Francisco wharf with a man in an ancient costume frozen in its center. A doctor scientifically thaws the body out and with a shock of electricity starts the heart beating again. When supplied with pen and ink, the recently-frozen man begins writing in an incomprehensible language. He is measured for clothes and lessons start in the instruction of English. The entire story is presented in the science fiction hoax tradition of Richard Adams Locke and is convincingly done. Like most of the hoax-type stories it just trails off without a surprise ending.

There was scarcely anything novel in the idea of "Ten Thousand Years in Ice," but envious of the positive reaction to the story some suggested that Milne had taken the idea from the French author Edmond About, who had written a suspended animation novel utilizing a similar method titled L HOMME A OREILLE CASSEE, printed in America in 1883 as A NEW LEASE ON LIFE from J. W. Lowell, New York. The same company had published W. Clark Russell's THE FROZEN PIRATE in 1887, a truly excellent adventure which involves a pirate thawed out after having been frozen for 48 years. Though Russell was and would become a popular novelist and biographer, this was to be by far his most renowned and successful story. THE FROZEN PIRATE was the most likely candidate for Milne's inspiration, though a science short titled "Revival After Freezing," as far back as the May, 1880 issue of Fred Somer's *The Californian*, reporting on an alligator which had been frozen solid in a block of ice and restored to life after thawing, cannot be discounted, since Milne was not only contributing to the magazine at the time but might even have written the item himself!

All that being said, the journalistic method of narration that convinced so many people that "Ten Thousand Years in Ice" might actually be true was a quality which none of his predecessors had succeeded in doing as well, including Mary Wollstoncraft Shelley, who attempted to perpetrate a hoax with her short story "Roger Dodsworth: The Reanimated Englishman," about a young man frozen in the ice for 166 years, posthumously published in 1863.

The people of San Francisco enjoyed it and chalked down another "good one" for Milne, and waited for a sequel that might or might not come. Time passed and then, according to Hart, "One morning the Argonaut's large mail was abnormally swollen by a bunch of letters from Vienna, from Budapest, from Belgrade, from Prague, from Bucharest, and from various other cities and towns in what used to be Austria-Hungary and what is now Czechoslovakia, Rumania, and Yugoslavia. A few of these letters were in English, some in German, Hungarian and other languages of the defunct polyglot empire. They came from people in every station of life — Magyar noblemen, military officers, professional men, actors, small shopkeepers, and what not. All wrote breathlessly, demanding further particulars concerning the gentleman who had been so long frozen."

The story had been printed in the Hungarian paper *Pester Lloyd* for February, 1889 with the translation done by Mme. Fanny Steinitz of Budapest. She had dubbed the author *Sir* Robert Duncan Milne to lend a little more authority to the account, but the results had been totally unexpected. The editor of *Pester Lloyd* had been bombarded with letters from readers asking if the story were true. Unable to answer he had given all those who wrote in the address of the *Argonaut*. A deluge of letters followed. When Jerome Hart issued a paperbound book ARGONAUT STORIES in 1906, containing representative selections from his magazine, he reprinted "Ten Thousand Years in Ice" as well as eight of the letters received with full names and addresses.

Coincidentally, in a sequel titled "The World's Last Cataclysm," run in the February 25, 1889 issue of the *Argonaut*, the man thawed from a block of ice, whose name is Kourban Balanok, is passed off as "A Hungarian friend of my son's" by a benefactor who is keeping him as a guest, while teaching him English. With his newly-gained command of our language, the man from the ice tells a remarkable story of coming from an advanced civilization nearly 10,000 years past, located on the rim of what is today the polar sea. Air flight was commonplace, electricity was the key to the technical functioning of their cities and intellectual progress was such that they even felt they were in contact with spirits of the dead. A great comet sweeps into their ken, with a magnetic head so powerful that it spins the crust of the earth on the fluid interior, drowning the world of his time and leading to a reversion of mankind to barbarism. Milne's delineation of the background of this strange man and the events leading up to the destruction of his civilization are nothing short of superb. He writes with an intellectual power, logic and intensity that is admirable, extraordinarily imaginative and convincing.

XXXV. MORROW MOVES INTO HIGH GEAR

Almost as if feeling the need for a change of pace, "A Female Highwayman" *(Argonaut,* March 4, 1889) by Milne had a woman hold up a stage with a shotgun for the sole purpose of obtaining enough money from her parsimonious husband to visit San Francisco. It is an interesting commentary upon the outlook of the period, that any story about a woman performing any job or act usually associated with a man was regarded as bizarre enough to lend novelty to a story without any additional exercise of ingenuity.

The same issue contained a crudely written, grotesque translation from the French of J. Montet titled "The Clown in Tragedy." A jealous clown cuts the steel wire of a tight-rope performer who is his lover, because she is about to leave him. As she falls, he catches her, preventing injury, but she leaves him in disgust after observing in the hospital how horribly smashed up he has become in the process. The only reason this story is worth mentioning at all is to compare it with the grotesqueries of W. C. Morrow, where horrifying subject matter is handled with the skill and vividness of near-genius.

Hart rarely put blurbs on any of his stories but in "A Peculiar Case of Surgery" by W. C. Morrow in the February 4, 1889 issue of the *Argonaut* he had good reason: "This powerfully written sketch is, as the title indicates," he opened, "a detailed account of a most extraordinary surgical operation. People with delicate nerves had better refrain from reading it. If after this warning they read it, they have only themselves to blame."

A man discovers his friend lying on his bed in a hotel with apparently the handle of a dagger protruding from his chest. A doctor states that if it is removed he will die in minutes. A surgeon called into the case offers the opinion that the weapon is a stiletto, whose pointed, round circumference has pushed the tissues aside, not cut them, and even though the weapon has penetrated the aorta the victim may live, provided the stilleto is never removed. An operation is performed removing the handle of the stiletto and sewing the skin over the portion remaining. Anti-coagulants are given the victim to prevent a blood clot, and also chemicals that might gradually dissolve the metal. It also has been deduced that due to the nature of the weapon the wound has been inflicted by a woman, the identity of whom the victim does not care to disclose.

Five years later the surgeon returns with his wife, whom he introduces to the still-living victim. She develops to be the woman who stabbed him because he had refused to marry her. At the shock of the meeting, the victim is so excited that he imagines the blade has slipped from his aorta and the blood is pouring into his body cavity. He quickly dies. An autopsy reveals that the muturic acid taken daily had dissolved the blade and the tissues had healed. This story was a favorite of Gertrude Atherton who said of it: "A more dramatic opening to a story has seldom been written . . . a strong and curious study of a man who lived for years with the blade of a stiletto embedded near his heart."

With revisions, this story has been collected and frequently reprinted under the title of "The Permanent Stiletto," but noteworthy as it was the blurb warning away the faint of heart applied more pointedly to "The Rajah's Nemesis" by Morrow in the March 11, 1889 issue of the *Argonaut*. Few who have read this story under his later title of "His Unconquerable Enemy" will argue the fact that it is one of the most blood-chilling tales of horror ever to appear on the printed page and unquestionably ranks Morrow extremely high on the all-time list of masters of the genre as well as among the greatest American short story writers.

A servant, as punishment for a series of murders and attempted murders, including the death and mutilation of the son of the Indian Rajah for whom he worked, is punished by having both arms and legs amputated at the stumps. The man is also to be kept alive and tortured at intervals for the rest of his life. The story is told by a surgeon who was involved, witness to and attending at much of what transpired. The basket case is kept in a metal cage 10 feet off the floor in one of the Rajah's favorite summer rooms, so that he may gloat at the mental and physical agony he has inflicted on his enemy. The details of the escape of the prisoner with no other tools than his teeth, the incredible ascent to a balcony and a drop to the sleeping chest of the Rajah, culminating in the death of both, is an epic of narrative horror possessing few equals.

The real marvel was that a magazine like the *Argonaut,* which was a regional publication, primarily circulated in one city, could command the production of original fiction on a sustained basis of such brilliant performers as Robert Duncan Milne and W. C. Morrow in the field of science fiction, supernatural and horror, along with the retinue of other fine writers previously described as contributing within the field of fantasy, as well as a score of others who were as distinguished at regional fiction.

XXXVI. ARGONAUT'S FANTASY QUOTIENT RISES

Morrow had another tale in the April 29, 1889 issue of the *Argonaut* which differed sharply in essence from those he usually wrote, titled "The Type-Writer* Exposed." It dealt with a man who is brought a group of type-written letters to analyze. Scientific proof positively identifying them with a single individual could make possible a breach of promise suit on the part of an unidentified woman. It is really a scientific detective story, for in several thousand words, given in the form of a report, Morrow, in a manner more typical of Milne than himself, breaks down the hundreds of elements by which an individual may be identified through his type-writing as easily as through his handwriting. It is more an exercise in procedural logic than a story, but in a day when type-writers were still uncommon, it was quite ingenious.

Hart's model in the later *Argonaut* was admittedly the work of the French writer Guy de Maupassant, and he periodically translated and ran one of that author's tales. He liked best those that included an element of horror and typical of that style was "The Gospel of Murder" in his June 10, 1889 issue, where a French judge gets to enjoy the executions of those he sentences so much that he begins murdering people for the thrill of it. Then, when in one case, a nephew of the man he has murdered is accused and brought to trial, he takes great delight in sentencing him to death and watching the blood spurt from the guillotine as the execution is carried out.

Then Hart scheduled one of Milne's most adroit tales, a scientific detective story "The Silent Witness" in the July 1, 1889 issue, in which a machine for cutting phonograph records is accidentally left on and records a conversation involving a murder. Protests are raised against offering "such a monstrous and unheard innovation" as evidence, but the judge rules that it be heard without prejudice. The recording reproduces the conversation ending in the murder. While the legal aspects of the validity of this evidence is argued, the murderess confesses. A wrongly accused man is released and "In the fervor of his heart after liberation, he wrote a characteristic letter to Edison expressing unbounded gratitude for that distinguished scientist's last invention having been the means of saving his life." If not the earliest, this must have been one of the earliest uses of the phonograph or any recording device as a means of obtaining evidence which solves a crime.

The ability of Hart to read French held him in good stead, for whenever he did not get enough off-beat stories from his local authors he authorized the translation of one he happened to run across in foreign publications. "The Fatal Rope" by Celieres, translated by E. C. Waggener, who had done others for the *Argonaut*, was a particularly good supernatural tale, appearing in the July 15, 1889 issue. At an army camp five men successfully hang themselves from the same rope with no apparent motivation. The captain, determined to destroy the superstitious belief of his men that ghosts are responsible for the deaths, stands sentry in the room with the suspected rope and is barely cut down in time as he, too, succumbs to the compulsion towards suicide which that particular rope invokes.

If there was not something suitable in the French publications, Waggener could do as well by translating from the Russian Sacher-Masoch's grim tale of horror "The Grave-Digger's Daughter" for the July 22, 1889 issue. The revolution has broken out in Russia and peasants are fighting rebels and both are dying. The grave digger is sick, but his powerful young daughter accepts unit pay and bonuses to bury in trenches the bodies of the dead. She buries them all, the instigators, the brave defenders, the innocent bystanders, and finally she comes to one still living, a former lover who had despoiled her and left her. He pleads and struggles, but she avers she is paid to bury not to succor, rolls him in a ditch, fills the dirt over him, and pats it solid.

Humor is one of the most difficult of all elements to incorporate successfully into fiction and non-fiction though almost all authors, no matter what their bent, try it at one time or another. Edgar Allan Poe had an entire body of humorous short stories which survive in his collected works, including such titles as "The Angel of the Odd," "Literary Life of Thingum, Bob, Esq.," "The System of Dr. Tarr and Prof. Fether," "The Man That Was Used Up," "Loss of Breath," and a number of others. These were, if anything, superior to the average run of humorous fiction of the time, but who would prefer these when he knew the same man was capable of writing "The Black Cat," "William Wilson," "The Pit and the Pendulum," "The Tell-Tale Heart" or "The Fall of the House of Usher"?

"A Suggestive Suggestion" in the August 5, 1889 issue of the *Argonaut* was one of W. C. Morrow's fortunately rare attempts at humor. The entire story was written in the form of a legal brief filed on the part of a 75-year-old multi-millionaire wishing to marry an attractive 19-year-old, asking that the court rule on whether this marriage would be legal and free of all claims by the women with whom he had enjoyed affairs and illegitimate children over the past 30 years. The humor derives from the petition and the wording of the court in rendering its view that "Fractional, incomplete and conditional marriage have never found high favor in the courts of this country, and rather than encourage polygamy in California, I adjudge all these alleged marriages to be void."

Modestly diverting as this piece may be, the readers were more interested in seeing stories like "The Surgeon's Experiment," "The Rajah's Nemesis" and "A Peculiar Case of Surgery," all ranking among the greatest horror stories ever written.

In 1887 Robert Duncan Milne had written the story "The Man Who Grew Young Again" concerning years being shed as a result of obtaining a blood circulatory rapport for a period with two younger men. The August 19, 1889 issue of the *Argonaut* carried a translation from the Spanish of R. B. de Bengoa by Osmund Warde on a similar theme titled "An Animal Elixer." A Spanish scientist exchanges the blood of a young boy with that of an 85-year-old man, whom he has reduced to a living but almost bloodless condition of suspended animation. When circulation is revived, the heart sends the blood surging in the opposite direction. As a result the man day by day grows younger instead of older, finally dying as a near-embryo, not able to take nourishment of any sort. The story was straight science fiction and originally written sometime after the year 1870, because that date is given in the context of the narrative. This story, for the time it was written, is superior science fiction and was later reprinted in England's *Short Stories* for January 2, 1897, crediting the story to the translator Osmund Warde. It should be obvious to all that the plot of this story is identical with that of one of F. Scott Fitzgerald's most famous novelettes, "The Curious Case of Benjamin Button," first published in *Collier's*, May 27, 1922.

In just two weeks Robert Duncan Milne followed up in the issue of September 2, 1889 with "The Centenary of the Elixer," which seemed unquestionably to have been inspired by Bengoa's "An Animal Elixer" for it was based on the social impact of a longevity serum extracted from animals and made available to the masses. The development of the story was such as to leave no further basis for comparison. A clairvoyant is hypnotized and ordered to pick up messages from the future regarding the discovery of Dr. Brown-Sequard which can prolong life.

His mind tunes in on 1989, 100 years in the future, when the world is celebrating the centenary of Dr. Brown-Sequard's longevity discovery. In addition to San Francisco's population of three million, two million have assembled, brought in by innumerable flying machines (the larger ones capable of flying across the continent in six hours). A talk at the unveiling of a statue in memory of Dr. Brown-Sequard gives the history of the past 100 years. Mass extermination of animal life has taken place to provide enough of the long-life serum. During the early years haste and inept preparation resulted in millions dying from improper injections. The Catholic Church had threatened excommunication to anyone who took the serum but in 1989 the Pontiff had reigned for over 80 years, so the faithful had begun to suspect hypocrisy.

Early in the 20th century a devastating world war broke out in Europe, which ended with the Federation of European States and a single government in 1920. In the United States the unions had grown immensely powerful and actually began to give their members military training. Giant trusts seemed to own everything in the United States, so the unions organized a coup d' etat in which they seized Washington, D.C. and overturned the government. The middle class refused to accept the new government and created their own army, launching a strange type of civil war. The unions were eventually defeated, but the trusts were also broken up and cooperatives, where the means of production were owned by the workers and the profits shared, were formed and worked.

Successful transmutation of metals destroyed the value of gold and silver and resulted in a paper money economy with the redemption value backed by the government. Africa was brought into the community of civilized nations and the Sahara was irrigated, making it possible to support a much larger world population, now at 2.5 billion. Automation makes it possible for man to work only one day a week to get enough to live on. However, the world will shortly run out of animals from which to make serum.

This was unquestionably the most socially conscious bit of science fiction written by Milne, who had previously been much more interested in what happened than what was done with it.

A writer cannot go on for a decade, producing scores of ingenious yarns in a popular publication without having a definite influence. Geraldine Bonner had virtually rewritten his story "Into the Sun"; W. C. Morrow in his scientific approach to the man kept alive without a head in "The Surgeon's Experiment" could have gotten it from no one but Milne; and even Ambrose Bierce in his jumps into the future to provide a setting for a bit of satire probably owed something to Milne. Now, came a Los Angeles writer named Charles Dwight Willard (best known as C. D. Willard) with "The Restored Palimpsest" in the September 16, 1889 *Argonaut*, who was also an unquestionable disciple of Milne's.

A palimpsest is a parchment from which a previous inscription has been erased and a new one penned over the erasure. Willard told of the invention of a believable scientific apparatus which could restore the memories that had apparently been erased by time. The staging of the story is pure Milne, starting out with a chance meeting, the discussion of the feasibility of pseudoscientific topic — in this case phrenology — and then the revelation that one of the men is a brilliant scientist, with a well-equipped laboratory and a completed invention just waiting to be tested. Overpowering his confidant by physical strength, the scientist lowers a metal cap over his head, attaches two electrodes to his subject's forehead, and by controlled impulses sends the man's mind racing back to his memories of childhood. The machine's potentialities seem to be greater than that, for the subject is being carried back into the realm of *ancestral memory*. Just at that moment, the room is broken into, the experiment is terminated, and the scientist carted off to an insane asylum.

Willard had come to Los Angeles in an effort to recover from a series of hemorrhages related to advanced tuberculosis. He was working as a reporter on the *Los Angeles Herald*. A wealthy man was planning to publish a quality West Coast magazine out of Los Angeles to be titled *The Pacific Monthly,* which was to be edited by Charlotte Perkins Stetson. The story by Willard in the *Argonaut* so impressed him that he negotiated with the author to write fiction for his new magazine. Willard would write a variety of stories, including science fiction, and also continue to contribute to the *Argonaut,* for *The Pacific Monthly* was to expire in 1891. Willard would later go on to publish *Land of Sunshine,* a weekly that would eventually challenge the *Argonaut* as the literary leader of the West, but that was still years away. There is another point of interest about the name C. D. Willard that brings us to the early days of the science fiction pulp magazines. *Astounding Stories of Super-Science,* published by Clayton Publications beginning with January, 1930, featured the science fiction novels, novelettes and short stories of a competent and readable veteran pulp writer named Charles Willard Diffin. When two stories appeared by C. D. Willard, "Out of the Dreadful Depths" (June, 1930) and "The Eye of Allah" (January, 1931), they were credited as being the pen name of Charles Willard Diffin (Charles Diffin Willard). Since Diffin also had stories in the two issues in which the name Willard appears and since the style of those stories was typical pulp of the day, they quite probably were pen names of his, but the coincidence is worth noting.

That Frederic Somers even from the ivory tower of *Current Literature* continued to follow the *Argonaut* was amply attested to when he reprinted "The Grewsome Waiter" by Thomas J. Vivian

(October 21, 1889) in his February, 1890 issue. Vivian was a long time contributor to the *Argonaut*. "The Grewsome Waiter" was a tale of the supernatural, about a man who becomes an agent, unwillingly, of The Grim Reaper, transmitting death by touch to those near and dear to him. Vivian had been a reporter and dramatic critic on *The San Francisco Chronicle*. Most of his material there appeared anonymously, but he apparently was an early science fiction writer. It was said of him that "Vivian was gifted with a vivid imagination, which enabled him to conceive the impossible and describe it as an actuality in a convincing manner."

John P. Young in his book JOURNALISM IN CALIFORNIA became more specific about this in regard to the *Chronicle:* "It is astonishing to note in running through the files how often room was made for a bit of imaginative writing at the expense of crowded-out local. A case of this kind was presented when some reporter was permitted to describe the exploits of a flying ship which made regular trips between San Francisco and China, consuming only three or four days in the passage. The writer located the station for arrivals and departures on the corner of Montgomery and Clay streets, and, in his mind's eye, he saw a big business doing. The article was unsigned, but it was probably the product of the pen of Thomas J. Vivian, who had a fondness for the fanciful and could make the seemingly impossible appear very probable."

To keep his ideal short story writer before the eyes of his writers as well as readers, Hart had a translation of Guy de Maupassant's little-known "Why He Married" published in the October 28, 1889 issue. The story opens with a man giving the reasons why he is to marry. He is going to marry to have another human being around the house, to minimize his unreasonable fear. This fear had been engendered by arriving home one night, finding his door open and the figure of a strange man lounging in an armchair with his back towards him. Reaching for the man's shoulder he finds the chair empty. He never sees the apparition again, but whenever and wherever he is in the house he has the constant *fear* that someone is watching him. "He haunts me — it is folly, but so it is," de Maupassant writes and the reader knows it is not fiction but is the lowering shroud of madness, that was so classically depicted in his masterpiece "The Horla" *(Gil Blas,* October 26, 1886) and the kinship of the themes of both stories are linked and horrifyingly foreboding. Today, when de Maupassant is thought of as a classic writer, it must be remembered that his short stories were written for newspapers and weeklies of France, that his career began in 1880 and he was dead by 1893 and the *Argonaut's* translations were very soon after the original appearances of his stories, and frequently their first appearance in English.

De Maupassant was not the only French short story writer whose supernatural fantasies Hart favored. The November 18, 1889 issue brought to the readers of the *Argonaut* Catelle Mendes' work translated by L. S. Vassault titled "The Mirrored Demon." Well written and atmospheric, the tale told of a phantom image that enticed a girl to her watery death in a disease-ridden pool and the appearance of her ghost to reenact the tragedy. Mendes was a highly regarded publisher, poet, novelist, dramatist and short story writer, much admired by Fred Somers, who would also publish "The Mirrored Demon" in a new translation by Alice Ballard-MacDonald as "The Shadow of the Reed Pool" in the December 1889 issue of *Current Literature,* and follow it with another supernatural story "The Laughing Springs" in his April, 1890 number.

"The Electric Hand" by Charles L. Mosher in the December 2, 1889 number of the *Argonaut* seemed to represent a timid attempt to explain extra-normal powers in pseudo-scientific terms. A character in the story has the ability to sense the presence of living creatures within miles of his position by the intensity of a tingling in his right arm. Under certain conditions that right arm is capable of building up a discharge of electricity powerful enough to kill humans — in this case Indians — by a sheer touch. There is always a withdrawal involving intense pain to himself. Not enough was done with the idea and the story sort of petered out.

Far from timid was Robert Duncan Milne in his tireless campaign to reduce the supernatural and supernormal to the most explicit scientific explanations as in "An Experience in Telepathy" for the Christmas, December 23, 1889, issue of the *Argonaut.* He launched into the scientific basis for the reception of "visions" by certain individuals, asserting it a form of telepathy that could be rendered stronger and be repeated at will with the amplification provided by electrical apparatus. With their foreheads crowned by metal hoops and their hand grasping crystal rhomboids, two subjects set electricity cracking into their temples and by mutual, concentrated will create an image of a friend of theirs who is visiting Mexico, but he is in somewhat of a fix, tied hand and foot by bandits. By exercise of tremendous will they render the bandits unconscious, transmit a message to their friend who extricates himself from his bonds and escapes.

Within a month this was followed by one of Milne's more brilliant stories, "The Eidoloscope" in the *Argonaut* for January 27, 1890. This story was similar in theme to his "The Palaeoscopic Camera," which takes photos of the past, and is about a device that recreates images of the past from the heat emanations of the walls of the rooms in which they had occurred. The suggestion is made that this instrument may prove either a toy or possibly an excellent device for solving crimes. We are brought face to face with the undeniable fact that what the readers of Milne obviously wanted and delighted in was not the adventure which resulted from his imaginative inventions but the utterly ingenious, fascinating and learned scientific convolutions of their theoretical possibility and practical construction. Just as the followers of Erle Stanley Gardner's Perry Mason stories are most interested in the unexpected courtroom strategies that ferret out criminals and less interested in the crime, so Milne's readers were most interested in the means and least in the ends. "The Eidoloscope" is one of the most dazzling exhibitions of Milne's peculiar aptitude as he seems to plausibly delineate the theory and construction of a piece of equipment that can capture images from the past, and the utilization of this instrument to uncover a woman criminal is merely a literary excuse to have employed it at all. Perhaps the readers enjoyed stretching their imaginations to supply their own ramifications of the utilization of such a device.

Milne would not appear in the *Argonaut* again for another 18 months, and that would be the last original story by him in that magazine. Part of the reason was that he was working on *The San Francisco Examiner,* and a few more of his stories would appear there during the coming years, but more than that, in a profession that was noted for its drunkards, he was regarded by his co-workers as the champion alcoholic of them all. In the mornings he would awaken without a hangover but so debilitated that he found it difficult to work and before the afternoon had progressed many hours he was too far in his cups to work. His body revolted and he found that from waking until noon he could drink nothing stronger than beer but as the day wore on he could resume imbibing more potent brew.

XXXVII. MILNE IN THE EXAMINER

Fiction under Milne's *byline* had begun appearing in *The San Francisco Examiner*. The earliest was "A Pharmaceutical Revenge" in the Sunday, October 20, 1889 edition. This occupied almost a full newspaper-sized page, but was pretty mild stuff for Milne, who again assumed his frequent role as narrator. He tells of striking up a friendship with a wealthy Englishman, half Italian, who has spent a good part of his life tracking down a relative who paralyzed him with a drug, embezzled money from him, and ran off with the girl he was engaged to marry.

The Englishman turns the tables on the culprit by giving the man $100,000 for a valuable mine, paralyzing him with the same drug placed in a glass of claret to close the deal, removes the money from the man's pocket, and then with the signed deed to the mine leaves the country.

Milne's second story for the *Examiner* was "A Hypnotic Mystery" (March 2, 1890) and this was made more effective by being related in the form of depositions, similar to the technique utilized by William Henry Rhodes' "The Case of Summerfield," and which device Milne had previously employed in "A Theft of Seventy Millions." Milne again used hypnotism or mesmerism as the basis of his plot. A San Francisco capitalist with the gout permits an electrical therapist to ease his miseries. During the "treatments" he falls under the man's hypnotic power and in that state endorses the marriage of his daughter to a character of low repute, signs over $500,000 in cash and an undetermined amount of stock to him, and the entire matter was accomplished with such ironclad legality, impeccable witnesses of the finest character and general correctness that it is almost unchallengeable and must stand, because who would believe the story about those precisely correct actions being carried out against his will?

While working on the *Examiner* Milne had made numerous contributions to the *Argonaut* and these could be easily and clearly differentiated because they were predominantly fiction and overwhelmingly science fiction. What remained puzzling was his association with *The City Argus* and its publisher Robert E. Culbreth. An editorial comment in their issue for December 27, 1890 spoke of "Robert Duncan Milne who has been connected with this journal for the past twelve years as literary editor and a member of the editorial staff . . . " An examination of the publication page-by-page bears no signed contribution by Milne until the March 8, 1890 issue where they reprint from the *Argonaut* the poem "A Shifting World," by "special request." It is provable that during 1891 Milne was in the employ of *The San Francisco Examiner,* yet the *San Francisco City Directory* for 1891 listed his occupation as "Literary Editor, City Argus," (his residence was then at The Washington Hotel).

The December 24, 1890 edition of *The City Argus* printed his poem "Clades Variana" in *Latin,* which he had composed at the age of 16 while at Trinity College in Scotland, and which had won him the Knox Prize for Latin verse. Three poems in English appeared in the January 3, 1891 edition, "Drogenes Liquiter," "The Russian Captain's Story" and "Twin Jewels." "The Russian Captain's Story," which Milne notes is based on fact, is a grim and exceedingly well-done narrative poem of a Russian soldier who has been skinned alive except for his hands by the Turks and begs his friend for the pistol shot that will end his misery.

The one story Milne had published under his own name was titled "What Might Have Happened" and eventually appeared in the June 3, 1893 issue of *The City Argus.* The Geary Act provided that all Chinese who had not been registered as of May 5, 1893 were liable to deportation and the Supreme Court had ruled that the law was legal. This law only affected a few cities like San Francisco, Newark, N.J., and New York which had large Chinese populations. Newark had the second largest Chinatown in the United States at that time. It later deported thousands of Chinese and though there was still a small Chinatown after World War II, today it has disappeared entirely.

Milne wrote a fictionalized version of what might happen if

San Francisco attempted to enforce the law. The marshalls face 6,000 armed Chinese ready to resist and early attempts to register them are repulsed. Finally, the entire area is surrounded by soldiers and the Chinese given the alternative of registering or being deported. The affair was carried off smoothly and a mass clash averted. Milne did an excellent job in his fictional hypothesis and had it not been subtitled "If the Authorities Had Undertaken to Deport the Chinese under the Geary Act," delving historians might have thought it factual.

Milne's last original contribution to the *Argonaut*, for which he now had written scores of tales, nearly 50 of them science fiction, was "An Artificial Mirage" in the issue for July 27, 1891. This had all the strengths of his best stories. A scientist constructs a huge circular device that will create mirages to order. Actually it can be used to bring views of events occurring in many distant points close up. Milne's lecture on the theory of mirages and the construction of his device for creating them at will is nothing short of magnificent, the reader almost feels like clapping in acknowledgement of his intellectual achievement. The weakness is that there is no story, the characters are invited back to view a test of the device, but Milne never obliged with the sequel that was unquestionably intended.

Part of the reason for Milne's not appearing regularly in the *Argonaut* may have been *The Wave*, "A Journal for those in the swim," published by Hugh Hume and J. O'Hara Cosgrave. The weekly had originally begun publication in Monterey in 1888, stressing society, music, sports, books, pictures and "the merrie life." It moved to San Francisco and became a popular journal there in 1891.

Its change in location also resulted in recruiting some of the best writers in the area including Ambrose Bierce, W. C. Morrow, Harry Bigelow, G. A. Danzinger (Benjamin deCasseres), Frank Norris, Arthur McEwen, Percival Pollard, Frank Bailey Millard, Emma Frances Dawson doing translations, and Robert Duncan Milne. This was a formidable, sprightly and illustrated competitor to the *Argonaut* and obviously must have paid for contributions or it would not have boasted so stellar a lineup.

Milne's short story "Brain Transference" appeared in the

January 17, 1891 number and took place in a private mental institution. Before a hypnotized witness, the doctor removes a portion of the brain from a man who regards himself as a king and a similar-sized portion from another patient who feels he is the most humble of saints, transfers them and sews them up. Some months later the man who felt he was a king has disposed of all superior airs and has acquired traces of humility whereas the other has gained considerable self-esteem and discarded most of his self-effacement.

"The Artist's Spectre" by Milne in the June 27, 1891 issue of *The Wave* relates the tale of two men who visit the apartment of a late artist who has vowed on his death bed to return. While eating supper they see his indistinct apparition appear in the doorway for a brief time, then fade away. They bring a friend the second night and the apparition reappears at the same time in the same place, but the friend walks through the "ghost" and finds there is a portrait of the dead man reflected on a concave mirror, from which light of the setting sun filtering through the shutters causes the illusion of a ghost when the light strikes it right.

These stories were light compared to the work that Milne had previously been doing. With the appearance of "A Question of Reciprocity" serialized in the November 15 and 22, 1891 issues of *The San Francisco Examiner*, he returned to the top of his form. It now becomes more understandable why editor J. O'Hara Cosgrave had made it a point to comment on the story. Milne was also one of *his* contributors, one of the family so to speak, but the quality of the story that appeared in the *Examiner* was a local *tour de force*. Milne had written for him pleasant fillers, but the *Examiner* had obtained a real circulation grabber.

Milne seriously considered collecting his best stories into a book and wrote his uncle Duncan James Kay* that the book would be dedicated to him for past kindnesses. Touched by the idea, Kay

---

*When Duncan James Kay died at Drumpark in the Stewartry of Kirkcudbright, Scotland, April 7, 1903 his personal estate was set at 242,124 pounds, 13 shillings and 9 pence. The dollar was roughly valued at $5.50 to the pound in 1903. In terms of purchasing power, that amount was easily equivalent to $10 million today.

sent Milne $2,000 for the dual purpose of publishing the book and making a visit home. Milne made serious preparation for his trip to Europe and booked passage. The day of sailing, he started for the ship, stopping on the way to tipple a few. He never made the trip to Europe, never published the book and never, apparently, returned the money. This probably was the incident that dimmed his uncle's enthusiasm for sending him more in the future, though acquaintances said that the uncle never completely deserted him, despite all, but contributions did become infrequent.

There were reputed to be two days a year when Milne remained cold sober and was on his best behavior. Those were Thanksgiving Day and Christmas Eve. He spent them as guest of Mrs. Lottie A. Roberts at diverse addresses in San Francisco. These invitations had begun in 1879 and continued every year until his death. It was said of them: "Never did he attend these little family functions in a condition other than that which befitted a man. However self-indulgent he might have been before or became afterward, those two days of the year always found him sober and at his best. Then he would disclose all those charms of conversation and manner which men of his talents so often possess. His talk was bright, witty, thoughtful and showed that between drinks his mind was active and retentive." What Mrs. Roberts was to him has not been ascertained. She was widowed from George P. Roberts in 1897 while resident at 1213 Golden Gate Ave. She had at least one child also named George P. Roberts, who was a student. Her husband had worked for William Sparks Company. Immediately following his death she removed to 1425 Golden Gate Avenue.

XXXVIII. MILNE TAKES THE "CURE"

While until now Milne's literary contributions had been almost forgotten by the world, one special feature he was party to is still remembered, mainly as a testimonial to Hearst. During the early days on the *Examiner* Hearst's reporters performed many spectacular feats of not only physical heroism but great ingenuity in securing newspaper "beats." Among the most talked about men of the day was Dr. Leslie E. Keeley, who had invented a series of treatments, consisting predominantly of periodic injections of bichloride of gold in the patients, which allegedly cured them of all desire for alcohol, drugs and tobacco. These desires were asserted to be due to degeneration of the nerve and brain tissue and the pink fluid comprising Keeley's Cure restored these tissues to health.

As the single worst alcoholic on his staff, Hearst decided to have Milne take the "cure" and write a story about it, though Milne claimed it was his own inspiration. Leaving Mrs. Lottie Roberts' table after Christmas dinner, Milne asserted he had started on a glorious binge. In the process he met a friend who had taken the "cure" and was now drinking nothing but non-alcoholic beverages. Milne decided he would take the "cure" as a scientific experiment, but he didn't want to be cured. He enjoyed being a drunk and was particularly fortunate inasmuch as he didn't get morning-after headaches or hangovers. To him it was a contest, a challenge to see if his will could prevail against Keeley, who claimed to have only a 5% rate of recidivism for those who undertook his treatment.

Keeley had opened up a Pacific Coast Branch of his Institute at Los Gatos, a town only a few miles south of San Jose. Accompanied by a friend to make sure he did not change his mind, with money obtained from the paper, Milne traveled to Los Gatos. He was interviewed by O. N. Ramsey, business manager, and Dr. G. E.

Sussdorft, resident physician, and enlisted in the "cure." There were two or three days of tapering off, and then the injections began at regular intervals of four hours. Milne found they not only turned him off liquor but off everything. He found himself virtually unable to eat anything the first three or four days there. Sleep was also extremely difficult. He found it difficult to do any physical or mental activity and was in a perpetual state of lassitude.

Milne was institutionalized 21 days and when he left he immediately wrote a full-page article titled "Thro' the Bichloride Mill" for Sunday reading in the January 17, 1892 edition of *The San Francisco Examiner*, detailing his experiences and those of his acquaintances. At the end of the piece he said: "My desire for liquor has departed, where or how it is hard to say, . . . Time and time alone must prove the permanancy of the bichloride of gold cure for drunkeness."

For about two weeks Milne remained abstemious. Then, he fell into his tipsy ways again, with Jerome Hart, editor of the *Argonaut* fairly certain that his fellow editors and reporters on the *Examiner* were responsible for his fall. An editorial implied that this cast doubts on the efficiency of the Keeley Cure. Dr. Sussdorft replied that Milne had no wish to be rid of his habit (which was true), "because according to his ideas, a state of drunkeness is preferable to a state of sobriety. . . . "

Apparently this did not immediately adversely affect Milne's employment with the *Examiner*, for the June 20, 1892 edition carried an extraordinarily prophetic feature headed "A Millennium Near at Hand." This piece chillingly catalogued the deadly devices immediately on the horizon which would work towards mankind's self-extermination. The opening lines lent some light as to why it was a Chilean ship that invaded San Francisco Bay in Milne's "A Question of Reciprocity" when the writer says: "Whoever it was, whether Blaine or Harrison, that kept this country out of war with Chile, the failure of a fight was a great disappointment to experts in warfare all over the world, who vainly sigh for a conflict that will afford some sort of test of the value of modern naval and military methods. There has been no battle on the sea since the days of wooden battleships, and rapid-firing weapons, fish torpedoes, high explosives, submarine destroyers and other devices for scientific and wholesale killing have had no chance for a practical trial."

One of the sub-heads declared: "War would mean the annihilation of the human race," and then the author went on to enumerate the devices that could bring this about including U.S. experiments with military ballooning for purposes of bombardment, smoke bombs to conceal the movements of troops, illuminating bombs to light up enemy terrain, bombs containing deadly poisonous gas, pilotless aircraft loaded with bombs proposed by Maxim, the inventor of the machine gun. The writer of the article then points out that this is identical with the proposal of Robert Duncan Milne in his story "A Question of Reciprocity," which used a machine called "The Vampire Bomb," which closely resembles today's "cruise missiles," except that it is propelled by a helicopter principle. An artist's conception of Milne's aerial torpedo was included with the story.

Suggestions did not end there, for the writer then went into detail on Maxim's deadly machine gun, the introduction of high-velocity guns of smaller calibre, which have great accuracy even over long distances, the introduction of exploding bullets, the torpedo boat and the deadly torpedoes themselves, submarines firing torpedoes, and floating mines above and below water to protect harbors. The article concluded by citing Lord Lytton's THE COMING RACE, which had a method of destruction so great it made war unthinkable. The prospectus set up here was in that class and the comprehensiveness of it and the fact that it referred to Milne raised the rather reasonable question of whether or not he might have written it.

XXXIX. THE LAST FLARING

Milne had long been the resident authority on comets, and their appearance seemed to inspire editors to ask him for copy on them and he apparently never failed to rise to the occasion. Holmes' Comet had come into view in late November, 1892 and was distinguished by the fact that the core and the tail were of the identical substance and contained no internal heat but shone by the reflected light of the sun.

Adopting the mode of hoax fiction, but placing his speculations several months in the future, Milne wrote a story for the December 4, 1892 issue of *The San Francisco Examiner* titled "The Great Comet of 1893." The subtitle of the story was "The Second Deluge," which conjures up visions of Garrett P. Serviss' masterpiece of the same title *(The Cavalier,* July, 1911 to January, 1912), dealing with a similar theme.

In unsurpassed reportorial style, Milne tells of the announcement of a comet in the papers of March 15, 1893, named Barnard's comet after one of its discoverers. The earth will pass through a fringe of its tail, but Prof. Barnard notes that this type of thing has happened in the past with scarcely any noticeable effect, and he expects the situation will be the same this time. Milne is not so sure and refers to Ignatius Donnelly's controversial book RAGNAROK: THE AGE OF FIRE & GRAVEL (1882), presenting a theory that the earth once passed through a comet's tail composed of gravel which left a layer on most of the earth's surface, followed by internal heat from volcanic action in the earth and external heat from the friction of the comet's transit, forming a strata on the surface of the earth in which no fossilized remains are to be found.

Prof. Bernard reveals that this comet is composed mostly of hydrogen and under Milne's questioning prod concedes that under certain circumstances that hydrogen could combine with the oxygen in the air, forming water. The amount of water would depend upon the quantity of hydrogen and if the amount of water formed was excessive, it could deplete the oxygen reserves of the air, lower the energy level of human beings and even threaten their existence. The hypothesis proves correct and it shortly begins to rain, continuing to rain 24 hours a day for days on end. In San Francisco entire portions of the business section are under water, but the local problems are the smallest part of it. By the time the rain ceases, 300 inches later, the oceans of the world have risen eight feet. The entire city of New Orleans is no more. Part of Colorado has become an inland sea connected to the Gulf of California. In Asia 50 million Chinese drown and 30 million more natives perish in India. The food crops of the world are destroyed and famine threatens.

The only positive results are to be found in the Sahara, which has been transformed into a sea, and the inland deserts of Australia, which have become fertile. One seventeenth of the oxygen of the air is now locked in water, but the waters are receding and mankind will rebuild.

The splendid logic of the piece commands great respect, for it is superbly handled. Milne, as he is too frequently, is more concerned with what has happened and how it has happened than to whom it has happened, but he never leaves the reader in doubt as to why it has happened.

Just two weeks later, in the December 18, 1892 issue of the *Examiner*, Milne appeared with another remarkable story, "The Death Valley Mummy." A completely dehydrated, dessicated body of a man is found in Death Valley. Though the body has been reduced to but 40 pounds, there is no other sign of deterioration. A scientist removes the body to his apartments in San Francisco and begins a careful series of steps to resuscitate the "mummy." The body is placed in a tank which is sterilized, over a period of weeks, a steam engine slowly pumps water and chemicals into the tank and the "mummy" gradually rounds out and attains its normal weight of 160 pounds.

The contents of the stomach and intestines are pumped out and the arteries and veins are flushed with a special solution. Then the doctor gives the subject a massive blood transfusion from his own body, an electric needle shocks the heart muscles and starts it beating again. Gradually the body is brought to consciousness, is fed and cared for, but even though a remarkable technical success has been achieved, there has been such severe brain damage that the subject is virtually a vegetable. The physician places him in an insane asylum and leaves the country.

The story is extremely well written and the scientific explanations for the dehydration are acceptable as are the carefully explained and thorough medical procedures to restore life to the patient. In view of the medical knowledge of the period, it must have read with great plausibility to intelligent readers.

That Milne's stories obviously set well with the readers was underscored by the fact that this story was preceded by a biographical note on Milne's life and an artist's sketch of the author. The story also carried three illustrations on a single page.

Elements of both "The Great Comet of 1893" and "The Death Valley Mummy" are obvious in the gentle satire "How San Francisco Looked in 1893, An Archeological Fantasy," published in the *Examiner* for January 1, 1893. Utilizing Ignatius Donnelly's theory from RAGNAROK: THE AGE OF FIRE & GRAVEL, Milne has a comet break up and cloak the earth in fine dust up to a height of 100 feet. Several deep breaths of the stuff are all that is required to kill a person. Only a few survive, but a new civilization arises in Africa where in the year 3893 an archeological expedition is sent out to rediscover the site of ancient San Francisco. Excavating on an inland sea with the most modern equipment, bodies of thousands of the unfortunate inhabitants are found, who still retain their shape and clothes, though they crumble at the touch.

In "The Great Comet of 1893" the scientific hypotheses of how a comet-induced catastrophe could occur is the whole story. In "How San Francisco Looked in 1893" it is merely a device to permit the people of the future to observe something of a legendary city and to speculate on the meaning of much of what they see. There is humor here and the method is parallel to that of "Mellonta Tauta" by Edgar Allan Poe *(Godey's Lady Book,* February, 1849) which finds the people of the year 2848 trying to make sense out of the artifacts of 1848. The endings of both stories are very similar. In Poe's story, future man is trying to figure out who the hell this fellow named George Washington was, whose name is inscribed on a cornerstone, and exactly what did Lord Cornwallis surrender for and what happened to him. In Milne's story, a monument is found inscribed "James Corbett, Champion of the United States," and they'll be damned if they can figure out what he is champion of. There were six illustrations accompanying this story on a single page, several of them absolutely delightful, imaginative and inventive.

Comets were not all that intrigued Milne in the skies. Following a conjunction of the planets Mars and Jupiter he wrote for the January 29, 1893 *Examiner* a long article titled "Astrology as a Science." Actually Milne didn't think astrology was a science at all. His view was expressed in the lines: "In the olden times, when astrology was still widely practiced by leading thinkers, believed in by the vulgar and even dignified by the name of science . . . " He did acknowledge that many in the past and even the present did think of it as a science, and as a 16-year-old student he had studied the history and practice of the "art" carefully and then proceeded to give a very erudite exposition of its history, precepts and usage, and did not stop short of offering a practical description of how one might cast their own horoscope.

"Was It Justifiable?" published in the *Examiner* for April 9, 1893, told of an inventor in Ventura County who has fallen in love with and is soon to marry a Mexican girl from a very fine family. A long-lost cousin of the girl intrudes on the scene and appears to exert almost hypnotic powers over the girl, and there is no question that he intends to run off with her. The inventor has been giving the girl some rather strange gifts related to his inventions. He has discovered how to efficiently transmit electricity over a distance without the aid of wires. With a modification of his invention he builds a tiny working microphone into a locket which he gives to the girl and which is, in effect, a radio transmitter. The girl is bugged; everything that goes on between her and the "boy friend" is heard by him. He has given the girl a second locket with a tiny diamond-shaped light which can receive electrical currents without wires from a distance, and become incandescent. Every device he gives the girl is taken from her by her cousin. The locket with the light, her cousin is especially pleased with and wears around his neck.

When the inventor hears through his sound system that the two are going to run off together, he transmits a lethal dose of electricity which is received by the locket around the young man's neck and kills him instantly. The coroner's verdict is death due to heart failure and as the story ends the inventor will marry the girl in 30 days.

The last work of fiction under Milne's name published in *The San Francisco Examiner* was "The Midas of Granite Mountain" in the Sunday edition of April 8, 1894, almost one year short a day of the appearance of "Was It Justifiable?" Shipments of gold bars, two feet in length and weighing 300 pounds apiece are being delivered to the San Francisco mint on a weekly basis, usually 30 at a time, valued at $2,250,000 per delivery at the prevailing rate of $16 per ounce.

Curious as to the origin of this gold, the narrator traces it to a mine near Prescott, Arizona, which has been considered long played out and had been worked by one Professor Amos G. Hawley. A visit at the mine site finds the excavation of virtually worthless quartz in progress. Nearby there is a windowless building. A message is dropped from a disposal chute from this building by a man who claims he is being kept a prisoner.

It turns out that an old man named Winckler who has been living at the mine, saw a block of quartz shattered by lightning and the pieces were then veined with gold. He secured Professor Hawley to duplicate the effect with laboratory equipment, but both of them have been taken over by a gang of ruthless men. When the narrator arrives with the sheriff, the place is vacant and the hints are plain that everyone concerned has decided there is plenty for all and have taken off for parts unknown.

The scientific theory of gold making is very similar to the one that Milne used in his story "A New Alchemy" back in 1879. Milne did not again express his theories in fiction form for the *Examiner*.

Just when he parted company with the paper is difficult to ascertain. Hearst was extraordinarily liberal toward newspaper reporter irregularities and it took a great deal to provoke him to the point where he would dismiss a man. It is quite possible that Milne worked on the *Examiner* through 1895, for in that year two signed articles by him appeared on the Sunday literary pages. The first, in the April 7, 1895 edition, titled "Balderdash of the Day," was his acerbic comments in response to Bierce's remarks chiding a poet that "flashes don't fall;" his second, in the July 14, 1895 edition, titled "When I Heard Huxley," gave his impressions of many years past of attending the lectures of Thomas Huxley and Tyndall in London.

The day was over when Milne stood almost unchallenged on the West Coast as the greatest imagination of the era. It was not that he had ever been deposed; drunkeness had forced him to default. Papers and magazines would publish literally anything he would write in any format but he wrote little. The *Argonaut* had reprinted under the title of "The Men on Mars" in their August 15, 1892 issue his story "A Telescopic Marvel." In 1896 they would reprint three of his stories, "A Trip Through the Air" (September 14), which was "Philip Hall's Air Ship," its sequel "A Flight to the Pole" (September 21) and "A Surgeon's Miracle" (October 26) which was "The Man Who Grew Young Again."

He had come through for the December 22, 1894 issue of *The Wave* with a light society love story in "The Accomodating Phanchette." A planchette is a board with three corners and a pencil that is supposed to have mystical powers. If fingers are lightly resting on the pencil it will spell out messages on the board.

To bring a highly desirable but bashful prospect together with an amenable young lady, a planchette is fitted with a magnetic pencil tip and a magnet is placed in the boot of one of the matchmakers. Thus equipped, they cause the pencil to write without any hand touching it the names of the man and the woman in answer to leading questions, resulting in their engagement. This story, as did several others, seems to verify Jerome Hart's claim that Milne was capable of writing any type of plot or any type of story to order, for there was no question that "The Accomodating Planchette" rifled in on the young female society-conscious audience that made up a good share of *The Wave* readership.

That this was no accident Milne proved again when he did another story, a modern Arabian nights tale for the September 19, 1896 issue of *The Wave*, titled the "Mahatma and the Princess, Or, The Modern Palace of Alladin." The Princess Fatima in the year 896 is fabulously pampered and spoiled, every whim catered to, no matter how expensive and unreasonable. Finally she asks for a new palace containing all of man's arts and manufactures from every major country in the world. The only men in the world who can give it to her are some mystics and the price they demand is that she must wait a thousand years for them to accomplish it. She agrees on condition that she sleep for 1,000 years so that she can see it. When she awakens, the Mahatma takes her to a gigantic department store of the year 1896, where the wonders in the way of goods, services, scientific progress transcend her wildest imaginings. When the day is done she is sated with marvels and is glad to return to Bagdad.

This story is another twist on Edgar Allan Poe's "The Thousand and Second Tale of Scherherazade" *(Godey's Magazine and Lady's Book*, February, 1845). Scherherazade must regale the king with a fascinating story each night, and the first time she fails she is to be put to death. Judging his love for the fantastic, she tells him of all the modern advances of 1845. In utter disbelief and contempt, he has her executed. It also contains elements of Poe's "Some Words With a Mummy" *(American Review:* "A Whig Journal," April, 1845), wherein an Egyptian mummy is restored to life and given a description of some of the wonders of the modern world, which so depress him that he asks to be put back to sleep again.

XXXX. THE DESCENT

During 1894, Milne's address was given as 637 Stevenson Street, San Francisco; 1895 found him one number removed at 636 Stevenson Street, and in 1896 he was at 616 Folsom Street. There was no listing at all for 1897. It is probable that Milne had no address that year, nothing under his signature being found dated 1897. His fellow reporters state that he was often permitted to sleep in the offices of *The City Argus* and in the offices of *The San Francisco Vindicator*, "The Recognized Organ of the Colored Vote of California." The question might be legitimately asked, "What value would Milne conceivably have to a Negro paper?" The answer to that question is very interesting.

The *Vindicator* was an independent Saturday weekly newspaper, published initially by George R. Dennis, Jr., at 405 Sansome St., and edited by James E. Brown. It was supposed to have begun publication in 1884, but the true year was probably 1888, when it received a 2nd class mailing permit, and is believed to have given up the ghost in 1906, probably as a result of the earthquake. It was four pages in size, 18 x 24 inches, and sold for $2.50 a year. At the time Milne was involved with it, Brown was the sole proprietor and editor and printing at 622 Clay Street with editorial offices at 432 Clay St. Advertising rates were $15 a column and there were seven columns to a page. Only 22 copies of this paper spread among three libraries are known to exist. THE AFRO AMERICAN PRESS AND ITS EDITORS by J. Garland Penn (1891), a book on the Negro press published in the nineteenth century, fails to mention the *Vindicator*, probably because all entries were paid for and Brown's paper, malingering with a circulation of about 800 at the time, could scarcely afford it. The circulation would climb to a peak of 3,500 by 1898.

Brown's approach was evident from examination of one of the few available issues, that for October 27, 1894. There was virtually no news concerning blacks anywhere in the issue. The entire front page was devoted to biographies and line drawings of white political candidates for office. Their biographies were written with extraordinary skill and with a vocabulary of a Ph.D. in English literature. The editorial page was at the same level, a political defense of some of the candidates reading: " . . . decry the paltry and contemptible innuendoes which are always forthcoming in the heat of the storm, we must also protest against the scurrilous way in which Mr. Estee is being treated. Must it go down to posterity that California of all the States of America, cosmopolitan as it is, cannot conduct a political canvass in favor of one candidate without covering another with undeserved odium. In the name of all that is fair, we adjure our subscribers and patrons to stand by the simple record of men as they have known them . . . "

Obviously Brown received most of his financial support from the politicians on the premise that he could deliver the Negro vote. Equally obvious, they had no conception of his true circulation. Most of the candidates owned businesses, and undoubtedly their year-round advertising support could also be counted upon.

The paper was not written for Negroes, it was written for white advertisers. Milne could write in high literary style for this newspaper. Undoubtedly those nights when he could find no place to sleep and staggered in drunk, the next morning he would spend several hours writing copy for Brown in exchange for his "lodging." There was probably a similar arrangement with Culbrith of *The City Argus.*

The last two stories known to have been written by Robert Duncan Milne appeared in *The San Francisco Morning Call,* a competitor to *The San Francisco Examiner,* so it is safe to say he was no longer working for the latter. It is possible that he may briefly have been on the staff of the *Call.*

That paper was founded with the edition of December 1, 1856 by The Associated Practical Printers, composed of five partners. Among its early contributors was William Henry Rhodes, author of the famous science fiction hoaxes. It innovated the idea of running social news about everyone and not just the prestigious, which practice is now copied by most papers. It also took no editorial sides politically. The *Call* carried on a running feud with the *Argonaut* and never mentioned them in its pages, but the *Argonaut* reamed them out plenty. The paper was sold in 1897 for $350,000 to John D. Spreckels. Under the new regime big salaries were paid, features were added and color presses installed. Robert Duncan Milne appeared with his last work of science fiction, "The Passing of the Printing Press," in the December 18, 1898 number. That they considered him an author of some importance was evidenced by an artist's sketch of him writing the story — $4\frac{1}{2}$ inches high by $3\frac{1}{2}$ inches wide — on long narrow strips of paper, with the note below: "Sketched from life." The "story," because it really was the outline of a new invention, was fascinating. Milne would have a film made of material to be printed, using a special type of material. He then placed it in a holder beneath a cathode or X Ray with 5,000 sheets of light sensitive paper beneath it. The power was turned on and in seconds all 5,000 sheets were perfectly and identically printed. Milne also takes a crack at explaining why the paper prints only on the side exposed to the X Rays and not on the bottom sides, and is reasonably convincing.

Milne's final story for the *Call* and perhaps the final one he ever wrote, appeared less than a month later in the January 15, 1899 edition. it was a detective story, not science fiction, titled "The Mystery of Tokio — Masu Miyakawa"; subtitled "A Japanese Detective Story." It introduced a Nipponese hawkshaw worthy of being anthologized.

An American in Tokio draws $60,000 from the bank with which he is to close a deal at 7:00 P.M. that night. A telegram delays the closing until the next day. He is killed while asleep and his wallet taken and lowered out of the window to an accomplice. Another thief who has been after him insists on a share of the money from the one who has beaten him to it, only to be shot to death by a gun with a silencer for his pains. While dying he tells the Japanese detective Mr. Kato the whole story and the name of his assailant.

A rickshaw man delivers the dismembered body of the man who had used the gun with the silencer to the police in a bamboo hamper. It had been left by a patron who did not return for the property. Mr. Kato asks the rickshaw man whether his passenger might conceivably have been a woman dressed as a man, which is his suspicion. In a variety of disguises, going door to door pretending to distribute tea samples, Kato finds a woman suspect. He follows her as she meets with an actor friend. Claiming to have a message from that friend he calls at her house, but she only pretends to be taken in, for she tries to murder the detective, shooting at him from hiding after he has left. Fleeing back to her house with the detective following her, she enters and it almost immediately blows up. Neighbors remove all intact items from the house. Among them is a large trunk. Suspicious because her body has not been found in the house, Mr. Kato has the trunk removed to the police station and when it is opened she steps out. She murdered the American businessman, passed the wallet out of her window to her husband, who in turn killed the other thief. She murdered her husband so she could run off with her lover and was foiled by Mr. Kato. A highly involuted and clever story, revealing that in moments of sobriety Milne's mind was as agile as ever.

During the past 10 years when Milne was surrounding himself in an alcoholic haze, William Randolph Hearst became the leading proponent of science fiction in the United States starting with the *Examiner* and originating and reprinting material in other papers. Ambrose Bierce was a paid staff member who would write some of his most brilliant stories for Hearst and in the last decade had come in for considerable critical acclaim for his two collections of short stories TALES OF SOLDIERS AND CIVILIANS (1891) and CAN SUCH THINGS BE? (1893). W. C. Morrow had a minor best seller and widespread recognition for the collection of his best short stories in THE APE, THE IDIOT AND OTHER PEOPLE (1897). Even Emma Frances Dawson would have an outstanding collection of her stories, AN ITINERENT HOUSE AND OTHER STORIES (1896), which Ambrose Bierce promptly raved over.

The *Argonaut* developed an entire new generation of science fiction and supernatural writers, cumulatively leaving a marvelous legacy to the field. In the San Francisco papers, Jules Verne, H. G. Wells, H. Rider Haggard were among the regulars, as well as local writers. When Milne blew the $2,000 his uncle had given him to publish a collection of his short stories on a prolonged drunken binge, he had doomed himself to literary oblivion, for one hardcover book might have spread some portion of his regional reputation and caused at least a few of his stories to be anthologized and reprinted. His place in the history of the development of science fiction might then have been preserved.

There is no taking away from him the fact that he was the closest thing to the first full-time science fiction writer in America or abroad the field ever had. At least 60 bonafide science fiction stories published over a period of 20 years appeared, supplemented by a number of outstanding detective yarns with scientific twists.

Considering the closeness of his relationships with Ambrose Bierce and W. C. Morrow, it would be hard to deny his influence on their writings. It would be impossible to deny that he was instrumental in the *Argonaut* printing its excessively large portion of science fiction and fantasy and in contributing to Hearst's enthusiasm for it. He was a natural outgrowth of the hoax school of science fiction, but he possessed a fund of scientific knowledge beyond the scope of any of the others who wrote it. He could string thousands of words of involved scientific theory mixed with philosophy and his readers loved it. Yet he repeatedly showed that he was not merely a captive of science, for he could tell a story with a beginning, middle and an end, and do it well.

The diversity of his themes was remarkable. He did not take an idea and merely exploit it for the sake of adventure, but added adventure to illustrate the concept. There was much humor and satire in his works as well as stark drama. Charles Howard Shinn, a contributor to the *Argonaut* and the *Overland Monthly,* had begun to place promotional articles on the virtues of California in the national magazines. The October, 1899 issue of *The Forum* ran his article titled "Literature of the West Coast" in which he said: "Wonder-tales of the purely imaginative sort are perfectly at home in the soil of California. Some shorter stories in this vein seem to be destined to long life and wide fame. They can be compared to the best works of Poe, or of O'Brien, whose 'Diamond Lens' is justly reckoned a masterpiece. 'Caxton' wrote wonderful stories many years ago, and they still keep going the rounds of the newspapers. In more recent years, Robert Duncan Milne has put into short stories a genius quite equal in dynamite force to that of Wells; still later, Emma Frances Dawson, W. C. Morrow, Geraldine Bonner, Ambrose Bierce and others have told their weird tales with a short-story art worthy of long remembrance."

XXXXI. THE END

Did Milne ever enjoy the brief pleasure of reading that article before, befuddled by liquor and enfeebled from its ravages and poor nutrition, he spongily started to cross Market Street at the intersection of Montgomery Street, San Francisco, Friday morning, December 15, 1899, a few minutes after midnight? Philip Healy, grip man of the McAllister Street cable car 281, claimed he slowed down, rang his bell and began shouting at Milne, but was ignored. The conductor, Thurston, asserted the streets were wet and the tracks slippery. A witness, liquor-store owner Harry Dobie, said that Milne, who had cleared the track, suddenly fell backward, striking his head on the car steps. The grip man asserted that Milne fell backward, was struck on the arm, and hit his head on the pavement. Unconscious, he was picked up by some men on the scene and taken to the San Francisco City receiving Hospital, where his condition was diagnosed as a fractured skull. Drs. Bray, Starr and Heintz trepanned his skull to relieve the pressure on his brain shortly before 2:00 A.M. He appeared to rally, but his constitution was too weak to sustain it and at 3:40 P.M., December 15, 1899, he died without recovering consciousness. His body was taken to the morgue pending an inquest. The grip man, Healy, had been arrested by Officer Meyer but was released on his own recognizance at 9:00 A.M.

The San Francisco Examiner had gotten the story of his *accident* into their December 16, Saturday morning edition, headlined "Robert Duncan Milne a Cable Car's Victim." This story was undoubtedly read by his friend Lottie A. Roberts, whose residence was given as 2335 Bush St., for she showed up at the hospital with two woman companions only minutes after his death. She suggested that she would arrange for burial for the sake of the family. The

Examiner in their edition of Sunday, December 17, stated: "No relatives of Milne had appeared at the morgue last night to take charge of the body. Should the relatives not make arrangements to-day, 'The Examiner' will see to it that Milne is given a Christian burial."

An inquest into Milne's accident and death was held Tuesday, December 19, before a jury and Coroner Hill. Still another physician, Dr. Frank Drail, testified as to the medical procedures carried out on Milne, and the motorman, his conductor, and a witness told their stories. The jury deliberated only a few minutes, finding the death due to accident.

Mrs. Roberts made all the arrangements for his funeral. The first announcement was that the funeral would be held Tuesday, December 19 at 2:00 P.M. from the funeral parlors of the California Undertakers Company, 405 Powell Street near Post. This evidently was changed for a later news story very specifically read: "The funeral of Milne took place yesterday afternoon (December 19th) from the parlors of the Golden Gate Undertaking Company. Rev. John A. B. Wilson upon the request of Mrs. L. A. Roberts, a friend of the deceased, conducted the religious services. The remains were in the Masonic Cemetery in a plot owned by Mrs. Roberts."

Milne's death received VIP treatment in the San Francisco press. There were stories of the accident, followed by stories of his death, followed by publication of odds and ends found on scraps of paper among his effects. All these stories were laced through with fascinating anecdotes concerning his life and career. He was known to every newspaperman in San Francisco and while they could be candid about his drunkeness, since there were no relatives in the United States, they did not hesitate to give him credit for his achievements.

The San Francisco Bulletin said on December 17, 1899: "The fact is that Mr. Milne was such a good writer and such a smart man that if he could have held a tight rein on his inclinations a wider world would have proclaimed him great. He had a mentality which was a constant surprise to those about him and should have made him independent, perhaps famous. Frank M. Pixley, formerly editor of the Argonaut said that he was the best general scholar on the

Pacific coast. . . . Some of his stories were pronounced by his admirers as 'fine as anything ever written by Poe.' They attracted attention abroad and were the subject of comment of literary journals in London."

While research has failed to uncover the references to him in London journals, two reprints of his stories from the *Argonaut* were located in the British *Short Stories,* published by C. Arthur Pearson, which was a companion to *Pearson's Weekly,* where so much of George Griffith's work appeared. "A New Theosophy," subtitled "The Recent Startling Manifestations of the Pentagram Club," appeared in the March 7, 1895 issue *(Argonaut,* June 27, 1888) with six illustrations; and "A Modern Proteus" in the May 30, 1896 issue *(Argonaut,* March 24, 1888), with five illustrations.

The obituary further said of Milne's writing: "Great facility in writing was a characteristic that impressed the reader. Though very technical the narratives never seemed labored. They had an easy swing that was one of their chief charms."

About recent writing it said: "A few weeks ago he wrote and forwarded an article on banking for publication in an Eastern banking publication. He had been working for the City Argus for some months but had about finished that engagement when death overtook him. . . . His mode of life was such that many wondered that he ever lived, to say nothing of retaining the powers of his mind, but although he has done nothing notable for a long time, those who were in a position to know say that he was as capable of good work as ever."

On December 16th, in reporting on his accident, *The Examiner* said: "Milne had been a public character for years. He was a man of brilliant attainments, and had he been able to overthrow John Barley corn he would have made his mark in the world of letters . . . when in a more than usually ambitious mood, he would put his very best work into a contribution to Eastern magazines." None of these have been located. It ended by commenting on his range of education and stating: "despite the manner of his life, [he] retained through his career the habit of study." This piece also supplied the information on his relationship with Robert Louis Stevenson and ended with the sentence: "Robert Duncan Milne was a kindly man and was never known to injure anyone but himself."

Surprisingly Jerome Hart printed only a brief notice of his death in the *Argonaut* for December 18, 1899. Possibly the deadline was upon him for in his book IN OUR SECOND CENTURY (1931), Hart wrote at length with a warmth and admiration of Robert Duncan Milne. He also reprinted "A Wireless Telegraph" (October 20, 1902) and "The Lost Ship Marigold" (December 22, 1906). When Hart put together a collection titled ARGONAUT STORIES, a paperbound anthology issued in 1906, he included Milne's "Ten Thousand Years in Ice," and as an addendum, a selection of the letters he received from Hungary commenting on the story. This was the only story of Milne's known to have been included in a book. The only other item of Milne's discovered in hardcovers was his poem "A Dream of the Golden Gate" *(The Wave,* August 1, 1891) in SAN FRANCISCO * AS IT WAS * AS IT IS * AND HOW TO SEE IT by Helen Throop Purdy (Paul Elder & Co., San Francisco, 1912).

The New York Daily Tribune for Sunday, December 24, 1899, ran a notice on Milne in its column "Topics in California." It stated, in part, "He had a genius for the construction of intricate plots, and many of his short stories resemble those of the Englishman Wells in their ingenious application of some principle of science. Milne was recognized as one of the best Latin scholars on the coast, but he threw away all the advantages by excessive drinking." Then they had an unusual closing sentence which does not appear in any of the San Francisco papers: "Though he was a man of unusual mental capacity, Milne's brain was small and weighed only forty ounces and two scruples [a scruple is 1/24th of an ounce] but the convolutions were remarkably deep and well defined." Apparently the result of an autopsy.

"A bunch of copy paper partly covered with random notes dealing with heterogenous matters, a few letters and two small pocket combs constitute the effects of Robert Duncan Milne, the talented writer of unquenchable thirst," *The San Francisco Examiner* reported on December 20, 1899, under the headline: "Last Take of Copy Left by Robert Duncan Milne." Two ideas for science fiction stories were found, one based on the premise that there are times in life "when one has a clearer vision of things hidden from the ordinary sense; when one is struck with an intuition of events transpiring in widely remote portions of the earth," and the other "The mutual relations of mind to matter, of idea to fact, of sentiment to sense, are as yet a sealed book, as a luminous vision seen through a glass darkly. . . . Glimpses we indeed have of the existence of such relations, but we fail to comprehend the conditions under which alone it would seem to exist."

Two poems were found, and both published. The longest, titled "The Love That Failed," was a five-stanza poem, a sentimental bit of verse comparing the life of a man and woman to a ship at sea and using appropriate similes. The strange thing about it was that it was copyrighted in the name of Frank A. Busse, who was a bookkeeper for A. Repsold & Co., and resided at 633 Castro. What his relationship was to Milne and why the newspaper printed the copyright in his name is not known.

The second poem found was only five lines long and written in Latin with a free translation by Milne beneath it. It seemed almost to anticipate his final dissolution in its very personal message:

> *Soul of mine, pretty one, fleeting one,*
> *Guest and companion of my clay,*
> *Whither away, prithee, whither away?*
> *Pallid one, rigid one, naked one —*
> *Never to play again, never to play!*